Compulsion

Kymberlee Burks-Miller

DEDICATION

To the love of my life, Bryce Miller, thank you for twirling me that first night. The song Fearless says it all. I love you...

To our miracle, Connor-Bryce, you will always be mommys' little monkey.

You are both my entire moon~

To Charlotte Semones, you are the best BFF ever! Love you

To Sabrina Ford and Carly Anne Wallace, you are both so much more than just friends!! Love you xoxo

To the Burks' and the Millers', thank you for loving me

Mom~Thank you for loving me and teaching me how to be fashion forward

To my Angel in Heaven, Maryann Burks. Mommy I hope that I am making you proud. I love and miss you everyday ~me

CONTENTS

ACKNOWLEDGMENTS

Paperback cover by: Robert Hunyor

Edited by: Melissa Ringstead

I want to acknowledge a few more people: Candis Honey, Paranormal Reads, Alchemy of Anne's Anomolies, Muzna Shafi from IMPRINTATION, I Love Books, YA Book Lover, Rue Volley, Jenny Needham, Wanda Hart, Wendy "Lovetiggi" Gonzalez, 98 Rock, The UTZ Patriots Football Family, and so many more who continue to spread the Compulsion word!!

Dan Amos composed the music for the book trailer for Compulsion~Thank you Dan!!

Donnell Wallace is the artist who created Compulsions' original cover that will be gracing the hardcovers this summer. To the top we go!

CHAPTER ONE

I'm nothing spectacular. Not the girl that everyone turns and ogles as she passes by. Not the girl who is overly sexy, or sporty. For that matter not even a total brainiac. I'm just an ordinary girl, six feet tall, slender, long curly brown hair and weird blue eyes. Like I said, ordinary to the extreme! So why is he staring at me with those piercing green eyes? The man in the suit that is totally designer by the way. My guess…Armani. My phone vibrates and my ringtone, Galway Girl, plays loudly. What can I say, I'm Irish!

"Hel-lo," I say, my voice chipper as it always is when I'm at the mall. I recognized the hysteria in the familiar voice on the other end. It's my father and he's crying.

"Lily, sweetie you'll need to come home. Granny has passed."

My world has just shattered for the second time in my life with those three simple little words. I've gotten pretty good at hiding my emotions in public. When your mom dies of breast cancer when you're in your early teens, you feel like scratching someone's eyeballs out! And that really is not a socially acceptable public display of emotion, right? Random people come up to you with their sad smiles to give their condolences. Then, after a while, people continue to stare but their comments are usually behind your back. Especially where my family lives, in the small town of Hampstead in Maryland.

"Oh, that poor man and he has all of those children to raise alone," I've heard.

"Those poor girl's without their mothers' guidance, so young," was also said.

That's why when I applied and was accepted to Towson State University in Towson, Maryland, which is almost an hour from home, I jumped and took it! I started off as a Pre-Law major. I wanted to right the injustices of the world, but I'm not great at arguing my point because of my ADD, or attention deficit disorder. I tend to start off going down one path, and then BAM I see a butterfly and my attention is diverted. So, as of right now, my major is undecided. I left Towson Town Center with my poker face firmly in place.

I headed to the garage to get my Jeep, and allow myself the much needed breakdown, and phone call to Camden, my best friend. I got in my vehicle and the tears began just as I started dialing. Two rings and Cam answered.

"Lily, oh my God! Your dad just told me, I'm so sorry!" I started my Jeep and turned the radio off. Ironically, the song playing was something about living like your dying. That's exactly how I felt, like I was dying inside, but my body just wouldn't finish the death process. I rubbed at my eyes with the sleeves of my shirt, and spoke to Cam.

"I just don't understand how!" More sobs. "I just spent last weekend with her. She was walking in her garden picking herbs, and then she was in the kitchen baking about a million cookies, and pies. This makes no sense."

I pulled out of my space a little erratically. I almost hit a candy apple red compact car on my right. Crap! I tried to slow down a little coming around the turn that led down to the lower level and out of the garage.

Cams' voice carried through the speaker, "I know it's hard Lily, she's been like a mom to you for so long now." I was just about to tell Cam, like only a BFF can, to shut the hell up, when out of nowhere there was the guy from the mall in front of my Jeep. I slammed on my brakes, bracing for an impact and screamed, "For shit's sake!"

When I looked up he was glaring at me. My heart was beating out of my chest and all I could do was stare back. I felt like his eyes wouldn't let mine go. My thought process was wrong, I should have been thinking about what could have just happened, but instead I thought about how hot he was, tall, lean but muscular, and great hair, brown and a full head of it! It was those green eyes that captivated me. Cam's wailing brought me out of the thought of just how yummy this guy was. I looked at the phone as she screamed.

"Lily what's wrong? Did you hit something? Are you ok? Lily, answer me!" I turned back to look at him, but he was gone. Where did he go? I scanned the garage, but there was no sign of him. So, I answered my best friend.

"Yes I'm fine, almost hit a hot guy but, whatever."

The drive from Towson to Hampstead was weird, my body went into autopilot and I just let it. Cam stayed on the phone with me the entire ride trying to direct my attention to other topics to put off what I was inevitably going to have to deal with today, the reality that my Granny was gone. She really is the best BFF! So let the mind numbing psychobabble begin. We talked about everything from my only ex-boyfriend Mark, who is really not much to talk about, my classes, and how I was going to need to email my professor's, and Ash to see if I could borrow her notes. She's a girl I go to school with, not really a friend. Cam asked me about my crummy apartment and then my job. I worked the second shift at the emergency veterinary hospital. By the time Cam was done, she had emailed my professors and Ash, called my work, and talked me straight into town. I pulled up on the front lawn of granny's farm. Cam let me know she would see me in just a bit. She needed to call her husband and let him know what had happened. Cam married an incredibly handsome and sweet sailor in the U.S. Navy right after high school named Luke Myers. He and I had hit it off from the beginning. Cam said that we were like two peas in a pod, whereas Cam and Luke were completely opposite. You know the old adage, opposites attract. It's true. I couldn't picture anyone more perfect for her than Luke. They were like two puzzle pieces made exactly right for only each other.

I sat there unable to move just yet. I knew that I would never feel my grandmothers' arms around me as I walked through that door ever again. That thought brought on a physical pain in my stomach. I felt like I was going to be sick. After a few minutes I managed to pull myself together enough to face my family. I got out of my truck, and was immediately greeted by Granny's gray tabby cat Izzy. She purred as she wound herself between my legs. I bent down, and picked her up, nuzzling my face into her soft fur. She had to be as old as me because I can't ever remember her not being here. I kissed her sweet little nose, and put her back down. I looked at the house, and took a very long, deep breathe, and walked into my own personal hell on earth.

"There you are Lily! We were getting worried." My dad rushed over and hugged me. His eyes were red rimmed and puffy. He moved off to my side, and there was Granny on a stretcher with a white sheet pulled up to her neck like you see in the movies. A shiver that had nothing to do with the crisp September weather ran up and down my spine. I walked over to my grandmother. She looked different, asleep, but not peacefully. I bent down to kiss her cheek and the tears that had never really stopped from the phone call with my dad revved up into high gear again.

I whispered in her ear, "I love you Granny." I kissed her cheek knowing that it was the last time. As I was standing back up, with tears falling fast down my face, I noticed what looked like mosquito bites on her neck. Odd. Granny never got bitten. She always grew lemon balm, and every morning from April until the end of October, she would rub herself down with the leaves. She used to make me do it, and the leaves actually smelled like freshly cut lemons, so I never really minded. It was another one of her "old remedies". I can't complain. We were rarely ever sick growing up.

"We really need to be going now. I'm so sorry for your loss," said one of the men with the black jackets that had Medical Examiner written on the back. How many times were those words going to be spoken over the next few weeks? My sisters, brother, and cousins started coming up to me.

Cassie, the older of my two sisters grabbed me, "Lily they said she fell outside by the mailbox. I overheard the doctor tell dad that he thought it was a heart attack." I had to bend to hug my sister. She is about six inches shorter than me.

4

"We'll know more after the autopsy Cass." My heart sank at the thought of someone cutting my grandmother open. My Uncle Donal was standing closest to us.

He put his arm around my shoulder and said, "Sweetie there's not going to be an autopsy. That's how your grandmother wanted it." I was speechless. How the hell am I supposed to make any sense of this with absolutely no answers? They wheeled my grandmother in front of me. The men were taking her out of the house just as Cam pulled up. My lifesaver.

Cam got out of her car and ran dutifully to my side. She grabbed my hand and squeezed tight as the men lifted granny's lifeless body into the van and shut the door with a final bang. That is a sound that I will never forget as long as I live. A zillion things were racing around in my mind, but I had to focus, or at least pretend to, right? My family is huge, so I had to reintroduce my best friend to the Moon clan. She hadn't seen much of my family since I had started school in Towson.

"Now Lily who is the tan girl again?" Cam whispered as my cousin approached us.

"That's Uncle Donal's youngest, Riona but we call her RiRi and what can I say she gets the Native American gene more than the rest of us." I whispered back before RiRi got to us. My grandmother's family was from Galway, Ireland. My grandfather, who I never knew, was from the same small village in Ireland. However, after coming to the states his mother fell in love with, and married, a Cherokee Indian. RiRi is tall, about five feet nine inches, and slender. She has long dark hair, and the same weird blue eyes as me. She's the kind of girl the guys definitely stop and stare at. Just like the rest of granny's girls, she was also well endowed in the chest area. She's confident, loving and the female relative I was closest to.

"You ok, Lil?" She had a plate of food in her hand that she placed on my lap. Food that extended family, friends, and neighbors had been bringing since the van left earlier. "You have to eat something." RiRi's eyes were swollen, and red like the rest of ours.

"Thanks Ri. I'm fine. How about you?"

She broke down and sobbed on my shoulder. Cam grabbed the plate before it fell to the ground. In less than a minute Cassie, and our youngest sister Jessie, were at our side crying. Just a few seconds later there were arms everywhere! All eight of my cousins, and now my brother Declan, all six feet six inches and two hundred fifty pounds of him were tangled up in an embrace that resembled a football huddle. There were tears…a lot of tears, and love for family hit all twelve of us in that moment. We needed each other and we knew it! We all looked up at the same time at one another, looking into the same eyes…the exact same wildflower blue eyes…Granny's eyes. We smiled. Can you believe it?

We actually giggled while the tears still fell down our faces. Who knew that was even possible?

I was told later that my grandmother was being taken to Eline Funeral Home, on Main Street, to be prepared for a small service, after which she was to be cremated. The wake would follow immediately after, here at the farm. My family was finally starting to say their goodbyes. Tomorrow was going to be even harder than today. After just a few minutes the only people left were my dad, Declan, Cam and I.

"You guys go ahead. I need a few minutes alone." I whispered.

The protesting started with my brother, "Lily come on. We're not leaving you here alone. We need to stick together." He really does have a sweet heart.

"I'm good D. I just need a few minutes here alone. Do you know what I mean?" He nodded his head in affirmation. He walked over, hugged me, and turned his shaved head to get in my dad's car. That argument won, Cam started hers.

"It's ok Mr. Lochlan, I'll stay with her." I looked at Cam and she knew. Whatever I needed to find here, I needed to do it by myself. I didn't have to say it. Between Cam and I, it had always been like telepathy.

"Look you guys I'm fine." I said defiantly. How many times was I going to have to tell this particular lie in the near future? "I'll only be a few minutes behind you guys."

"Lily...I don't know about this." My dad, the only parent and protector that I had left from here on out, said. I walked over to my father and hugged him whispering, "Daddy, I really need to do this." He looked into my drained face. I could only imagine what he saw there.

"Ok, keep your phone on Lily." I watched them all leave.

I walked around the front lawn with Izzy at my heels. How did this happen? I'm here, and you're not Granny. You promised me that you would never leave me. A shadow moved in my peripheral vision over near the barn. Izzy hissed, positioning herself between any danger and me. Then she stopped just as quickly as she had started. I could have sworn that I just saw a person standing at the entrance to the barn. "What the hell... Izzy!" I jumped about a foot off the ground as her tail swished, and touched my leg. I looked back over at the barn, but there was nothing there. It must have been one of the animals that I saw. I was scaring myself. Did I think a scary monster would jump out of the dark at me? Get a grip Lily! I cried into the night, "Granny I need you! How am I supposed to make it without you!?" It came out in sobs, as I fell to my knees. I'm not sure how long I stayed in that position, dry heaving. My whole body ached from pain. I'm not really sure what I had thought that I would find here, but I certainly couldn't think here, not now…not without my grandmother. I locked up the house, got in my Jeep and drove straight to my childhood home, back to Dad's.

He was in the kitchen when I walked in the front door. "Tea pumpkin?" Yep, definitely back home…well for the night anyway.

"No Dad, but thank you. I'm just going to go to sleep if you don't mind?" He smiled, but not his usual smile. This one didn't reach his eyes.

"Of course not baby girl, sweet dreams." I kissed his cheek.

"Dad are you ok? I mean I know that's a totally ridiculous question…but I mean are you ok?" He just smiled again at me. I felt bad not just for myself, but also my Dad who had now lost his wife and both of his parents. I felt horrible for him. My father was a strong man, physically and spiritually, but the years since he'd lost my mom had been hard on him. He was once a tall and healthy looking man. Now he was starting to look a little gaunt. I was terrified what my grandmothers' death would do to him. I glanced back at my dad. He had his 'I'm fine' face on, and I didn't want to upset him any further tonight. So I turned, and walked down the hallway. I could hear Declan's radio going, so I passed his room without disturbing him. I stopped at Jessie's door and peeked in. She was sleeping, or pretending to be, so I quietly retreated from her room. Cassie's door was cracked, allowing the soft glow of her light to escape. I poked my head in. Cassie was sitting at her vanity. She lifted her sad eyes to meet mine in the mirror.

"You ok?" I stared at her reflection.

"I'm okay Lily, just tired." I knew exactly what she meant. I walked over to her, and kissed the top of her head, then turned to go, but not before she asked, "Lily…do you think that Granny's at peace?"

I nodded my head to her, afraid that if I opened my mouth to respond I would lose it. I walked out of Cassie's room and shut her door, leaving her to her thoughts. I made my way to the end of the hall and opened my own bedroom door. I used my hand to feel for the light switch on the wall. I flicked it on. Ugh, some things never change.

After I had moved out my dad had left my room exactly the way that it was. Everywhere that you looked were reminders of happier times, pictures of Cam, Kris, Jackie and I from all of our school years, my mom and dad, granny and the rest of the family all over the place. Stuffed teddy bears of every color, and North Carroll Panther banners (my high school mascot) were all over the room. Thankfully, I had left clothes here just in case of an unexpected overnight visit. I quickly changed into a set of my happy bunny pajamas and laid down in my bed. My mind was literally jumping around from topic to topic so fast, that I lost track of a thought as soon as it popped into my head. I was crying so hard that my ribs hurt from all the deep sobs. I felt like my heart would never heal. I couldn't get the image of Granny on that stretcher out of my head, finally after a couple hours or so I cried myself to sleep.

The next morning, after my shower, I pulled my hair up into a soft twist, the way granny always loved it. I grudgingly put on my black funeral dress that perpetually hung in this closet. I went out to the kitchen where no one was eating. The only thing on the menu this morning was coffee. That was fine with me, I needed an IV drip of it. No need to apply make-up today. What would be the point? It's all going to end up on the tissues anyway, right?

My brother rode with me, and in true Declan fashion he asked me as we came to a stop sign, "Lily, if we hit someone on the way to the funeral home and they tell us that they're not hurt. Can we beat the shit out of them until they are?"

I could not help myself, I burst out laughing and so did D! This was the purpose of his comment. It worked like a charm, let me tell you. My brother had a way to make you laugh at just the right times. I think that it was his dry humor. The funeral home was jammed packed with people of the community coming to pay their final respects to my grandmother. As we walked into the memorial room, we were seated with our immediate family and waited for the service to begin. A short, round man approached the lectern, and cleared his throat.

"We are all gathered here to say our final farewell to a woman who has been a pillar of strength to her family and this community, Aileen Fionna Moon, known to all as Leeny." The sounds of sobbing began, and yes I was one of the blubbering masses. The man called my father up to speak. My grandmothers' children were each taking their turn to memorialize their mother in the order of their birth. So next up was Uncle Donal, followed by Aunt Cathleen, Uncle Hugh, Aunt Brigid and last but not least Uncle Dillon.

As I drove back to Granny's for the wake Cam called my cell.

"Lily I'll be behind you a few minutes, I'm not feeling well." Her voice was weak and shaky.

"Cam you should go home, and lay down. You looked a little pale. I'll be fine. I'll call, and check on you in a bit." Cam and I had always been there for each other, from the bullies on the playground in elementary school, to our awkward, gangly pre-teen phase. Nothing had ever stopped us from being there for each other if we could help it.

"Lily I just need a few minutes, and I'll be there." After a small protest she finally agreed to go home and, rest. I got to the farm, and went inside to see what I could help with. My aunts were all in the kitchen, and everything was done. Great! Nothing menial for me to do. My mind kept trying to wonder about Granny's last moments, but I told myself not yet. I grabbed my ballerina slippers and wool sweater from my Jeep and threw my heels on the back seat. I walked around trying to avoid as many condolences as possible. I found myself meandering around the fields of the farm with no place in particular to go, very thankful that I had changed my shoes. Just to keep walking was the goal. Once I knew that I was far enough away from the house I just let my mind go, and before I could stop the deluge of memories, the flood gate opened and I was remembering things I had forgot ever happened.

Like the time Granny, my mom and I were supposed to bake apple pies. OMG! We had gotten up early that chilly October morning walking out to the orchard to pick the last harvest of apples. Granny and my mom were always very close, and that morning I got to be a part of their little group. We got to the trees, and Granny explained to me where to put the crate under the tree.

"Lily-Bug, climb up that little step ladder and just have fun," she told me as my mom looked on. I giggled. Hello I was ten. We were each at a different tree. Mine was a little farther away from my moms' and Granny's. But not too far, I could still hear them talking. I had picked about a half of a bushel before I jumped off of my little stepladder, giggling to myself. That's when I noticed the really tall man standing about ten or twelve feet away from me. He was watching me, with the most incredible eyes. They were bright red, and he had the most peculiar look on his face, kind of like he was hungry. I was staring back at him, and couldn't seem to take my eyes off of him. Like I had blinders on, and the only thing my eyes could see were his. That fast I heard Granny yell to my mom.

"Leighann grab Lily and get back to the house!" My mom was there lickety-split, grabbed my arm and ran toward the house with me in tow. I heard a loud muffled scream and Granny's voice shouting something in Gaelic. She was a proud Irish woman, so she was always trying to teach us the "old" language. A few of us learned a little but none of us spoke it fluently. However, Cassie did learn to read it. The next thing that I remember is Granny walking up the steps of the house wiping her "special" knife on her apron. After she cleaned it off, she put it back in its silver cover and slipped it back into her front pocket.

"Granny, who was that man? Where did he go?" I asked a little breathlessly when she walked in the house. She looked at my mom, and then to my curious little face, and spoke.

"Lily-Bug, he was just a salesman, nothing to worry about. I ran him off." She and my mom exchanged another look then mom said that we needed to get back home because she had to get supper started, which was weird because I thought we were spending the whole day at the farm. Granny kissed, and hugged us both good-bye and then we left.

Funny how I forgot all about that day, huh? When I looked up, I found that I had walked all the way out to the gazebo without realizing it. I wrapped my sweater closed more tightly as the chill set in. Sitting here reminded me of another recollection about two years after the last memory. I was twelve, and my mom had already been diagnosed with breast cancer. She had already had all sorts of treatments done by this point. She had both of her breasts removed which I found out later was called a double radical mastectomy. My mom had gone through radiation therapy and chemotherapy to no avail. The only thing that the chemo did was make her sick and weaker than she had already been. The doctors classified my moms' cancer as stage 4, and terminal. I was in the hallway outside of my parents' bedroom listening, c'mon I was twelve and that was the best way to find out what was going on with anything. Granny had come to see mom that day.

"Lochlan, they should know the truth." My moms' voice was weak with the effort of trying to put some force behind it. I could hear the bed squeak when my dad sat next to my mom.

"Sweetheart, let's not worry about this now, ok. All that matters in this moment is you getting better." My grandmother was in the room, but remained quiet. My mom asked my dad to leave her alone with Granny for a few minutes, and he grudgingly obliged.

"Please watch after them Leeny. You know I'm going to die soon." My mom sounded desperate, and I cringed at her words!

"Leighann, dear you need to rest." Granny said in her deep Irish brogue. She leaned in a little closer to my moms' head, so I really had to concentrate to eavesdrop. "Everything will be fine. The children will know when they're ready. It's their destiny. So now you see, we just need you to rest." I heard her kiss my mom.

One month later my mom had died. God. Would I ever have a normal life? I came out of that memory with renewed grief for my mom and a new ache for Granny. I started walking back to the house, to find that almost everyone had already left. Good. I needed some time alone to set things right in my head. I walked up the steps to the front porch where my dad was talking to one of my grandmother's friends.

"She would have been very thankful that you were here Ms. Lenore." My dad helped the little old lady off of the porch as she nodded her approval to him. A young man led her to a car, maybe her grandson. After she was securely in her vehicle she turned her head in my direction and smiled at me, then she drove off of the farm. I looked at my dad.

"I really have to get home. I have to go to school, and work tomorrow. Plus I still have to run over and check on Cam, she wasn't feeling well." My dad hugged me.

"Lily-Bug you need to stay a little longer. Mr. Hewitt, the Estate Attorney, is reading Granny's Last Will and Testament in just a few minutes."

Great. I'm already having a seriously shitty day. Let's add more.

"OooKay!" I drew the word out so that my dad would totally know that this is so not something I was up for. He just gave me that look that says, 'This is something that you have to do.' without saying as much. Fine. How long could this possibly take? My dad and I were the last two family members to enter the living room. I saw Mr. Hewitt, a tall but stocky man in a suit that was old and a size, or two, too small for him. He was seriously balding and had very beady, shifty eyes. The attorney was standing in front of the fireplace, obviously waiting for us. We sat down on the sofa (HE gave me the heebee jeebee's) and he began.

"As you know I am John Hewitt, Leeny's attorney and I am here to read her Will and to make sure that her final wishes are carried out." He was looking right at me. Only. At. Me.

.

CHAPTER TWO

"I'm going to commence with a letter that Leeny mailed to my office two weeks ago," began Mr. Hewitt's little speech. He reached into his pocket pulling out a handkerchief, and rubbed at his eyes. He cleared his throat and began to read my grandmothers' letter that was shaking in his other hand.

'To my sweet beloved family, I'm truly very sorry. If you're being read this letter than I have passed away. Please do not cry for me, I am in a better place and have joined all that have gone before me. Always remember that I love each and every one of you. I have chosen something special for each of you to remember me by. But before the Will is read, I wonder if you, my family, will join me in listening to my favorite song one last time together. Mr. Hewitt please play it NOW.'

It was just a moment later that the music started, and I giggled through the tears at Granny telling Mr. Hewitt when to start the music from beyond the grave, it was almost like she was really still here. I listened, remembering her sing this old country song through the kitchen, and outside in her garden. My grandmother had a very firm belief in strong family unity, values, and love. Until today, I honestly never understood what that meant, but now looking at the faces of my family I finally got it.

The music ended. There wasn't a dry eye among my family. The attorney stood up with a stapled group of papers and started reading.

'Aileen F. Moon does hereby leave to her eldest son, Lochlan R. Moon, one Lee-Enfield .303 rifle.' Mr. Hewitt offered my father a rifle that looked extremely old. My dad reached out his hand taking possession of the offered weapon.

"It's a British Enfield, this thing has probably seen both World Wars. Dark walnut wood stock nicked and marred from use. It's a bolt action, single shot. This was my father's rifle!" My dad started bawling like a baby. I reached up to comfort him, but he shook his graying head at me.

"Lily, its ok. I haven't thought about my father in a long time. This is good." With that, my dad sat down and started tinkering with his rifle. The attorney's eyes found mine.

'Aileen F. Moon does hereby leave her granddaughter, Lilyann K. Moon, her rainbow moonstone pendant and chain.' I felt the tears fall over my cheeks. Declan put his hand in mine, and squeezed. My father reached over, and handed me a tissue. Mr. Hewitt walked towards me, and handed me a simple white box.

I opened the hinged top to a sheet of paper with Granny's writing on it, the note read, 'My Lily-Bug, I'm so sorry. You must feel as though I've left you as well. But always know that I am with you in Spirit! It's your job now to take care of the Moon family. Your heart and soul are strong. Learn to believe in yourself, and your abilities. Follow your path in life wherever that may lead you. You have an inner strength that is rivaled by no other. Protect them! Please put this necklace on and NEVER take it off. I love you so very much. Love, Granny'

I stopped myself from crying any further, and like a good little girl I reached in the box and pulled out the pendant on the chain holding it up to the light. It spun on the chain and on the back it read in Gaelic 'Tuigim thu' isteach Spiorad', with the translation underneath, 'I am with you in Spirit'. I kept reciting my grandmother's words in my head trying to make sense of them. Surely she didn't think that I could do anything to really protect my family. And if she did what exactly did we need protection from? I reached up and clasped the chain around my neck. As my hand followed the chain my fingers touched the beautiful stones and knew that this necklace would never leave my body.

Next Mr. Hewitt turned his attention to Cassie, who looked so grown in that moment. She is only five feet four inches tall, and very thin. She pulled a lock of her sandy blonde hair behind her ear as she looked up to meet the attorney's beady eyes.

'Aileen F. Moon does hereby leave to her granddaughter, Cassandra K. Moon, her round rainbow moonstone necklace.' He finished by handing my sister the same type of white hinged box that he had handed to me. Cassie took the box and opened it. She read the note aloud that was included. 'My Cassie, I have loved you from the moment that you were born, and I always will. I say this not to upset you, but to protect you. Please listen to Lily. 'Talamh chosnaionn me' - 'Earth protects me'. I need you to put this necklace on, and NEVER take it off. It's my last request of you. I love you so very much. Love, Granny.' After she read the note Cassie put it back in the box. She put her new necklace on, meeting my eyes.

"I promise Granny that I will listen to my sister." Her voice broke at the end of her oath. I leaned across Declan, as did Cassie and we met in the middle. We had a short embrace before the attorney piped up again.

'Aileen F. Moon does hereby leave to her grandson, Declan R. Moon, one three stoned rainbow moonstone pendant with inscription.' Mr. Hewitt handed a smaller white box to my brother. He opened the box to a folded letter, the same type of letter that Cassie and I had received, which he read to us.

'Declan, you are the strongest of all of my grandsons, you get that from your father, and your grandfather. The day you were born was a great gift and treasure to me. I will love you always. As I have already told Cassie I need you to listen to Lily. I'm sure that everyone is getting pretty tired with my repetitive words, but I need them obeyed and you are the man for the job. 'Uisce chosnaionn me' – 'Water protects me'. Put the necklace on and NEVER take it off. I love you so very much. Love, Granny.' Declan put the note in his pant pocket, and pulled the chain over his head kissing it before tucking it under his shirt. This was going to take all damn night at this rate! At that moment my cell phone started going off, but we couldn't figure out where my purse was. So the phone kept playing Galway Girl. Finally Aunt Rae, Uncle Donal's wife, and my moms' best friend, found my Coach bag and handed it to me smiling sweetly. I truly love her. I checked my phone. It was Cam. I pushed the button to silence my phone, and immediately texted her. 'In middle of will reading call u when I'm done xoxo L', and promptly turned my phone off. Everyone in my family was watching me.

"Sorry," was my witty retort. All of my cousins, sisters, and D started laughing but with me, rather than at me. My brother was the first one to pipe up.

"Well Granny said we HAD to listen to you O' fearless leader. Therefore we accept your apology." After he said, all of us, even the adults laughed even louder and harder than before. Is this a will reading or a party? Whatever. Mr. Hewitt cleared his throat again and droned on.

'Aileen F. Moon does hereby leave to her granddaughter, Jessica R. Moon, one set of square rainbow moonstone earrings.' What is up with all of the moonstones? That was totally a Granny-thing. Jessie took the box that the attorney passed her, and opened it to a note that we were all anticipating at this point.

'To my youngest granddaughter Jessie, I know you already know what I'm going to say. So, I'm going to what is it that your generation says, oh yes switch it up a little. Be patient, don't try to grow up so fast. And yes listen to Lily. Child, you have made my soul feel young. 'Nocht chosnaionn me' – 'Air protects me'. Place your earrings in your ears and NEVER take them out! I love you so very much. Love, Granny.'

Jessie did as she was instructed, but it was rather hard with her hands shaking from laughter at the image of Granny trying to "switch it up". Cassie pulled Jessie's long dark brown hair back as Riona helped take my youngest sister's pearl earrings out, Jessie managed to put her new earrings in, and I must say her face lit up as soon as they were in her ears.

Mr. Hewitt excused himself into the dining room for a moment. RiRi grabbed my attention.

"Lil what is up with all of the moonstone stuff?" I was just about to tell her that I had no clue when Mr. Hewitt, panting a bit with the effort of carrying something massive into the room, cleared his throat. He sat this huge mahogany piece on the floor in front of him. The old lawyer grabbed his handkerchief again, and wiped at his brow. He was definitely earning whatever Granny had paid him tonight.

'Aileen F. Moon does hereby leave to her son, Donal R. Moon, an Edison Amberola V Phonograph.' Uncle Donal stood up and walked over to his newly acquired asset. He was tall like my father with the same warm facial features.

"This was mom's favorite player!" he exclaimed as a tear trekked down his cheek. "See, it plays these old cylinders. There must be over fifty of them! I wonder which ones she found." He sat down, while I wondered how in the hell he was going to get that thing in his house tonight. The attorney checked his pocket watch (yes, where I'm from older men still have pocket watches clipped to their vests) and carried on with the reading of the Will.

'Aileen F. Moon does hereby leave to her grandson, Ciaran D. Moon, one diamond shaped rainbow moonstone pendant.' Again with the moonstone, maybe she wanted us all to have something alike, to keep us together as a family? Who knows? My cousin Ciaran took the box and opened it. Just like Declan it was a flat disc shaped pendant with a Gaelic inscription on the front of it. He read his note to the awaiting audience

'My dearest Ciaran, you have always been my inquisitive and loyal one. There is no one in the entire world like you. Treasure our family and our history, the way only you can. 'Tri thine chosnaionn me' – 'Fire protects me'. Put this necklace on and NEVER take it off! Help your cousins, younger brother, and sister they are going to need you. I love you so very much. Love, Granny P.S. Help Lily.' Ciaran turned his sandy blonde head in my direction as he slipped his necklace over his head, and sat back down. Mr. Hewitt was ready with the next box and handed it to its new owner.

'Aileen F. Moon does hereby leave to her grandson, Aidan R. Moon, one round rainbow moonstone pendant.' Aidan opened his box to a letter. The letters were becoming just as much, maybe even more, of a gift to each of us than the actual items that Granny had chosen. Aidan put his necklace on first, and then read his letter to all of us.

'My laddie Aidan, always my best helper, and yet you are a natural leader. From the day you were born you have only brought light into my life and heart. I know that my requests must seem odd to everyone, but I do have a reason for them, so please help the family adhere to them. 'Talamh chosnaionn me' – 'Earth protects me'. Please put this, wait you already have, haven't you? Yes of course you have. NEVER take it off. I love you so very much. Love, Granny' When Aidan looked up at us we were all having a serious fit of the giggles again. He smiled sheepishly.

Honestly this had to be the reason my grandmother had done things this way, so that we could all smile again, huh? Maybe we could make it through this after all.

Riona was sitting back like she was nervous, which was strange because RiRi was one of the most confident people that I had ever met.

'Aileen F. Moon does hereby leave to her granddaughter, Riona C. Moon, a heart shaped rainbow moonstone ring.' Ri leaned forward to accept the small white box being handed to her by the old lawyer. She traced her finger around the edge of the box before opening it. She finally took the slip of paper from the box and sniffled into her tissue. She looked at the sheet of paper and began to read.

'My little angel Riona, you're my feisty one. That's a good thing, and don't let anyone ever tell you otherwise. Your family is going to start to rely on you. Pay attention to what you see, hear and feel young one. 'Amharc a'ta' se' croi cinnte go na firinne' – 'Look in your heart to see the truth'. Place this on your finger now and NEVER take it off. I love you so very much. Love, Granny'

Riona took the ring and placed it on the index finger of her right hand. She held it up to let the light dance off of the moonstone. Apparently I wasn't the only one who noticed that Riona's letter, like mine, was slightly different than the rest. Everyone was staring at Riona now, as the attorney excused himself again.

"Why do you think Granny wrote something different for you and Riona?" Shannon asked me, in what sounded like a very hurt tone, but her mom answered before I could.

"I haven't got the slightest clue about anything your grandmother is doing, or has done, wait how do I phrase this?" Aunt Cathleen said. She was as confused about the correct grammar at this point as the rest of us.

"Shan, let's wait and see what your note says, I bet it's awesome!" Like my words had summoned Mr. Hewitt, he appeared with three small white boxes in the doorway. No heavy burden this time. The old attorney looked relieved. He cleared his throat and proceeded.

'Aileen F. Moon does hereby leave to her eldest daughter, Cathleen W. Moon, her wedding ring set.' Aunt Cathleen jumped up a little too enthusiastically. She basically ran to grab the box out of Mr. Hewitt's hand, and in one foul swoop she had the box in her hand, and opened, gushing, "Oh my... Mothers' rings, I never would have dreamed that she would leave these to me." Aunt Cathleen sat down (she's the drama queen of our family) as she dabbed under her eyes with a tissue. Today, even I couldn't doubt Aunt Cathleen's authentic emotions towards her mothers' death. Mr. Hewitt called us all back to attention with his next words.

'Aileen F. Moon does hereby leave to her grandson, Braden B. Moon, a three stoned rainbow moonstone pendant.' Braden quietly walked up to the waiting box, and took it from the man offering it to him. He opened the box and unfolded the note inside reading softly, 'My boy Braden, I am so proud of the man you are becoming. I know that you are more reserved, but now is the time to open your mind and try something new and different. Look after your mother, sister and cousins. 'Uisce chosnaíonn me' – 'Water protects me'. Please put your necklace on and NEVER take it off. I know it's not the coolest thing, but it is from your old Granny. I love you more than you even know. Love, Granny.'

Braden pulled his necklace from the box. He let the chain fall between his fingers, as he admired the disc. Like all of the other boys' pendants it had what looked like a backward crescent moon touching a full moon touching a forward crescent moon. Under the moons were three moonstones set to look like a W, with an inscription underneath it in old Irish, and the English translation on the reverse side. He wiped his eyes and slid the chain over his head, where his necklace would stay. My cousin Braden sat next to his sister Shannon as the attorney spoke again.

'Aileen F, Moon does hereby leave to her granddaughter, Shannon B. Moon, one square shaped rainbow moonstone, and silver bracelet.' Shannon was handed a hinged box like the rest of the girls. She opened the box and reached for the letter after a quick glance and a small smile at her bracelet.

'My sweet Shannon, you have always reminded me of my mother back in Galway. She too had a very precious heart and often got her feelings hurt over things that were never meant to hurt those feelings. I'm assuming that you're wondering why Lily and Riona's letters are a bit different than the rest, well my sweet, that is a question that will be answered in good time and you have to trust me that it is NOT because you are NOT as special to me. You ARE so very important to me! I love you all the same. So please take good care of this bracelet for me, I left it to you because like you, it too is special to me. 'Nocht chosnaíonn me' – 'Air protects me.' Please put your bracelet on and NEVER take it off. I love you SO very much sweetheart. Love, Granny.' Shannon lifted her beautiful eyes and gently smiled to the room at large. I stood up and walked over to her.

"Shan, may I help you put on your beautiful bracelet?"

She handed me the piece of jewelry and her arm. I laid the bracelet on her wrist and hooked the clasp. I kissed her forehead.

"Beautiful, just like my cousin wearing it." She wrapped her arms around me and whispered, "Thank you Lily." I smiled as I crossed the floor back to my place dutifully in between Declan and my dad. Hmmm dutifully, it really does feel like I am responsible for them all now. No, that can't be right. I am too young for that much responsibility.

Izzy came prancing in from the kitchen and jumped onto my lap, crazy kitty! I ran my hand through her fur. Pieces of my hair fell forward as I leaned down and whispered to her, "Where have you been all day, huh?" She proceeded to purr like a freight train. Mr. Hewitt, who had just walked back into the living room, started to speak, but stopped abruptly as he noticed the late arriver in my lap. Izzy turned her head in his direction and began to stare the shifty attorney down. Mr. Hewitt turned to my uncle Hugh, who was smirking because of Izzy's reaction to the lawyer.

"Yes…well… 'Aileen F, Moon does hereby leave to her son, Hugh K. Moon, an Ansonia Cosmo Crystal Regulator Pendulum Mantle Clock.' Uncle Hugh stood up and gently took possession of the antique.

"This clock was made in 1914, mom took very good care of it. Hey Lochlan, Don, do you guys remember how many times mom caught us after curfew with this thing? It keeps perfect time." All of my aunts and uncles, even my father, was laughing remembering a different time in the same space. My cousins, sisters, brother, and I started laughing trying to imagine our parents as reckless kids. As if!!

'Aileen F. Moon does hereby leave to her grandson, Cormac A. Moon, one round rainbow moonstone pendant with inscription.' That shut us all up. Cormac looked up and was surprised to see Mr. Hewitt standing in front of him. Obviously he was just as anxious to get home as the rest of us, and thankfully just a few more family members to go. Cormac fumbled taking his letter out because of his muscular hands. We let Granny's words envelop us all. 'My dearest Cormac, what can I say, everything that you touch turns to gold! It's the luck of the Irish for you my boy. Please stay sweet, sincere and honest. Don't forget to have fun! Help your family. Lily and the girls will always need you and your cousins, just as you and your cousins will always need Lily and the girls. 'Talamh chosaionn me' – 'Earth protects me'. Please put your necklace on now and NEVER take it off. I love you so very much. Love, Granny.'

Cormac, just like all of Granny's kids, did as he was told. He pulled his new chain over his head. At that moment Izzy hissed in the direction of the room that Mr. Hewitt had just vanished into. Her body puffed out and her tail fluffed just like last night.

"Izzy what the hell is wrong with you?!" I snapped at her as she jumped off of my lap, taking a strip of my leg with her. "Damn it!" I yelled. Declan ran into the kitchen and grabbed a wet washcloth. He brought it out and pressed it to my gaping wound.

"What is up with her today?" D asked. I looked at him.

"Why? Has she been acting up? When she came in here and sat on my lap was the first time that I've seen her all day." My cousins Ciaran, Aidan, and Cormac walked out to the room Mr. Hewitt had just come from to check on Izzy and whatever may have got her going. My aunts helped clean, and bandage my leg. We got the blood to stop, it was only a deep scratch, it would heal. They walked back into the room that we were all still in.

Aidan announced, "There was nothing out there to get her all riled up. Maybe it was one of the other animals out by the barn. That was the direction she was running in. She IS temperamental!"

I laughed at Aidan, he was right of course, that's why Granny loved her. Mr. Hewitt spoke up again with even more urgency in his voice to leave this house. 'Aileen F. Moon does hereby leave to her daughter, Brigid L. Moon, one oil painting titled "An Evening Walk" by Joseph Kennedy.' Aunt Brig walked up to collect the painting.

"Mr. Kennedy is from County Tipperary in Ireland. Mom adored his work. She always said that his paintings made her feel like she was home." Aunt Brig carried the painting back to her seat. Everyone said that Aunt Brig looked most like Granny, and that Riona and I looked just like them. Right now I could see that in her face (not in the height though Ri and I are tall and she is only five feet two inches) it made me feel very close to my family.

"Yes, well, if we may proceed," the stocky man inserted. 'Aileen F. Moon does hereby leave to her grandson, Liam C. Moon, one square rainbow moonstone pendant with inscription.' Liam is my youngest male cousin. He goes to high school with Jessie and they're both seniors. He is the golden child, literally. He has blonde hair, tall, and muscular. Go North Carroll Panthers. Liam took his box and opened it, reaching for the letter that we were all waiting to have read to us. Without delay he gave us what we wanted.

'My little Liam, you're my youngest grandson, and the most mischievous of the bunch! But that is the reason that I admire you so much. You're not afraid of trouble and that skill may be needed in the future. But wait for the right time! 'Nocht chosnaionn me' – 'Air protects me'. Put your chain on and, not even for football games, NEVER take it off. I love you so very much. Love, Granny.' The sparkle in his eyes showed us the same thing that my grandmother had just made plain in her letter, Liam could be a "bad" boy if he wanted to be. He slipped his chain over his head, just like his cousins before him and sat back down next to Aunt Brig.

Uncle Dillon got ready, but Mr. Hewitt asked us if we would join him outside. This threw us all for a loop. We all got up and walked single file outside to the front lawn. This attorney was seriously working my last nerve. I was the last one out and the last one to see that there was something underneath an ugly old tarp. It was making the front lawn look like a junkyard. Fabulous.

'Aileen F. Moon does hereby leave to her youngest son, Dillon D. Moon, one Harley Davidson EL motorcycle.' Uncle Dillon was obviously in heaven. He, along with every other male member of my family, was fawning all over this death trap. I'm not a fan of motorcycles.

"It's a 1936, three years after Harley Davidson put the Eagle on the gas tank," I heard one of my male relatives say, I think it was Liam. I was suddenly distracted by Izzy. She was sitting on top of a heap of leaves purring, and staring into the dark confines of the barn.

Cassie nudged my arm and asked, "Do you see Izzy? What is she staring at in there?" All I could do was shrug my shoulders. Izzy was certainly not acting like herself. Cassie and I were not the only ones staring at the old cat. All twelve of us, my cousins, sisters, Declan and I were all watching her. Mr. Hewitt gained our attention for what I was sure was the last time before I was permitted to go home, to Towson, not my Dad's.

'Aileen F. Moon does hereby leave to her grandson, Seamus D. Moon, one diamond shaped rainbow moonstone pendant.' Seamus walked past his father, uncle Dillon, to retrieve his box. He promptly removed the letter, and began reading to us by the porch light.

'My little Seamus, you're my thoughtful one. You always analyze every situation, before you speak. Your intellect is what makes you, well, you. You have always been a beacon of strength for our family. Help take care of them now that I am gone. 'Tri thine chosaionn me' – 'Fire protects me'. Please put your necklace on and NEVER take it off. I love you so very much. Love, Granny.' Seamus swung his chain around his neck, holding onto the pendant. It's time to go home, right? Wrong. Mr. Hewitt spoke up quickly before anyone could delay his final words.

"I know that all of you are wondering about what Leeny wanted to happen with the farm. So let's proceed so that we can all get home since it's getting rather late." I was ready, name whoever and let me go. I was still watching Izzy as he read the final words from my grandmother.

'I know that my family wants to know who I am leaving the farm to. Well, I have decided to leave the farm to someone that cares about what happens to it as much as I did. I know that each and every one of you care about the farm and I do not want you to misunderstand me. It's just that she is the one who has shown the most concern for the animals, my orchards and my herbs.' I noticed all of the girls looking around at each other. I smiled and continued to watch Izzy's weird behavior as the attorney finished the letter, not really paying attention to the rest of the information. I was ready to start my hour long drive back.

'Aileen F. Moon does hereby leave her farm, animals, vehicles, and all contents not previously distributed to selected family members to.................................Lilyann K. Moon.' My head whipped around to find everyone staring at me. The only thing I could manage to summon of my vocal chords was, "What the HELL did you just say?"

CHAPTER THREE

The phone was ringing as I unlocked my little apartment door. I heard the usual greeting from my machine.

"Hi you've reached Lily, I'm not home so please leave a message after the beep and I'll get back to you as soon as I can, Bye." Cam was frantic.

"Lily if someone has not heard from you by nine o'clock tonight I am coming down there with the police!" I'd call her later. As I scanned my living room, my eyes found the bag that I had packed last night. Since returning late Tuesday night, I had avoided all phone calls. I couldn't concentrate on classes and I had had to call out of work. I didn't even have the energy to log onto the internet and check my Facebook page. I needed to re-evaluate my life, and I needed to do it without any distractions. I needed to go where no one would find me.

"Well it's off to the farm then, isn't it?" I spoke out loud for the sole purpose of exercising my voice. I probably hadn't said more than a few sentences in three days. I pushed the button on my cell phone that would display the time and date, 3:40p.m. Friday, September 24th.

"For shit's sake!" I yelled at myself for forgetting that it was my mom's birthday. When I looked up I caught a glimpse of my reflection in the framed mirror above my sofa. Dark circles. So I grabbed my weekend bag, purse, cell, and keys and headed out to my Jeep. I needed to hit the Starbuck's on campus before embarking on my hour drive back to Hampstead.

I threw my bag on the back seat, purse on the front seat, dropped my cell in the cup holder, put the key in the ignition, turned it and my Jeep hummed to life. It was ready to take me anywhere my heart desired, or in my case today where I had to go, but first to the York Road coffee house that would make my drive that much easier. I pulled up to the curb, grabbed my wallet, yanked the cell out of the cup holder, and turned the ignition off pulling my keys with me. I had not thought about the will reading since I had gotten back to Towson but my mind just sort of went back there now without my permission as I was walking into my favorite haunt.

"Lily, this is good!" Uncle Dillon said hugging me. Declan came over and put his arm on my shoulder.

"Yeah, sis, think of the parties we can have here!" A couple of my cousins murmured their agreement with D. Morons!

"Look there has to be some mistake, Mr. Hewitt." I pleaded, looking at my dad instead of the old lawyer; my dad was just beaming at me.

"No, no mistake Miss. Moon. Your grandmother and I had this discussion several times and she was always adamant that it had to be you. I need to be going, but I will have the papers sent to you here at your farm by the weeks' end." I physically cringed at those last words 'your farm'. He had his coat hanging over his arm as he started to turn to leave, but turned back to face us all.

"I truly am very sorry about losing Leeny. My God that woman was my favorite client.....and my friend." He rubbed at his eyes again, turned and got in his car pulling away from the farm. I would never think of this farm as mine, its Granny's! RiRi walked over to me.

"Lily, Granny had a reason for leaving the farm to you. I think that she knew that you would keep us all together. That this place would stay the heart of our family." She put her hand in mine and smiled at me. Had RiRi always been this wise?

I hugged everyone in the family, opting to leave my dad until last, telling everyone, "I have to get back to classes and work. I'll talk to you guys tomorrow. I love you." My dad hugged me and walked me to my Jeep.

"Lily I know it feels like a big responsibility but your grandmother has always been an excellent judge of character and if she thought that you could handle this, than you can. I'm so proud of you Sweetheart!" he said. I needed out of here bad!

"Daddy I have to go, I still need to check on Cam, I'll call you when I get home, ok?" My father knew I was serious when I called him Daddy.

"Ok as soon as you get into that apartment, but Lily," he waved his arm at the big house and land that it sat on and said, "this is your home, always has been." I got into my Jeep waving to everyone again driving off of the farm. I rummaged through my purse for my phone. I found it, and called Cam.

I rushed through everything that she had missed and when I had finished all she could say was, "Hmmm, that doesn't surprise me, Lily. I mean about the farm, not all the moonstone jewelry business. I have absolutely no clue what the hell that is all about. But you have always been happiest at the farm." Ugghh was no one going to understand? No, probably not! The farm was Granny's not mine. It would never be a happy place for me again. Not without her there. So I let the subject drop and told Cam, "I'll call you when I get home." She told me she would wait up to make sure that I got to Towson safely. And that was the last time I had spoken to anyone close to me in days.

I felt like I had walked into a wall. I came out of the memory only to find that I had smacked right into some guy! Great! I dropped my wallet and keys, "Shit, I'm so sorry. I wasn't paying attention." I looked at the man who stood up with my wallet and keys in his hand. OMG!! It was the yummy guy I had almost killed from the parking garage. I stood there for a moment unable to speak, looking like a total ditz.

When I finally recovered the use of my voice all I could say was, "Hey, you were at the mall, and the parking garage on Monday, right!" It came out as an accusation instead of a question.

"Yes, that was me." He replied. His voice was so sexy.

"I'm really sorry." I managed to choke out. He handed me the wallet and keys.

"I couldn't take my eyes off of you. You were very happy and then the next moment you looked very sad. Although I must admit you hide your emotions better than anyone I have ever met," he said. Seriously nobody pays attention to me, but he did.

I started stuttering badly, "I...I...I, my grandmother died." Wonderful. I felt like such an idiot. He held his hand out to me and looked directly into my eyes. I met his amazing gaze.

"I'm Mason Shaw." I couldn't take my eyes away from his. They were unlike anything I had ever seen before, emerald green with gold around the edges.

"I'm Lily, umm, Lilyann Moon." I shook his god-like hand. My stomach started acting like I had about a million Monarch butterflies fluttering around in there. "I'm sorry, I have to get going." I blurted out and turned to face the counter. I sounded like I belonged in a mental institution.

"Can I have a large caramel Frappuccino and a large white chocolate mocha latte' please?" I ordered from the barista, paid and waited for my drinks, he was still in the shop waiting to order, I think. My drinks were ready; I grabbed the little disposable tray and turned toward the door.

"It was very nice to meet you, personally, Lily."

I looked back and said, "Yeah, I mean yes, you too, Mason. See you around campus." Wait was he a student here? I don't remember ever seeing him on campus. I didn't have time to find out either and if I was being perfectly honest with myself why would that Adonis-like man want anything to do with me? I acted like an idiotic little child with a schoolgirls' crush! I made my way out to the Jeep, put everything in its place for the drive, and hit the speed dial button for Cam, placing it on speaker. Cam had to be waiting with phone in hand. She answered after only one half of a ring.

"Lilyann Moon, you better have a very, and I mean a very good, reason for ignoring me!" I'd hurt her feelings and she was worried about me, that was obvious.

I had an hour long drive ahead of me, with a lot of explaining to do. "Cam, I'm sorry. I just needed to think, which didn't happen, and I don't know. This is all a lot to take in, but I am very sorry that your feelings were hurt. That was not my intention."

Cam sniffled. "Oh Lily, I have been so worried about you! Just promise me you'll never not talk to me again!" I am a horrible person!

"Cam I promise. How about I pick you up tonight and we go out to a pub? Just a girls' night out, I'm on my way back to the farm, but don't tell anyone yet. I still need some time to think. You can tell them that you have talked to me. But just please don't tell them I'm going to the farm, ok?" Cam hesitated. Something was up with her.

"Lily of course. I promise. I, uh, I need to ask you a question." Yep! Something is definitely up.

"Anything Cam, you know that." I could hear Cam flicking her nails. That was her nervous habit.

"Lily, will you be the baby's godmother?" Was she telling me what I think she was telling me?

"Cam, wait are you....you're...what...pregnant?" I didn't give her a chance to confirm my suspicions. I rattled on. "Oh my God Cam!! Of course, I would be honored! But when did you find out?" Cam and her husband had been trying to have a baby for a couple of months now; she was going to be an incredible mother! My best friend was crying into the phone.

"Lily I found out Tuesday after the viewing. You didn't need anything else on your plate. Plus I knew you were also going to have to deal with your moms' birthday." My mom. After a good forty minutes of baby talk, I couldn't and wouldn't get into my mom just yet. I let Cam in on the Mason meeting earlier as I was still sipping on my yummy caramel frap!

"Wait, Lily so did he give you his number?" I rolled my eyes through the phone.

"No Cam, why would he? I was a babbling idiot and he is a GOD! And to top it off I almost killed him remember."

Cam was my biggest supporter so she proceeded to inform me, "Lily, my God, I can't believe after all this time that I actually have to say the words out loud but honey, you look like a runway model! You're tall, awesome hair, a great chest, and your eyes! What I wouldn't give for your eyes!" Cam giggled. Pregnancy hormones had obviously affected her head!

I finished my coffee just as I pulled up to the farm; thankfully someone had remembered to leave the porch light on. I told Cam I would call her tomorrow, I had to promise on our blood sister oath that I would not just disappear. It was like we were ten again! I grabbed my stuff and walked up the steps to the porch, I noticed a courier package addressed to me propped up against the front door. Huh? I picked it up, and was greeted by Izzy as soon as I got in the door.

"Hey, Miss Attitude, you any better?" She purred at me and ran up the steps. Yep, she's back to normal. I put my bags down in the front room and walked slowly into the kitchen. I turned on the teakettle, and came back through the front room to grab my bags. I snatched up the still unknown package and headed upstairs. I had thought about this while Cam was talking about the baby, and decided that I needed to sleep in Granny's room. It still didn't feel right, but I needed to feel close to her. I grabbed a set of fuzzy pink pajamas out of my bag, and changed my clothes. I found a scrunchie, and pulled my hair into a ponytail. I grabbed the box that had my name on it and, pulled the tab to rip it open. I reached in and slid the contents out onto the bed. I picked up the letter with the attorney's name at the top, and read it to myself. Apparently Granny also had a half million dollar life insurance policy that had been left for the farm. Well, at least the bills would get paid even if I wasn't staying. Mr. Hewitt had transferred the remains of my grandmother's account into a new one with my name on it. He had also deposited the insurance money in the new account. In the paperwork, now lying scattered on the bed, was the deed to the farm now addressed to me, and everything that I needed to access my new checking account, which included a box of checks and a debit card. I put everything in my purse and tossed the box in the wastebasket.

I decided to look around Granny's room, but first I needed to go make my tea. I walked back down stairs with Izzy at my feet. The teakettle was whistling as I got to the kitchen. I went over to the counter where Granny kept the fresh chamomile and scooped out two tablespoons into the steeper. I opened the cabinet above my head and grabbed my favorite mug, put it on the counter, and then I grabbed the honey from the other side of the room and let a teaspoon drizzle into my cup. I put the honey back where it belonged, and went to the stove. I grabbed the kettle pouring the hot water over my chamomile and honey. I turned off the flame, leaving the little stovetop light on for guidance tonight, as I would most certainly need more tea, grabbed a spoon and headed back upstairs.

When I got into Granny's room I shut the door easily, and turned around. Izzy was perched on my grandmothers' bed watching every move that I made. I stared at her vanity. I sat in her chair picking up her hairbrush. It was sterling silver, and part of a set that included a comb, and a mirror. My grandmother had told me a couple of years ago it was a gift from her own grandmother. I ran my fingers over the bristles gently, knowing that the last person who had touched this object was the one person I was missing most in this moment. The tears were already slipping down my face.

On her vanity she had pictures of all of us in beautiful ornamental frames, several perfume bottles, and a glass jar that looked almost like a small vase that held an array of make-up brushes. I sipped at my tea. Mmm… Granny had always told me that chamomile was great for relaxing a person. She was right. Granny's bedroom was amazingly furnished and decorated. She had an antique walnut bedroom set with a queen sized canopy bed. The most beautiful bedding decorated sporadically with light pink roses, centered on the longest wall of the room. The nightstands encased the bed, like two magnificent bookends, that had the most ethereal crystal lamps on them. They cast a soft glow through the room. It made it very easy to sleep in here. I had often slept in bed with granny when I was a little girl, what with me always afraid of every bump in the night, which granny assured me was just the house settling.

Granny had a walk in closet next to the vanity, stocked with her clothes, shoes, purses and coats. I was definitely not ready to go in there. In the opposite corner from the closet she had a long mirror that was encased in the antique walnut. I caught a glimpse of myself; I looked thinner and paler than normal. Great!

"Some runway model I make." I laughed at my own stupidity. Izzy meowed her disapproval at me. I set my mug down on the long dresser, turning around to look at the purring cat on my grandmothers' bed. Out of the corner of my eye I saw a picture that I knew on the tall chest of drawers. I walked over and took the frame from the top of the dresser and sat down on the closest window seat. It was my mom and I on my twelfth birthday, the last one that my mom was alive for. I felt the tears falling harder, and let them.

I whispered, "Happy Birthday Mommy. I hope you and Granny found each other up there. I miss you both so much. How am I supposed to make it here without either one of you?" I kissed the photograph and put it back in its place. I needed tissues.

Something caught my eye outside. I could have sworn I saw…….a man, no it was just an animal. My imagination is at an all-time high right now. Great! Crazyville here I come! When I picked up my mug I turned back to Izzy and she was sitting on top of the cedar chest at the foot of the bed. Rather than setting my tea down again, it had cooled already, I just chugged it. I placed my empty mug on the vanity and went back to the cedar chest trying to open it, but it was locked. I went back over to the vanity searching each drawer, no key. I had always been curious what Granny kept hidden in that thing. Now I have the ability to find out, and I can't find the damn key! After opening a few dresser drawers, to no avail, I kicked the cedar chest in frustration. I regretted it as soon as I felt the pain in my foot! I started jumping up and down holding my toe.

"God damn it all to hell!" I screamed like a banshee. I was shocked that the neighbors weren't banging on the door. Wait, the closest neighbor is a couple of miles away. Okay, not a great thought if someone breaks in the place. Maybe I would call an alarm company tomorrow. Now that my toe was only throbbing, and my deluded thoughts were in check, I went to Granny's side of the bed and decided it couldn't hurt to ask the cat. Okay so maybe my insanity was not under control.

"Izzy, do you know where Granny kept the key to the cedar chest? Okay Lily talking to animals is one thing, expecting a response, you're certifiable girl!" At that moment Izzy started meowing like crazy and walking up the bed towards me. When she got to the nightstand she put her front paws on the book laying there.

"What's wrong kitty?" I started to scratch behind her ear. She began to swat angrily at the book. "Okay, let's move the..." I looked down to see what book it was. "The book of Crystals and Rocks, hmm." When I lifted it up to get a better look, I heard a clink on the floor, and OMG, there was a key. "Holy Shit!"

Wait, did the cat just show me where to find the key? I was in shock! This couldn't be the key, could it? I bent down, and picked it up. Before I could get too far in my thought process, she agilely jumped from the bed and purred by the door.

"I'm coming." I opened the bedroom door, and she ran out. My mouth just hung open. I left the door open for her. I placed the key in the lock and turned it. I heard it click. No way! I practically fell to the floor in front of the chest. I adjusted myself so that I was right in front of the chest, and opened the lid. There was a big book on the very top and it looked super old! The binding was a greenish-black color, and it had a funny smell to it. I lifted it out of the chest. An envelope fell out of it onto the floor. The only thing written on it was Lilyann.

I put the book down beside me and, grabbed the envelope from the floor. I could smell my grandmother, her perfume. I gingerly slid my finger under the tab, and pulled out honest to goodness parchment paper. My eyes zoomed back and forth reading her words.

'My sweet Lily, let me start this letter by telling you how proud I am of you. You will lead the Moons' with grace, strength and love. Our family comes from a long, strong, proud line in Galway, Ireland. Oh my dear, you have no idea what you are capable of. All the good that you children will do. But first if I am gone before my birthday on October thirty first, then there are two issues that you must deal with. First, take a deep breath Lily, I was killed! I did not die of natural causes. I have been keeping the vampires at bay with the wards around the property. Yes I said vampires! Second, the wards are a magical security gate, which vampires can't cross. The bad ones at least. Yes sweetheart there are a few good ones. But the wards will start to wane until they are completely down at midnight on Halloween. You and the rest of the Coven must reinforce them before they fall. If not, every dark vampire will be on the property to kill you. Our blood is strong, and they want it. The book that this letter was in is your Book of Shadows. It has been passed down from the beginning of our line. Your answers lie within, study it, and make them study it. Lily, do you understand what I am telling you? I was a witch and you, your sisters, brother and cousins are all witches. The most powerful coven of witches in all of history. All of our power is with you. Yes, look inside yourself, you are a Witch. You are the most powerful witch in over five centuries Lily. I'm sorry that I can't be with you on this journey my Lilybug. I love you, and know that you can handle this sweetheart. I am with you in Spirit! Blessed Be, Granny.'

The letter fell through my fingers. "Son of a Bitch!"

CHAPTER FOUR

The letter lay in my lap where it had landed after falling out of my hand. I'm a witch. That is totally insane! I flipped through the Book of Shadows, seeing recipes that weren't for food. They were called potions. This one was titled: To Erase One's Memory. Use only herbs harvested during the waning moon, light the cauldron and add one red and one white rose, equal pinches of Chamomile, Black Horehound, Valerian Root and White Sage. Mix potion until it bubbles, when it's ready, add 2 or 3 drops into the drink of the persons' memory you want erased. After they are away from you recite the following spell, 'Hear the words I send out this night. I call to you Goddess with all my might. I call the wind to blow away his memory. Let it be as if he's never met me! Blessed Be!'

"I'm a witch!" I wasn't having any trouble getting my head around this now! It made perfect sense. Everything about Granny screamed witch if anyone was really paying attention. The way she always just knew things. The way she had to pick her herbs at certain times. The statue of a Goddess that she would never talk about because I wasn't old enough yet. The biggest clue should have been the way Granny was able to make people do what she needed them to with just a look, or so I had thought. But it was magick, real magick. I had not really known my grandmother at all. I started flipping through the pages again, there were rituals, potions, spells and ......

"Oh my god! I'm a Witch!" The reality of the letter hit me like a sucker punch to the gut! I sat there on the floor reading through the book for what felt like an eternity until something registered in my head. The vampires were going to come for us and Halloween was a little over a month away.

I jumped up, grabbed my cell and dialed my cousin. Two rings and Riona answered.

"Lil, everyone has been looking," but I cut her off.

"Ri, I'm at the farm and I need everyone here NOW! Can you do that?" Ri giggled.

"Leave it to me. We'll see you soon. Love you." Good! The adults have some explaining to do and they're going to do it tonight!

"Love you too. Hey, I'll call my Dad! Bye." I punched in my dad's number and hit the speakerphone button so I could talk as I changed. He answered a little sleepily.

"Lilyann, where have you been?" I slipped a new shirt on and answered him.

"Sorry dad, I needed.... Dad look I'm at the farm can you bring Cassie, Jessie, and Dekko and come here.... now. I need to talk to you guys!" I called my brother by his Irish nickname so that my father would not hear the malice behind my intent. He perked right up, as I knew he would and let me know that they were headed over immediately. Perfect. Just a few minutes to put the kettle back on and set my stage! I walked over to pick up the book and something caught my eye when the light hit it in the cedar chest. It was Granny's special knife. My heart began to ache for her again. I reached down picking it up gingerly running my fingers over the handle, and stuck it in my jeans pocket smiling to myself. I grabbed my cell, mug and the book.

"I hope I'm making you proud Granny!" I shot up a quick prayer to her and made my way back downstairs.

I walked back into the living room with a fresh mug of hot chamomile after turning on the coffee pot because this was going to be a long night. I stashed the book on the stairs behind me, when I saw the line of headlights pulling up to the farm. They were here, and I was ready. I remembered that I had the pendant on and ran my fingers over the cold stones. They sizzled with electricity under my touch. I couldn't stop myself from giggling.

The entire Moon clan walked into the house with looks of concern on their faces. My dad grabbed me and gave a tight hug.

"Lily are you ok? What's this all about?" I almost felt bad about what my dad, aunts and uncles were getting ready to deal with. Almost.

"I'm ok...well no that's not entirely true, but why doesn't everyone sit down, and I'll explain." I started fidgeting and biting my lip waiting for everyone to find a spot. Cormac spoke up.

"Lilyann we have all been trying to reach you for days...what's going on? Are you in trouble? Is it Mark?" Cormac walked over, and put his arm around my shoulder and continued. "We'll kick his ass!" My cousins were all protective over me. I hugged Cormac around the waist with one arm, still holding my pendant with the other.

"No, no it's nothing like that, but thank you, the sentiment is really sweet." Izzy was now perched on the railing looking over my shoulder. I began my interrogation. I looked right at my father making direct eye contact. "Dad is there anything that you need to tell us about Granny?"

My father fidgeted (his nervous habit, I got it from him). Uncle Donal snapped his head around, looking from me to my father, and back to me. Like he was watching a ping-pong match. If this hadn't been a deadly serious matter it would have been comical. Like I said before, I almost felt bad.

"Lily what are you talking about," was Aunt Brig's response. I never took my eyes away from my father.

"Well, I would like to know if there is anything that any of my aunt's, uncle's or my father would like to tell us about our grandmother. Something that maybe we don't know yet, but perhaps you do?" All of the adults were looking at each other casting nervous glances back and forth. I knew in that moment that they had all known all along. My guilt totally disappeared.

"Well, Daddy anything?" I refused to look anywhere but at him. Cassie spoke up obviously confused.

"Lily what the hell is going on?" I ignored my sister, and turned my back to my family.

"Last chance Daddy!"

Nothing. It became perfectly silent. I grabbed the book and slammed it on the coffee table in front of my father. That made all of the adults scurry like cockroaches when you flip on a light. Except my dad. I heard the sharp intake of air. Ciaran stood up and hurried over to his own father.

"Dad what is it?" I turned my head and watched the future coven's confused faces. I suddenly felt bad for them (not the adults!), this was going to change all of our lives tonight, and I was sure not for the best.

"Lily what the hell is wrong with you? You just about gave Uncle Donal a heart attack by the looks of it!" Braden looked mad. Shannon and Riona scooted over on the floor and began to open the book. That got my Dad's attention.

"NO! Don't touch that book girls!" My dad bellowed, scaring the living daylights out of them by the way they jumped. He rounded on me.

"Lilyann Moon you have no right touching that book! I demand you put it back where your grandmother had it!" This was the first time in my life that my father had raised his voice to me. Something inside of me felt like it was ripping at the seams to get out, and I let it! Good-bye sweet, passive, obedient Lily.

"NO! You told me to accept the fact that Granny left the farm and its contents and responsibilities to me. I didn't want to, but I did! That book belongs to me now...well it belongs to all of us, and they have every right to look at it!" I yelled at him. I could hear the ring of authority in my own voice but was totally shocked when my family jumped. Seven candles lit themselves at that exact moment.

"Holy Shit!" Jess screamed.

My father with fury in his voice said, "Oh my god, you're just like my mother! Your one of them!" I didn't understand why he said that to me.

"I didn't light those candles! I was over.......here." The realization that without my permission or a trained action I had made those candles light. I felt something inside of me, buzzing. Oh man...how did I do that? I reached in my pocket and pulled out the letter that I had already read and handed it to Seamus. He was standing closest to me and told him to read it aloud. When he had finished I had regained some of my composure and turned to my father in a more alarming tone, one of fear said, "You knew all along. You do realize that they're looking for us now, don't you? They killed Granny. They will pick us off one at a time." My father cringed at those words but didn't back down.

"We didn't accept that lifestyle and we are all fine Lily." I searched the eyes of my family and found them all confused.

Ciaran was the first to speak, "Lily, wait a minute, does this really mean that WE are witches?" I just nodded at him while staring at my dad. With that little gesture all hell broke loose! Everyone just started screaming at the same time but nothing was decipherable. I was still trying to figure out how I had lit the candles, but had to push that thought away for later and focus on what my dad had said to me.

Ciaran lifted his sandy blonde head yelling, "Quiet!" Finally everyone fell silent.

"Dad, yes, you guys are fine but you had Granny protecting you. You guys choose a different path and Granny let you have that choice. We don't. Who's going to protect us now that she's gone?" He sat down looking defeated. My dad, the protector, couldn't save us. He had walked away from destiny, and now we were being forced into ours. I walked over sitting next to him on the couch, steadying my voice.

"Dad, according to Granny's letter, the wards that protect us will continually get weaker until they are completely gone. I don't like this anymore than you, but I don't have a choice. I didn't wake up this morning and say Umm…I think I'll be a witch today, and have hordes of hungry vampires try to kill me, and my family. I can't let them die without a fight." I pointed at my confused family. "I won't lose them or you. You guys are all I have left." I sat up straight and looked him in his tear filled eyes, putting it as straight as I could. "Dad we either accept our birth right, and fight or we don't, and die. It's really just that simple." My dad took my hand, and kissed the top of it nodding to all of us.

"They have to defend themselves." My dad looked at his brothers and sisters, who were all now nodding their approval. I was completely caught off guard when Cassie stood up tapping her foot at me.

"Lily for real, what kind of drugs are you on? Witches and Vampires, my ass!" Aidan and Cormac stood up with Cassie and looked at me.

"Come on! Lily this is the most ludicrous thing I have ever heard. You're making a mockery out of our grandmothers' memory!" Cormac accused. I just stood there, rooted to the spot, unable to speak.

Thankfully Declan came to my aid, "You heard the letter! And…and look at my dad. Hell, look at your own father! Does he look shocked or scared?" Everyone turned to look at Uncle Hugh. Uncle Hugh was as white as a ghost…or as white as I had always seen vampires on television, which brought something else to the front of my already crazy mind. I looked at my dad.

"Have any of you ever seen a vampire...I mean how do we know who they are?" My father looked as if he were going to answer when Aidan jumped back up.

"All right, enough! I have heard enough of this bullshit! I'm out of here, who's coming with me?" He headed to the door, after a quick glance around the room Cormac and Cassie followed him out.

Aunt Rae jumped up and came beside me. "No worries, sweetie. Your mom and I had this all figured out before she passed, I'll talk sense into them. But the rest of your coven and you need to get started on protecting us all." She kissed my cheek and she was off. It was clear why Aunt Rae and mom were best friends; they were two peas in a pod. I smiled in spite of myself.

"Good, they're too stuck up to be witches!" Riona giggled. Great, a third of my family thinks that I'm on drugs or drinking or crazy, perhaps a combination of the three. Another third of my family doesn't want us to fight for our lives, and the remaining third thinks that this is some fun after school activity!

"Listen to me carefully! This is not a game, there are real vampires out there and they want to kill us!" I spoke each word clearly and carefully as if I were talking to a room full of three years olds, which sobered everyone up fast! "And from what little I read in that book, we're going to need a full coven, that's all twelve of us! We need them! We need to figure this ward stuff out and after we have an initiation ritual to a goddess I have no clue about, try to activate our......power or powers or whatever it is that we have? And we only have until Halloween at midnight to figure all this out!" I said as I rubbed my temples. I was only twenty-one, but I was working on a major migraine and a nervous breakdown tonight!

My cousins and I stayed up all night long going over the book trying to find anything that would help us. I was still in shock. I couldn't believe that our heritage had been kept from us, and now we had to fight to save it. I had no idea whether or not we would be able to become the witches we were destined to be, but we had to try. Our lives depended on it! A few of the adults stayed just to get us coffee, and help in any way that they could. I think they were trying to repair the damage done to all of us with the huge secret. It was a start. We were able to fully understand the moonstone jewelry mystery. At least I knew that sitting through that will reading truly had a purpose! Granny had used one large piece of consecrated moonstone to make all of our jewelry. So when we came together as one it did as well. According to the book it's more powerful together as are we. Finding that piece of information made us go on a search throughout the house looking for books on herbs, crystals and divination. Riona found them on a bookshelf behind her from another room.

When I asked her how she knew where they were, she just giggled and said, "I have no idea, I just knew." I would definitely be reading the Book of Shadows, or as we were calling it the BoS, for any clues about how Ri did that. During our hunt we had learned that the knife in my pocket was actually called an Athame, and it had been passed down through the generations of Moon witches. We had also found Granny's cauldron, ceremonial bowls, and altar. My aunts and uncles were exhausted from the evening's events so they went home with promises to return helping us as much as they could. We found the initiation ritual spell which was going to take a lot of work to prepare for. Then we found the complex potion, spell and crystal combination for the wards.

My head was spinning! We had so much to learn, and only five weeks to get ourselves ready. When the sun had started to come up everyone started falling asleep on their feet. I told them to lie down for a couple of hours before we delved back into our search. While they were sleeping I had found something interesting in the book that I would need to share as soon as they were all awake about our powers. I had just poured my fifth cup of coffee, and sat back down at the breakfast nook with the book when the back door opened. Cassie, Aidan and Cormac came in looking ashamed. My sister began.

"Lil, look we're sorry for the way that we acted last night. Aunt Rae told us everything, but you have to admit it does sound crazy when you first hear it." She looked around for help from the other two. All at once they said, "We're in!" I took a sip of my coffee trying to compose myself, because one of the many things that I had learned last night, but had kept to myself until this moment, was how to trigger my elemental power. We each had an element that we could wield for protection and mine was fire.

"You guys do not have to apologize to me for your feelings." I looked at the fireplace in the kitchen, and flicked my wrist towards it watching the three faces of my family jump in shock. A full roaring fire sprang to life, and I continued. "But for our ancestors, for the witches that came before us, for Granny you will respect our Wiccan heritage!" I hadn't noticed the audience that had formed in the doorway until I heard their screams of delight at my instance of magick. Declan was right there with a witty response.

"Awesome Sis! You're going to come in mighty handy for campfires!" Everybody started laughing. After that there were no more questions about what we were. The only answers left to find were how to use all of our powers, how to strengthen the wards, how to identify and kill vampires, and how to protect ourselves.

"Alright, now according to the book you have to let everything go, accepting who you are, and focus your energy on your element." I told everyone what I found out about activating each of our elemental powers. Cassie was actually the first after me to activate her element of earth. She made the floor shake so badly that I had to hold onto the counter! Maybe doing this inside was a bad idea. My grandmothers' dishes, knick-knacks, and books started falling everywhere!

"Cassie, pull your element back inside of you," I yelled holding the plates so they wouldn't break. The house stilled, and I put the plates back on the shelf.

After that we decided to work outside sparing the house from further damage. Ciaran grabbed candles from the living room for the fire users to practice with, and we all went outside. The best thing that I can say about our first attempt of working with our magick is that we were all able to call the elements, and they answered. We had lots of practice ahead of us! We spent the remainder of the weekend doing just that, and going through the book, cupboards, closets and old trunks searching for all the crystals, herbs, and anything else that we would need for our task. We were seriously going to need to learn how to do this, but first things first. Initiation, and then cast new wards! Cassie found most of the crystals that we needed for the ritual.

"K, I found three clear quartz, two rose quartz, one moldavite, one lapis lazuli and one obsidian, now we still need a Selenite, Mandrake root, Valerian root, and Witch Hazel." With preparations for our ritual underway, and everyone onboard, I had other things to tend too.

I needed to go back to Towson to make the necessary arrangements that were sure to cause a fight between my father and me. I needed to take a semester off from school, work and anything else that could pull my attention from learning the craft. My life had become too complicated to worry about something that wouldn't even matter if I didn't survive this ordeal. I didn't feel like myself. Last week I would have run screaming in the opposite direction, today I was readying myself to face this threat head on.

I left my coven at the farm, telling them that I would call them later, and headed back to the college town that had become my home. The hour drive flew by. I hadn't really listened to the radio in the past week, but before I knew it I was jamming to everything that hit the stations. Singing to the top of my lungs, smiling, but my caffeine withdrawal was seriously on DEFCON 5. I sought out my little coffee spot. I swear my nose could've gotten me there while my eyes were blindfolded. I parked, grabbed my purse and headed to the door. I was looking down so I didn't see him at first, but when the door opened he greeted me.

"Hi Lily, it looks as though we have the same coffee habit." I giggled, not wanting to sound like a total moron, as I looked up.

"Hey, Mason right. I'm sorry about the other day." I was smiling, again captivated by his eyes. Something about those eyes made me feel safe, and terrified all at the same time. He smiled in return.

"Could I persuade you to join me for a few minutes? We are in a coffee shop?" I needed to get moving, but I wanted to know this God! There goes my whole getting rid of things that could distract me from the craft! Ah hell! I nodded my head, and we stepped up to the counter together, but before I could say a word he was ordering for both of us.

"A large caramel Frappuccino and two large white chocolate mocha lattes. The beautiful young lady enjoys one hot and one cold coffee." I just looked at him biting my lower lip, how did he remember that? Oh my Goddess! That is totally killer sweet! But really he had only been in the coffee shop with me once, and he knew my order? Mark and I had dated seriously for over a year and he couldn't tell you that I liked coffee, period! Mason paid for our coffee. I tried to give him money for mine, but he looked insulted.

"How about a seat at the window?" Mason asked. I nodded again, unable to speak yet without a fit of hysterical giggles.

He pulled out a chair and waited until I understood that it was for me. He is amazing, so why the hell is talking to me? "Thank you," I said sitting in the chair as he pushed it in. He was smiling at me. Those eyes…I was biting my lip again.

"I'm happy to see that you are in much better spirits Lily. And I'm very sorry about your grandmother." Mason and I sat across from each other, as he helped me with my coffee. How in the hell am I supposed to speak when in the presence of this incredible man? Breathe, Lily. I reached for the frap and took a healthy pull on my much needed caffeine supplement. I looked up, and found his eyes searching me. Damn, I needed to speak.

"I'm really glad that we ran into each other again, well…. not literally again. I just meant that it's great that we're able to talk. I'm sorry I babble a lot when I'm…… Do you go to school here at Towson?" I took a very deep breath gathering my thoughts and pushing oxygen to my brain! He laughed at me slightly.

"My, you do babble, but you make it look adorable. And if talking constantly is your only flaw then I think we'll get along just fine." I bit my lip, while giggling this time and cut it.

"Damn it! I always do that, my lip biting habit is worse than my babbling problem." I sucked on my lip to stop the bleeding. He continued to stare at me with a look of intense concentration that only lasted a second. His expression had changed so fast that I was sure that I had imagined it. He was grinning at me when he next spoke.

"I would love to take you out sometime if that's something you would be interested in. In this day in age a woman can never be too careful, so instead of asking you for your number I'm going to give you my cell number with the truest of hopes that you will indeed call." He handed me a slip of paper with his phone number written on it. I didn't understand why he would be interested in me, but I'm totally calling him! We talked for another half of an hour, about random stuff like my grandmother, the farm, my family, school, and my BFF Camden.

I glanced at my watch, "Shit!" I jumped up. "Mason, I'm really sorry, I have to get going, talking to you is so easy I lost track of time. But I swear I will call, would...... would tomorrow night be too soon?" I asked in my flirty voice. Holy Hell, I was flirting! After clumsily gathering my things, he opened the door for us, and I notice a totally killer looking ring he was wearing with a kind of bird on it. "That is a really neat ring," I said to Mason.

He winked at me, and said, "Maybe someday I'll tell you the story behind it." I smiled as he walked me to my Jeep. He is a total gentleman. "By the way tomorrow night would be perfect," he said as he left to go home or school or where ever it is that he was going. I still hadn't figured that out yet. He was smiling at me as I pulled out of my spot. I didn't know how, but he was definitely going to be mine! Wait, when did I get so confident?

When I got back to my apartment it was so quiet. I stood in the middle of my tiny living room with my overnight bag in my hand, feeling incomplete. "I don't belong here anymore," I said, my voice was again confident because it was the first thing that crossed my mind. I practically ran to my bedroom dumping my dirty clothes in my hamper, reaching for a fresh pile to replace them. Not hesitating I called the coven. I needed to get moved back to the farm A.S.A.P! I had already had this conversation with them before leaving the farm.

On the drive back to the farm all I could think about was Mason, his lips, those eyes and for the love of all that is holy I wanted to see if his chest was as hot without his shirt! My conscious was berating me for having those thoughts but I told that little part of my head to shut the hell up! He was hot! When I pulled up to the farm it finally felt like home again. Nothing could wipe that goofy smile off of my face except my father, who just happened to be pacing on the porch when he caught site of me. Great! This is not how I wanted this to happen, but I'm a big girl now and needed to handle this like an adult.

"Hey dad, what are you doing out here? It's too cold, let's go inside." I tried to turn to walk in but he gently grabbed my wrist.

"Lilyann, can I have a word with you out here? Everyone else is inside, and I don't want to have this conversation in front of them." I could see the restraint that he was attempting, so I put on my most innocent face pushing the thought of Mason to the back of my mind.

"Sure Dad, is everything ok?" He made his I already know what you're doing face.

"Lily are you sure this is the right decision for you? You fought so hard to get into a good school, and get away from here." My answer came to my lips without any thought.

"This is where I belong dad. Granny protected us, she kept our magick going making sure we were safe. Now she's gone physically, but her spirit is here, and I need to be close to it, so I can protect us now. It's our responsibility now to keep ourselves, and everyone else, safe. That's what I want. All of my life I have tried to find where I fit in the grand scheme of things. Now I know, and it makes me happy, actually ecstatic! Stop worrying and come inside. You can help me get moved back home. Just think about it Dad, you get to have your little girl back. You can't run away from family."

That brought a little smile to his face. Well... it was a start.

CHAPTER FIVE

All in all it only took six hours with my family's help to move everything that I owned into trucks and head home. Wow! Who would have thought a week ago that I would be able to refer to the farm as home? Certainly not me. Things can change in a heartbeat and I still didn't know how many of those I had left. The girls and I had everything washed and put away with in less than four hours. Cam was just leaving for the night.

"Lily it's so good to be able to drive five minutes to get to you again!" Her smile was genuine and it set off her hazel-green eyes.

"I'm really glad to be back. What's wrong Cam! Look at me!" Her face had gone stark white and she was staring off in the direction of the barn, trembling! She finally turned her head slowly towards me rambling about seeing my mom and Granny.

"What?! Cam, no you couldn't have seen...let's get you home. I think that your hormones are getting the better of you again."

I didn't believe that. If Cam said that she saw something, than she did! However, there are very few certainties in my life and one of those devastating facts is that my mother and grandmother were very much dead. I wouldn't let Cam drive herself home, and she wouldn't let me drive so we met in the middle calling Luke. He arrived at the farm a few minutes later. Cam had told him what she thought that she had seen. He refused to leave me at my home alone until he checked it out. Luke had become like another cousin to me! He decided that my land was secure. They left her car behind till tomorrow. She and I needed to talk about this but tonight wasn't the right time. She was pregnant and needed her rest. Now that I was alone I had a phone call to make.

I grabbed my cell phone from the kitchen counter and dialed the number that I had memorized already. My bravery was starting to fail me, I almost hung up the phone. Goddess! I needed to hear his voice, and I did on his machine. 'You have reached the voice mail of Mason Shaw please leave a message.'

I was completely tongue tied and started babbling, "Hi Mason, this is Lily...uh...Lilyann Moon, we met at the coffee shop and..." Beep! That damn machine hung up on me! I tossed the phone on the counter and turned the teakettle on. What the hell was I thinking? Obviously he wouldn't answer when I called, he was beautiful, and I was not. I had gotten my hopes up that I would hear from Mason again. I had allowed myself to believe that he was actually interested in me. I needed to call Ciaran so that we could try to figure out where we could get our hands on the rest of the herbs, and crystals for our ritual, but the phone rang, nearly giving me a heart attack. I grabbed my cell and answered my tone a little abrasive, "Hello?" I instantly regretted it.

"Hi Lily, it's Mason. I'm sorry, I couldn't get to the phone before it went to voicemail." The goofy smile plastered on my face was so huge I was sure he could hear it.

"No. There's no reason for you to apologize Mason, I'm sure you were busy," I said biting my lip, and twirling my hair around my finger.

"I'm so glad that you called me tonight. I was afraid that you didn't like me." Wait…he was joking right?

"You can't be serious, of course I like you. You're funny, smart, handsome, and a total gentleman." Okay calm down, maybe he really was into me. "You must be busy studying or um…please don't think that I'm being rude or nosy, but do you go to TSU?" I had to know.

There was a moment of silence before he replied, "I pop in and out of the art department sporadically, but in the recent weeks I have become a fixture, I'm sure that you've seen me Lily, because I have certainly seen you, and all of the guys watching you." Whoa he's noticed me?

"What guys Mason? Nobody notices me, I'm way to plain." I giggled as if this were obvious.

"You, Lilyann Moon are far from plain. The way your eyes sparkle when you're excited, the way you babble when you're nervous and for me especially the way your hair falls in your face just the right way. Or the cute little way that you bite your lower lip when I talk to you." I think that I'm talking to an angel.

"Thank you," was all I could say without basically throwing myself at him through the phone!

"What about that dinner?" he said softly, and without hesitation my mouth opened and the words tumbled out.

"I'm game, what did you have in mind and when?" Holy Shit! Again with this new confidence? He laughed that soft airy way of his that was now becoming a wonderfully normal sound to me.

"Tomorrow night around seven, I'll pick you up at your apartment?" Oh crap!

"Mason, I…uh…I moved back to my Granny's…. I mean my farm. I could meet you somewhere." He actually sounded relieved. But why? I was farther away from him now. Mason calling my name brought me out of the conversation I was having with myself.

"Lily, I don't mind at all picking you up and bringing you home afterwards. Two things though, I need the address and wear something sexy, just not too sexy. I really don't want to have to kill someone on our first date for trying to steal my girl." Ahhhh yep I've died and gone to Heaven!! He actually called me his girl!

"Ok Mason, see you tomorrow."

After Mason and I hung up I called all the girls, even the aunts! At the crack of dawn the troops all rolled in. We had to pick the right dress, sweater, shoes, purse, jewelry and everything else that I would need to make me look the part of Masons' date. This was going to take a lot of work on everyone's part. Aunt Brig had me take a shower so they would have a clean canvas to work with. Jessie found an aromatherapy treatment for nerves in the BoS. She set everything up in my bedroom.

"Lily just lay back and let the smell calm you down!" I did as I was told. Riona put some sort of white cream on my face, and said that it would make my skin flawless. I closed my eyes, and someone put slices of cucumbers on my closed lids.

"Are all of these things really necessary?" I asked. I heard giggling coming from every direction. Apparently I was a hot mess, and my family was just too nice to tell me. Awesome. I finally started to relax. I could smell rose, cinnamon, and chamomile weaving its magickal spell all around me. I didn't know if what I experiencing was real. I was enchanted by all of the magickal smells, and feelings. It was amazing at first, and then, "Ouch!"

I sat bolt upright and was eye to eye with my aunt Rae and a bowl full of hot wax.

"What the hell is that?" I half screamed, and half laughed. My hands found the throbbing areas above my eyes.

"We waxed your eyebrows," Aunt Cathleen said smiling. Oh Goddess. I had to check the mirror!

"Holy crap! Waxing is more painful, but totally effective!" Cassie gave me a manicure and a pedicure. She painted my nails a dark purplish-red color. It was hot! Riona pulled my hair into a soft bun with Granny's pewter and diamond pin that aunt Rae found. It let little pieces just naturally fall out in all the right spots. Cam did my make-up. My skin looked like it had been airbrushed. She gave my eyes the smoky, dewy look. Had my eyes always been this bright? I had the perfect iridescent lipgloss. I had picked it up on my last trip to the mall with Riona. My youngest sister had a bottle that she sprayed all over me causing my skin to glisten. Shannon picked a killer halter dress in shimmering black, holding it up for me to step into. I filled the dress in with my body and aunt Brig held up a pair of heels, lace up the calf black heels. My amulet set perfectly at my cleavage and I knew that my magick was all around me, adding its own little touch of fire. I had taken a moment to admire in the mirror what my family had created. I couldn't believe the reflection I was seeing, a beautiful version of myself. Everyone cleared out at six thirty and made me swear I would give major details in the morning.

I met Mason at the front door after two knocks and welcomed him into my home. He reached for my hand and kissed it.

"My, my, my let me see what I have here," he said, giving me a gentle twirl. As we faced each other the smile emanating from him told me what I needed to know, but that didn't stop him from voicing his opinion.

"Lily, you are breathtaking........ I am not usually at a loss for words but...being in the presence of an Angel has rendered me speechless." I was biting my lower lip from his compliment when he leaned in giving me a soft little kiss. Amazing! He reached for my black knit sweater on the arm of the chair and offered me his hand, which I took without hesitation, beaming. I didn't care where we were going as long as I was with him, but I still asked.

"So...what do you have planned for us this evening?" He was leading me out of the house when Izzy jumped up on the porch hissing, and then purring at him. "Izzy what is wrong with you silly cat?" Mason reached down and scratched the top of her head, and then she jumped down. Before she had ran off I could've sworn I saw Mason nod at her like she was telling him something and he understood? With everything strange going on around here lately, I would file that little quirk away for later. "You must be really good with animals, because Izzy doesn't like strangers."

He just gave me that dazzling smile and said, "Well Miss Moon I am really good at a lot of things and this evening I hope to illustrate that to you." I pulled the door shut and we were off.

We arrived at Phillips in Baltimore's Inner Harbor. "Reservations for Shaw," he spoke to the host without taking his eyes off of me and I blushed big-time! As we were being lead to our table I noticed a few men staring at me, and the way he rested his arm around my waist let me know that he had also noticed. This was totally a first for me! Dinner was incredible. Maryland crab cakes are the best! The Chardonnay was perfectly chilled, and I was enjoying another sip when the waiter came back to the table with the check that Mason had requested. He paid, and we made our way out of the restaurant.

When we were outside something inside of me just had to feel his lips against mine again now. He was holding my hand, and I turned into him. I reached my free hand behind his neck pulling his lips down towards mine. When they met it was like an explosion went off inside of me, warm, sensual, and familiar. Those lips were my lips to kiss, and only mine! Mason kept hold of our intertwined hands and with his free hand reached down pulling me even closer to him. It felt like we were one. This kiss continued for a few minutes longer. The passion between us was totally palpable to anyone, but to me this was new. Mark had never kissed me like this, and I in return had never initiated a kiss between him and me. What I was feeling for Mason was deeper, spiritual, passionate and primitive! How could I have fallen so fast for him? When we finally started to come up for air, he started giving me gentle little kisses on my lips, my cheeks, and my forehead.

I looked up into his eyes, "That was....I don't know." A worried look crossed his face, but before he could say anything. "It was perfect!" I leaned in to give him another little kiss. "I've never felt this way about anyone, it's like you've known me, my entire life." I looked down and blushed at how corny I sounded but his index finger found my chin and tilted my head up.

"I feel the exact same way Lily. Please believe me." And he kissed me again before laughing. "So now that we are officially on our way to being a couple, I am taking you dancing!" The sound of his laugh filled my heart until I thought that it would explode, but it didn't! He refused to let me walk the couple of blocks necessary to Lux Nightclub, so we headed to the parking lot to retrieve his car.......Whoa!! I have to say at this point that I had been too preoccupied by the chemistry between us to even know what kind of car he had! It's shiny, black and very expensive looking and with my extent of vehicle knowledge being about Jeeps, my question came out a little squeaky and awed.

"Mase, what kind of car is this?" He opened my door and I slid in. He leaned down. "It's an Aston-Martin V12 Vantage. Do you like it?" I could only nod, and then he laughed and kissed me. Like I said I don't know much about cars but this car I had heard of from all of my male relatives! Very expensive and very fast!!

Before we had even gotten to Market Place the music was pumping. The thumping club beat that was filling the night was amazing. I felt like Lux couldn't handle what was going on between Mason and I right now, but we were getting ready to find out! I grabbed my ID out of my purse as Mason held out an expectant hand. Mason took my ID and when we got to the entrance he flashed the bouncer both cards. When we walked in the same song was still playing, and playing loud! I loved it! The neon strobe lights worked the room deliberately finding a mass of gyrating bodies. I hadn't been here in a few months, whenever the gang came I never danced, everyone said I was great but I totally disagreed. They were my friends and family, they had to say that, right? Mason found an empty little table and I sat on the stool.

He leaned over me, kissing me, then whispered in my ear, "What would you like to drink Angel?" I smiled at him.

"You pick I trust your judgment." I stole another quick kiss before he headed off to the bar. I kept thinking to myself 'what if he asks me to dance?' That's when the butterflies started in my tummy again. Funny, I only felt insecure when he walked away. He caught my eye heading back to the table and OMG! I am so lucky. And my luck continued because just then my favorite song came pulsing through the speakers. The DJ had remixed it, so now it was a longer, sexier version. Mason handed me a shot glass that held a clear liquid, and a Long Island Ice Tea. I grinned at him.

"How did you know I love Long Islands and what is that a shot of?" He took a drink from his glass.

"I am drinking Irish whiskey, my drink of choice, and you are having a shot of vodka. And to answer your other question, I just took a guess. I am glad I choose correctly, now my lovely take the shot." He arched his eyebrow waiting for me to comply. I did and followed it with a drink of my Long Island. He looked at me with this devilish smile.

"Good, now we're going to dance." Uh-oh!

"Mase, I can't dance." He stared into my eyes not blinking or anything.

"But you'll dance with me, won't you? This is your song."

I rose from the stool, letting my sweater fall off of my shoulders, and down my arms in one graceful movement. I laid my covering on the seat that I had just vacated and felt the beat of the music start to move through me. I stood in front of him, taking the hand that he held out for me. I noticed nothing but Mason, and the way my body wanted to perform for him and only him as he led me out onto the dance floor.

Standing face to face I reached up putting one hand on his chest, and started to seductively circle his chiseled body. I was brushing my fingertips from his chest, around to his back, ending in the same spot that I had begun my little dance. I reached up, and pulled the pin from my hair and my brown curls tumbled down to the middle of my back somehow still framing my face. I started to move my hips to the beat. I ended up purposely with my back to his chest and let my body wiggle against his, going downward and back up. At this point I realized that all eyes were on us, and I didn't care. I was singing to the song and Mason had his mouth on my neck, gently kissing that receptive little spot. I felt like I was losing control of myself from his touch.

His hands were so fast that I didn't know what the hell was happening until I heard Mark's voice yell, "What the hell are you trying to do Lily be the town whore!"

Mason had seen what I had just spotted. Mark was coming towards me, aggression written all over his persona. With one arm Mason managed to get me safely behind his body, out of harm's way, with the other hand he struck Mark in the center of his chest sending him flying through a few dancers! Marks' body slammed back first into the side of the bar. Mason looked at my frightened face.

"Lily we have to go!" With that he had gathered our things and had me by the arm heading for the car that would certainly get us out of there at top speed. My mind raced in drunken haze, I kept seeing Mark fly through the crowd like he was part of a really bad circus act! Who gave him the right to berate me anyway? I was not his girlfriend anymore! He had always treated me as if I was just there for his convenience anyway! Why should he act any differently tonight? I stole a glance at Mason, and found him watching me.

"Are....are you ok Lily?" Of course I'm ok. I should speak though.

"I'm fine. Thank you for standing up for me, but it wasn't necessary. I should probably get home." I couldn't look into his glorious eyes, afraid of what I would find there. I looked up as we were pulling over on route 795, which meant that he had gotten us there in like ten, fifteen minutes tops! That drive should have taken at least forty minutes. Damn this car is fast!

"Lily I'm sorry that I hurt him because I see now that it hurts you." He just stared at me. "I do understand if you no longer want to see me." At this I started laughing hysterically!

"Mason I was upset, but not because you protected me, and certainly not because HE was hurt! All night long you've called me Angel, and suddenly it's back to Lily." I admit I pouted slightly. He leaned over and kissed me. "Mason, you'll be in trouble." I left it as a statement because that's exactly what is was. There would be consequences for his actions tonight. He tilted my chin up so that we were looking into each other's eyes.

"Lilyann, I will deal with whatever happens, as long as you are safe." He was leaning in to me as his cell phone rang angrily! He looked at the caller ID and reluctantly answered. "I thought that I might hear from you tonight Inspector MacQuarie."

CHAPTER SIX

We pulled up to the farm and Mason helped me out of his car. My pounding head was spinning. To top it off I felt sick to my stomach. Great! Stressful situations always bring me out of drunken good time.

"Let me carry you Angel." Masons' hypnotic voice helped ebb away the pain for a moment.

"No, I can walk," I said hopefully, smiling. The truth was I was terrified that I was going to barf on him. He let me walk as far as the steps, but then I almost tripped over my own heeled foot. So he scooped me up, saving me from a trip to the ER, and much humiliation. With the heavy burden in his arms Mason had gotten me into the house, and laid me gently on the sofa, kissing my forehead. Goddess, if Granny was here she would make me her "special" tea for a hangover. It had Pennyroyal, Chamomile, Spearmint, White Willow Bark and Lavender. She called it "the party kids' tea" which was a nice way of saying that sometimes the Moons' could drink!

"How about I make you some tea, I know a really good recipe for hangovers. It consists of a lot of the herbs that you told me that your grandmother had planted." Mason was smiling and my mind was a little slow, after all it was still spinning. Mason had me point him to the kitchen, and I laid my head back down closing my eyes. Just as everything was starting to settle down, the pounding in my head started to reverberate in the room. No that wasn't my head, there was a banging on the front door.

"C'mon Mason laddy I'm waiting." I started to get up but Mason came in.

"Lay down Angel, I'll handle this, your tea is almost ready." He reached for the door and opened it to a tall, stocky older man. "Inspector MacQuarie, thank you for meeting me out here. I didn't want to leave Lily alone right now." Mason walked over and sat next to me on the couch.

Inspector MacQuarie looked at me and said, in a Scottish brogue, "Ay so this is the lass that has caused yet another of your messes for me to clean up." I jumped up, head spinning and all, and stamped my foot at the Inspector.

"Yes I am the reason that you have to clean up another one of........wait Mason how many messes has he had to clean up for you?" I stood there with my hand on my hip, tapping my toe as the whole room spun in front of my eyes. Mason stood up next to me and tried to get me to sit down again but I looked at Inspector MacQuarie. "Inspector... I'm sorry what was it again?" The older man gave me a searching look and spoke.

"Lass, you may call me Duncan, I'm really not that formal with Mason." That deflated me a little.

"Well Duncan, it was my ex-boyfriend's fault really and I'll tell you whatever you need to know." I kind of leaned into Mason then, feeling really dizzy. Mason sat me back on the couch and motioned for Duncan to follow him.

"I'll take care of everything Angel. Just lay here and rest. I'll bring back your tea." He kissed my forehead and walked into the kitchen with the Inspector. I heard their whispers but nothing else because the jackhammer in my head was going to town again. I couldn't focus on anything. A few minutes later both men came back in the room. Mason had my tea and helped me sit up.

"Drink this love. It will help." I obeyed and after a few sip's my headache and nausea were finally gone and the room was staying still. Thank the Goddess!

Inspector Macquarie assured me that Mark would live, Mason would be in no trouble and that if he needed to reach me he knew where to find me. The best part was when Mason told the Inspector, "I'll be with Lily quite a bit so if you need me you'll likely find me here." After Mason walked Duncan out, he came back and helped me upstairs.

"I'll stay till you fall asleep love." I laid my head on my pillow, still fully dressed and started to drift off to sleep. The last thing I remember is a poem about an angel or a bird?

I woke up to my family's yells, "Lilyann Moon where are you? We want details!" I sat up. Shit! I was still in my halter dress.

"I'm getting in the shower! I'll be down in a few minutes! Turn on the coffee, please." I raced around, brushed my teeth and got into the shower. When I got out I yanked a brush through my hair and tossed my wet curls into a ponytail. I grabbed a pair of my designer jeans, and my favorite Aran sweater that I had gotten on our last family trip to Galway. I put them on, slipped my feet into my Ugg's slippers and headed downstairs.

"Well, Lil spill. What happened?" Ri was bouncing out of her chair. I headed to the kitchen, I needed coffee. Ciaran, mocking all of the girls, ran into to the kitchen and perched himself on the breakfast nook and in a totally fake girls' voice spoke.

"Yeah Lily! Is he a dish? Did he open the car door for you? Did he pay for dinner? C'mon we are waiting!" I smacked him with a tea towel, giggling myself.

"You do that really well! Have you been getting lots of practice?" I grabbed my coffee and sat down at the table, took a sip and answered them. "Yes he was a perfect gentleman! We went to Phillips and then we went to Lux Nightclub and then..."

I was saved from finishing that statement when Cormac walked into the kitchen and announced, "It's a good thing your new boyfriend took care of Mark, because I'm ready to kill him! Randy was at Lux's last night and called me this morning. He told me everything." Cormac walked over to me, "I like your new guy already!" He smiled at me. After a half an hour of explaining everything to everyone else and trying to keep all of my male cousins and my brother calm enough to not finish what Mason had started last night, there was a knock at the front door. Cassie came running back in from the living room.

"OMG Lily, I think Masons' here!"

I walked into the living room and opened the door to those amazing eyes and lips. I leaned forward and kissed him. It was a small kiss, but the electricity was still there.

"I'm happy to see you feeling better Angel." He took my hand and we walked into the kitchen where my family was trying to act nonchalant about Mason and me. "Everyone this is Mason, my...my...." I was fumbling horribly at how to phrase this. Mason spoke up.

"I am Mason Shaw, Lily's new boyfriend and hopefully her last." I didn't think he could take my breath away again but he just had. I was beaming! Ri, Shan, Cassie and Jessie were giggling. Everyone was watching Declan. He had a sour look on his face. Oh great! My family waited with baited breath. Then my younger brother smiled, walked over and shook Masons' hand.

"I like you already brother, after hearing about what that asshole said about my sister and how you handled him!"

After that Mason was just accepted. The boys all went outside to fawn all over the Aston-Martin and the girls stayed inside. We talked while we made lunch for everyone.

"He has the most incredibly full lips Lily. They're awesome!" Shannon said. I had to agree. When I kissed his billowy lips it sent shockwaves throughout my body! I nodded my head and knew that my cheeks had to be red as a rose. Riona came over and stood next to me while I sliced apples.

"So cousin is his chest as good without the shirt?" I almost sliced my finger open! Leave it to Riona to ask something like that!

"Well Ri to be totally honest I don't know, I haven't seen him without a shirt." I bumped Rionas' shoulder and reminded her to stir the tomato soup. Cassie was at the stove mulling cider.

"Lil, he seems really sweet." I winked at my sister. We had prepared a yummy lunch: grilled cheese sandwiches, tomato soup, apple slices with caramel sauce and hot mulled cider. Jessie called the guys in. We really needed to work on the ritual, but no one was in the mood to talk about it and honestly this was so not something I was even remotely ready to tell Mason. What if he thought I was a freak and ran away?

"A kiss for your thoughts?" Mason wrapped me in his arms and held me tight. It was such a secure feeling. I tilted my head up, kissing him gently.

"Just thinking how nice this is and how I hope that it never ends." I put my arms around him and snuggled my head in the crook of his neck.

"It will not." He reached up and rubbed his hand across my back comfortingly and reassuringly. Where had all of my new found confidence gone? I will not become a clingy girlfriend!

An hour later my boyfriend was getting ready to leave. "Mason it was really nice to meet you," Ciaran said while shaking his hand. I walked him out.

"Well I think everyone in there absolutely adores you! I also think that Liam is planning a spring wedding for the three of you." I said giggling. He gave me a questioning look. "Oh I'm sorry..." I was coughing from the deep continued laughter. "Yes the three of you. You, Liam and the Aston!" He grabbed me around the waist and pulled me to him.

"You are much more appealing to me." And then he let his lips meet mine. I swear even though it was October, and a late afternoon chill was making it frigid, things were definitely heating up around here! We ended our kiss and he promised to call me later. After he pulled away I walked back into the house and was greeted by my brother.

"Lily, Mason is totally cool. He knows everything about cars! We all voted and we dig your boyfriend!" Declan said standing next to me so I turned to him.

"So glad that you all approve!" I giggled a little more, sure my life was stressful, but whose isn't? I had Mason in my life now. He was everything that I could have ever dreamed of and so much more, but his best attribute was by far the fact that he human! Not a drop of paranormal to be found around him. That thought gave me such a content feeling. Now it was time for the coven to get down to work. Thankfully Seamus had the good sense to turn on the radio. Music has always helped me think more clearly. We were all in different little groups working on things for the ritual. My task was getting the spell and the hand movements down.

"Ciaran, I'm not sure that I've got this yet. What does the book say I do for the first verse again? Ciaran!" My cousin wasn't paying attention to me at all. He was glued to the book. Something had his attention. I tapped his leg with my foot.

"Oh. Lily, I'm sorry. Did you read this part about before the ritual? How the coven needs to elect a leader and what that leader needs to wear during the ritual? That dress has a slit all the way up the leg!" I sat down next to Ciaran and started reading where he pointed in the book.

'Lily, when you have told the others it is now time that you all elect a leader. They must all agree. Call the corners, cast a circle and each must pledge their loyalty to that leader. My sheath is in my closet along with the diadem, ceremonial cuff and garter. I presume that you are already in possession of my Athame. The initiation ritual has to take place the night before Halloween, then and only then, will you be able to strengthen the wards on Halloween. I'm sorry that I am not there to help you all. I believe in my young and powerful Moon Coven! Make your Granny proud! Love Always.'

"For shit's sake! Can this get any harder?" I whined. Ciaran and I gathered everyone together and read Granny's entry from the book.

"Sis the odds keep stacking up against us, maybe we should just run for the hills," Declan said in a joking tone, but he was just voicing what all of us were thinking and feeling to different degrees.

"No, we will not run! We are the most powerful, untrained witches in the history of time! We learn and we do what we have to do! We fight!" Liam bellowed.

"I second that!" I stood next to Liam, he was full of what Granny called "the Irish". Aidan stood up next.

"Between us we have brains, strength, courage, wits, spunk and the Moon blood! With that being said I nominate Lily as leader!" Wait, damn it what did he just say? I saw everyone nodding their heads in agreement. I pick THE best time to zone out and think about other things! Note to self, correct that habit! Ciaran spoke.

"Then it's unanimous, Lily you are our leader. Like Granny ever had a doubt." He winked at me. Note to self again kick Ciaran's butt!

"Ok. Then we need to really get on the ball. Initiation is the night before Halloween. We need to get everything together for the ritual and for casting the wards. And we still need to find out how to identify the vampires and HOW to fight and kill them before they kill any of us! Get some rest everyone we start acting like the witches that we are tomorrow." Everyone looked serious. Good, it's our lives on the line here.

Everyone headed home knowing what their part was and what they needed to bring to the table starting tomorrow. I went to the closet that was Granny's. I still hadn't had the nerve to open this door yet, but it was time. I gently grabbed the handle and turned. The door swung open towards me. I felt around on the wall just inside the room until my finger found the light switch. I flicked it on, and light illuminated the walk in closet. I started speaking to my grandmother.

"Granny I have absolutely no clue what I'm doing! How do I save our lives, our magick?" I felt the tears making warm tracks down my face. I could almost hear her in my ear telling me to pack up this old stuff to make room for new things. I laughed in spite of the ache in my heart. I went up to the attic bringing a few boxes with me, and began the daunting task of packing Granny's possessions. After an hour I had gotten all of her shoes, clothes, coats, and most of her purses packed. I had left a few of her bags, and all of her incredible hats out. I knew that I wouldn't wear them anytime soon, but eventually maybe. The last item hanging on the rod was a garment bag with a note addressed to me attached to the front.

'Lilyann, this is your sheath now. It has been passed down to each of the coven leaders of the Moon family. I had a feeling that you would be the leader so it is already hemmed to fit you. I wish that I could be there to see you take your rightful place at the head of our ancestral circle. I love you my Lilybug. Love always, Granny.'

I tucked the note in my back pocket and slipped the bag off of the white material. It was a strapless dress, a flowing, silky material that would caress the body beautifully when whoever wore it moved. I guess that person was now me. I pulled the hanger over my head to get an idea of what I would look like in the sheath. I could feel the magick emanating from the garment. I noticed an ornately carved wooden box on the floor where the bag had hidden it. I knelt down pulling the box to me. The triple goddess moon symbol was carved on top, our coven's mark. During our search the first night we learned of the magick that flowed in our veins we found out that the weird three moons on all of our jewelry was actually called the triple goddess moon. Our family's mark was everywhere we looked, we drew power from it.

I opened the lid, and sitting on top of green velvet were the blue leather garter, the silver arm cuff, and the silver and moonstone diadem. They were breathtaking! I excitedly jumped up, taking everything with me to the mirror. I clasped the silver fasteners of the garter around my thigh feeling more power filling my body. I giggled at the thought. I put the moonstone embedded diadem on my head, and held the cuff in its place at my bicep. I gazed at my reflection, and was overwhelmed by two facts. First, I was wearing articles that have been passed down through the ages that helped amplify our magick. Second, I still had no clue what the hell I was doing! I remembered that my Athame was in my pocket and pulled it out, raising it above my head and declared, "I am Lilyann Moon, leader of my coven, and the most powerful witch in over five centuries! Who dares challenge my power?"

At that moment Izzy came running into the room, and hit my leg causing me to lose my balance slamming myself to the floor. "Ouch!" I sat myself upright looking into the mirror and, again laughing, the diadem sat crooked on my head. I looked like a princess ready to lose her title.

"Well, hmm. Izzy, I think that I need a Wiccan makeover! What do you think?" She meowed at me. I continued to laugh at myself as I put those prized possessions away. I stacked the packed boxes in the hallway, deciding to wait until tomorrow when I could get the boys' help taking them upstairs.

I had just turned off the kettle and was settling down with the book and my tea when the phone rang. I answered, "Hello?" It was Mason. "Hi beautiful. How was your evening?" I don't believe that I will ever get tired of hearing his voice. I answered him, "It was good. We all just hung out and talked for a while. Like I told you before, they all love you." I was still wondering about how Mason would react if he knew what I really am, when something else came to my mind. "Hey I meant to ask you earlier. How is the Inspector?" I heard Mason sigh.

"Oh, Duncan is fine. I talked to him after I left your house, and he said to tell you hi." That was a relief! I wanted to double check that there would be no trouble for my new boyfriend because of my ex-boyfriend. After a few more minutes we said our good byes and I got off the phone. My love life was looking up! I was just heading up the stairs when my phone rang again. I smiled to myself thinking that it was Mason again, but I didn't recognize the number on the caller ID. I answered anyway.

"Hello?" No one answered. "Hello?" I said again.

"Ahhh, the lovely Lily. I am going to enjoy draining you dry now that Grannnnnny is gone." Click. The only sound I heard then was the dial tone. I am so screwed!

CHAPTER SEVEN

No time like the present to tell your best friend that you're a witch, right? Cam walked in the front door. "Lily?" I came in from the kitchen.

"Hey Cam, how are you feeling?" Cam put her coat on the chair with her purse. Then she walked over and hugged me. "Not as good as I would like just yet but the doctor says this is normal for the first trimester. Oh that reminds me…" Cam went back to her purse pulling something out and handed it to me. It was a black and white picture of what looked like a peanut. "It's the baby's first photo, an ultrasound scan. This copy is for you to keep." Whoa. I just plopped down on the couch and started to cry a little while looking at the picture.

"Cam…oh my…she's so beautiful." Cam looked at me.

"Lily what did you just say? Did you say she? Because I keep feeling like it's a girl too." I had absolutely no clue where that feeling came from, but I was positive that I was correct. We just looked at each other and reality hit!

"Oh my God, you're having a baby!" Cam smiled at me, and nodded. I hugged my best friend feeling very excited for her. "Let's go into the kitchen, I want to put this on fridge until I can get a frame." We both walked into the kitchen, and Cam sat at the table while I tinkered around.

"So where is everyone? I thought that your family would be over here all the time now that you're home," Cam said. I walked over to the table and sat down with my family's Book of Shadows in my lap.

"Oh they'll be over later, I'm sure." I mumbled. Here goes everything. "Cam there is something that I need to tell you about my family and me. And it might wig you out a little or in all reality it WILL wig you out a lot." I took a deep breath. "My…my grandmother was a witch and so…so am I, I mean so are we. My family." I put the book on the table, and waited for her to go screaming from my house! Alerting the good townsfolk that the witch lives there, pointing to my house. But she didn't, she pulled the book closer to her and then spoke.

"Is this the book that Ri told me about? And I want to see you light a candle!" What the hell! No screaming, no raving, nothing! Just a request to see me light something? Huh?

"Cam you talked to Ri, you already know that I'm a witch, that my family are all witches?" Cam got up and walked over to the cabinet and grabbed a box of crackers nodding.

"Ri said that you had a lot on your plate, and that you needed me. She also told me about you being a witch, but that it needs to be kept quiet. Lily we've been best friends for years! Sure we don't talk everyday anymore, but I'm always going to be here when you need me. Now, how about that candle?" She said smiling at me. I flicked my wrist at the fireplace.

"Fire!" and watched the reflection of the flames dance on my best friends' face. Well this was much easier than I had anticipated.

"What I want to know about is Mason! Did he really send Mark flying through the club?" Cam asked. Just hearing his name sent my heart fluttering again! I smiled, and walked to the fridge to get some more munchies for us.

"Yes, he really sent Mark flying, and he deserved it! Mason is the most…the sweetest…when I hear his name or see his face or just think about him all I know is that I want him to be mine and mine alone!" I said laying an assortment of foods on the table. Cam was staring at me with a strange expression on her face.

"Lilyann Moon! You are in love with him! I have never seen you act like this about any guy ever! Mason must be amazing to have you feeling like this," she exclaimed. I grabbed a celery stick and started crunching on it. I thought to myself that she was right! I just met this man, this GOD, and I honestly believe that I am in love with him. Damn it! However, I was not going to admit this fact just yet to anyone. Not even my best friend. I grabbed a vitamin water from the fridge and took a drink, clearing my throat and laughed.

"Cam I just met him. I'm not in love with anyone! Let's pig out while we talk about the baby!" That distracted her. Nothing works better to derail a conversation that you don't want to have with a pregnant girl than offering her food!

I told Cam all about the crazy phone call. She agreed with my theory that the vampires had killed Granny, and now they were playing with me. We were smothering our veggies in our favorite thing since ninth grade, French onion dip! We talked about her morning sickness and constant fatigue. I knew that we needed to broach the subject about the other night by the barn so I pursued the topic. "Speaking of the paranormal and weirdness that is my life."

She stopped eating and replied, "I'm not talking about the paranormal anymore." She put her head down and pulled her arms into her lap. I started again.

"Well we need to. What exactly did you see by the barn Cam?" She started playing with her nails. I knew that meant that she was nervous.

"Lily, it's just the pregnancy hormones like you said." My best friend said looking at the fireplace. She wouldn't look at me so I got up and walked over kneeling in front of her.

"Cam I just told you that I'm a witch. I'm getting really good at weird. I know that you saw something, I was there remember. The look on your face that night…I need to know. Were…were they together, my mom and Granny?" She looked down at me and started crying.

"Lily, I feel like I am going crazy! Ever since I found out that I am pregnant, I have been hearing things in my head and seeing people that I know are dead! When I saw your mom and grandmother I honestly thought that I had lost it! Luke has no clue what is wrong with me or how to help…what do I do?" I grabbed Cam and held her tight, trying to reassure her.

"Cam I will find out what was going on. I promise you!" My plate was filling up faster and heavier than my fathers' on Thanksgiving Day! "Cam I want you to keep a journal for me, okay? I need you to write down anything weird that you see or hear. If my grandmother or mom comes to see you again, I need you to call me immediately." My entire existence was becoming a paranormal nightmare! All except for Mason. I stood up and grabbed a box of tissues handing them to her. My phone rang. I checked the caller ID it was Mason. A huge smile crossed my face, Cam had spotted it and mouthed his name. I nodded my head as I answered the phone. "Hello?" I was rewarded by hearing the voice of my own personal safe haven.

"Hello Angel, I'm almost at your house. I've missed you." Yep, I have fallen for this man hard!

"I've missed you too. I'll see you in a few minutes." We hung up and after Cam heard that he was on his way she tried to leave to give us time together, but I insisted that she stay and finally meet my mystery man. Mason arrived at my house just a few minutes later. I introduced my best friend to my new boyfriend and just like with my family they hit it off perfectly. We all sat down for a bit, talking about life in general.

"Congratulations on your baby Camden," Mason offered. My best friend beamed at me. I could tell by the look on her face that she approved of my boyfriend. After a few more minutes Cam excused herself to go meet Luke for dinner.

"Remember what I said about the journal, ok?" Cam hugged and kissed me goodbye whispering in my ear, "Now I know why you fell so fast! He's fantastic!" She waved to Mason and walked out of the front door. That left Mason and I alone. We kissed as we walked into the kitchen. I had my hand around his neck as he gave me soft, gentle kisses. As we parted from our affectionate embrace Mason started sniffing the air.

"What is that heavenly smell?" he asked. I smiled shyly and answered him.

"I am trying my hand at cooking. That smell would be our dinner, mint lamb chops with caramelized shallots, and a pea puree. It's my moms' recipe." He smiled his approval to me. I grabbed his arm and pulled him away from the oven towards the refrigerator. "However, Mr. Shaw that is still roasting so help me with those." I pointed in the fridge to the cheese, and fruit plates that I had made earlier. He carried them to the living room while I grabbed the wine and two glasses. We spread out a tartan blanket on the floor for our fireplace picnic dinner. We sat in front of the glowing warmth of the fire and opened the bottle of wine. We talked about everything from our favorite foods, books, music and movies. I laughed when Mason said his favorite movie was Damsel in Distress with Fred Astaire and Ginger Rodgers.

"You don't' like that movie?" he asked. I sat up a little and answered.

"Actually I love that movie but my favorite Fred and Ginger movie is by far Top Hat." He leaned in and kissed me, and there were fireworks! He gently pulled away to look in my eyes.

"Lily just when I think you couldn't amaze me anymore, you prove me wrong." I smirked at him.

"Let's see how dinner turned out, okay." I went into the kitchen and prepared two plates and rejoined Mason on the floor. I have to say that I rocked my moms' special dish! We finished dinner while finishing our conversation about movies. Mason leaned into me again.

"Lilyann, I have never met anyone like you. I would do anything to protect you, give you anything just to see the smile on your face." I looked into his eyes and saw my feelings for Mason mirrored back to me. Was this really and truly happening to me? I thought that this kind of happiness was only real in fairy tales. I leaned into him and kissed him again. When I pulled back, just slightly to rest my forehead on his lips, I spoke softly, "The only thing I wanted you to give me, you already have…you." We laid on the floor cuddling into each other, just listening to our heartbeats. It was beautiful.

When I woke up, it was still dark but somehow I was in my bed. The clock on my nightstand read four thirty a.m. I flicked on the lamp and it cast its ethereal glow all around the room. I noticed a note and a little glass with lilies in it next to the lamp. The note read, 'Angel, I only left after I knew that you were sound asleep. I will call you in the morning, but if you need me before then call me, Mason.' Izzy meowed at me. I scratched my crazy kitty's head. My mouth was as dry as the Sahara.

"Izzy, do you need a drink too? What do you think about Mason? Huh?" Izzy jumped off of the bed, and followed me downstairs to the kitchen. I got her a saucer of milk and turned the water on for my tea. My phone was on the counter blinking that I had a missed call, so I checked it and again an unknown number. My entire body shivered, I really hope that I grow into my super-witch powers soon! I put the phone

down as it started ringing, and Izzy started hissing at the same time!
Jeesh! I answered the phone aggressively.

"Hello!" This time he replied immediately, "My, my, my Lily that's
no way to talk to the vampire who holds your future in his fangs." He
laughed and it made my skin crawl, but I was NOT going to let him know
how terrified I was.

"You want me Sucker than come and get me! Oh that's right you
have to wait until the wards come down! I have my powers now and I
WILL kill you!" I hung the phone up. I probably shouldn't provoke
crazy vampires, but he was really starting to piss me off! I started pacing
the kitchen floor trying to figure out what to do! I could call Mason.
He's strong, fast and totally smart but he's not a witch. He has no power.
Realization hit me, I can't get Mason involved. They would kill him, and
that would kill me! I needed to call my family, so I grabbed my phone
and dialed Ciaran's cell phone number. After a few rings he answered
sleepily.

"Hey Lil, what time is it?" I tried to stay calm.

"Ciar, I need you. I'm home and I'm scared." I could hear him
moving around. When he spoke his voice was clear and alert.

"Lily stay put. We're on our way!"

When the front door opened the entire coven was there.

"Lily what's wrong?" Declan ran over and hugged me, I was still
shaking from the phone call.

"Sit down guys. Just a few minutes ago was the second phone call
that I've gotten from the same vampire." Everyone looked shocked and
nervous. I recounted both phone calls to my family. Jessie was the first
to speak up.

"Umm, I think that maybe he called me too. Yesterday my cell rings
and I totally don't know who it is, right. So I answer anyway and this guy
says, 'Little Jessie, I think I'll make everyone watch me drain you first.'
And then he so hung up! And, well Halloweens' right around the corner
and I thought that someone was totally trying to scare me like in that
movie Scream. But now...I think it was a real vampire." Shannon was
touching her bracelet, Ciaran and I looked at each other.

"Shan did you get a phone call too?" Ciaran asked. Shannon
continued to play with her bracelet as she spoke.

"I just thought one of my friends' was playing a joke. But how do
the vampires know about us?" Shannon had asked a very good question,
one that I needed to find the answer to. Jessie asked the coven, "Has
anyone else gotten a phone call?" We all looked around at each other and
to my surprise everyone was shaking their heads, yes. Well Hell! I stood
up and felt electricity crackle through me. It was power. This feeling was
becoming very familiar to me. The candles lit again!

"Ok so somehow they've found out about us, each of us! So now we need to focus, remain calm and figure out how to defend ourselves!" Everyone stared at me. Aidan was the one to voice what was written on each coven member's face.

"Uh…Lily, you lit the candles again. Remember what you just said about remaining calm."

I smiled at Aidan and spoke, "Yes I did light the candles. But this time I meant to do it. The damn jerks are pissing me off badly!" We were hitting the books. All of us needed to start learning how to direct our power. "Fix your schedules guys. I want everyone here." Where we could work together and watch out for each other. I started to walk into the kitchen but Ciaran caught me.

"Lily, Jessie and Liam still have to go to school but I say that we take them and pick them up." I looked at the youngest two members of our coven who were just about to protest.

"Ciaran I agree, we take no chances." I instructed everyone go home and pack. We were going to have a good old fashion Moon sleepover which meant the coven was moving into the farm until further notice. Everyone left to gather their things and I headed into the kitchen. It was still early, seven a.m. I made a pot of coffee and started gathering books. I was just stacking them in the living room when my phone rang and I checked the caller ID. Mason. That brought a slight smile to my face.

"Good morning." I knew that I didn't sound right.

"Angel, what's wrong? I'm on my way!" He cannot come here right now.

"No, I'm fine just tired. Izzy woke me early this morning. I'm cranky when I don't get enough sleep. I'm sorry." Masons' voice sounded only slightly calmer.

"Angel, there is nothing to apologize for. I just worry about you when I'm not around. Too overprotective?" That made me giggle. If he only knew, I was a witch and I can take care of myself. It is sweet that he cares though.

"No, not too overprotective. It's nice to have someone feel the same way about me as I do about them. Thank you." Declan, Cassie and Jessie walked back in with their things.

"Love I hear Declan, I'll let you go spend time with your family and I'll see you this afternoon." How did he hear D? I got off the phone with Mason. I started directing the coven as they trickled in to their new rooms. I gave Liam and Jessie their own rooms because they still had school, but everyone else was going to have to double up. Once they were settled in, I pointed to different stacks of books that I had made. Everyone started grabbing different ones and began to read. I had found my grandmother and great-grandmothers' Grimoire's earlier and decided that's where I would start. I didn't know if I was mentally ready for what I was about to read, but the time had come for me to allow the anger towards the vampires to fuel the fire inside of me, instead of trying to run, and hide. I opened my grandmothers' Grimoire first, and began to read.

CHAPTER EIGHT

The difference between a Book of Shadows and a Grimoire is that a Book of Shadows has all of our spells, rituals, potions and instructions from the witches that went before us. The Grimoire is like a journal that a witch keeps of anything that he or she wants to remember. That's why I needed to start there. What did Granny notice the first time she saw a vampire? How did she know it was a vampire? Did she have any special tricks to kill them? I wanted her knowledge of the supernatural. I needed answers so I started reading. The first mention of a vampire came soon in an entry I found.

November 20, 1947

I can't yet fall asleep after the evenings' events. Me ma told me earlier that it was time for her to start my initiation training. She had us both drink some lovely rosehip tea to keep us warm on our walk. Me da and sisters stayed home, this was just for me and ma. We went walking the cobblestones. Ma was asking me all sorts of questions to check my knowledge of crystals. When a man, at least I thought it was a man, until ma pushed me out of the way and yelled, "Stay back child while I kill this vampire!" Me ma pulled a piece of sharp wood from under her apron and went after the beast! He has crazed red eyes! He tried to bite me ma but she was too fast for him! Just as he brought his face close enough to her to touch she shoved the wood deep in this creature's chest and he crumpled to the ground. I was so scared but ma just told me to get myself together. That one day I would have to defend myself against the vampires. She had me watch the process of the vampire turning to ash after its death. I am still shaking from viewing this. Ma told me that there are good vampires and bad vampires. I don't think I want to ever see another vampire not even a good one. Blessed Be~Leeny

I looked up for a minute to give my eyes a break from Granny's girlish writing. So there are good vampires too. I smirked to myself. "We need one of those." Seamus was sitting next to me going through the Book of Shadows.

"Lily, what do we need one of?" Seamus was looking at me curiously. So I told him what I had just read. I began thinking to myself, so according to Granny, there are good vampires out there too. We could use their help. If we could figure out how to tell the difference between them! That seemed hard though, seeing as how we still don't even know what a vampire looks like. Oh, except for the red eyes. Seamus had already started reading his book. I approached the Grimoire with more anticipation than before. After a few more minutes I found a series of entries written more recently that the previous one.

October 31, 1982

I truly cannot believe what gift the goddess has bestowed to me on my birthday, after all of these years fighting with the light against the darkness of the vampires. I went out to the edge of the property, to the orchards to collect the last of the apple harvest and saw a young man lying on the ground. He was beaten and bloody. I saw the beasts that had attacked him just off of my property. I crept around a tree and had one lined up in the crosshairs of my bow, but I had to make sure that I was also in range to finish the second. I moved silently a little closer, and then shot my bow. I hit my target. The other one saw me but a little too late, and to his disadvantage. I sent my other stake flying through the air, forcing my power to give the stake speed and strength. I may be old but I made easy work of those two!

I turned around to the young man to offer my assistance, but to my astonishment, it was me that the young one was afraid of. I had known from the first sight of him that he was one of the good vampires, with those green eyes. It took a little coaxing but I managed to get him back to the house. He told me his name was M, so I left it at that. It was clear that he didn't trust me. I fed the poor thing and made a reviving potion, which he was hesitant to take. I finally convinced him that it would help. I had never seen a good vampire before tonight, but this young one is something else altogether. He looks like he stepped out of the television. He is very handsome, tall, dark hair and those green eyes. He has perfectly chiseled features. I don't think that I've seen that color green since leaving Ireland. He finally started to talk a little. He's been drinking very little blood. But when he does its animal blood. He told me he's from Scotland. He and I spoke in Gaelic for a bit. It felt wonderful to have someone to speak the old language with. I have him resting downstairs in the secret library. Thankfully, none of my children know about that room. I hope he stays there until I can learn more about him and he's strong enough to fend for himself. Maybe I should spell the door. BlessedBe~Leeny

November 1, 1982

M was still in the library in the morning. I asked him to join me for a bit of breakfast. He has gained a little strength. He thanked me for helping him. It must be hard for the good ones, just like it is for us witches. He told me that he had been hiding for a while trying to find a certain witch. When I asked for the witch's name, it was me! A friend and ally sent him my way from Galway. When he realized he had indeed found me he almost dropped his fork from shock and relief. We talked for hours! M is very interesting, and honest! He told me about his beginnings when he did drink from humans. How it haunts him every day of his life. Around 5:00 this evening I had to send him back down to the library because Lochlan and Leigh Ann came over for a spot of tea. After they left I brewed another batch of reviving potion and M drank it straight away. He's down in the library now. We put the cot downstairs and agreed that's where he needed to stay to keep him hidden from my children. I didn't need to spell the door this time. I feel so guilty about doing that last night! It's off to bed for me. Blessed Be~Leeny

"Goddess!" I sighed. I looked up at the room, everyone had a book of some sort in their hands. "Hey guys listen to what I found!" Everyone stopped what they were doing and listened to me reread the entries to them. After I finished Riona spoke up.

"I think I know where that secret room is!" She told us that earlier she continued seeing a room in her head. "I think it's in the kitchen next to the fireplace. If I'm right we still need the spell to open the door." We were so close to figuring all of these secrets out. I could feel it! "Damn it! Ok I'll keep reading this," I said in an aggravated tone as I thumbed through the book. It looked like there were a couple more entries about M. "Seamus will you keep going through the Book of Shadows, see if the spell to open the secret room is mentioned in there?" I asked. Seamus put on his down to business expression, and nodded. Everyone got back to work. I jumped up with the Grimoire to grab another cup of coffee, and continued reading my grandmothers' written words.

November 2, 1982

M and I went outside for a little walk around the farm. Isadora joined us. I was shocked by her reaction! She hissed at him, and then became civil. I now see that she can sense the difference in him. He finally told me why he was sent to me. M has two brothers and a sister who are the worst of his kind, according to him. He was told about my powers and that I might be able to help him destroy his siblings. It would be nice to rid the world of such monstrous creatures! I made another reviving potion. A bit stronger this time and M again drank it straight away. This one seemed to help loads! Goddess! If only my children would have stepped into their destiny, we would definitely have the combined power to destroy them. But alone I am not sure I have what will be required. I will of course try. Blessed Be~Leeny

November 10, 1982

Lochlan and Leighann came over last night and told me that they are expecting! I felt that child's power already! She is going to fulfill the prophecies foretold about the Moon Coven! After they left M came upstairs and told me more about the meaning of his ring. It is quite exquisite, it has an Onyx stone, with a golden phoenix outstretched, an eye and the letter M in the top corner. The onyx is amazing as it represents strength, the stone used to be a ruby M told me. But after he turned his back on his nature of hunting humans the stone turned to onyx! Remarkable. The phoenix outstretched symbolizes M's rebirth. The eye stands for the all seeing eye used by the Freemasons. And the M is obviously for M, himself. He has gotten so much stronger and is helping me a great deal in hunting vampires. I didn't know if he would truly be able to kill one of his own kind, but he did. Many times over! He and I are going out tomorrow in hopes of following up on a lead! Blessed Be~Leeny

I finished reading. What prophecies? In 1982, mom got pregnant with me. Oh lovely, as if I don't have enough on my plate! I'll have to put that on the back burner for right now. Something wasn't sitting right with me about this vampire. "Hey guys, I couldn't find the spell. But look at this Lily. I found out about the vampires!" Seamus handed me the Book and Ciaran came over sitting next to us. We read where Seamus pointed.

Vampires

The vampires have been roaming our earth for many moons. They feast on the blood of humans, but they prefer witch blood. These beasts have been taking the blood of all the Covens, but we have a remedy to their attacks. There are only four types of wood that will pierce the heart of this creature, Ash, Pine, Oak and Rowan. The spears must be sharpened and blessed. Raise the spear above your head and call to the Goddess. "Goddess come to your daughter and bless this wood with your power!" You WILL feel the favor of our Goddess.

Now, how to identify these foul creatures. They are incredibly fast, unfathomably strong and their greatest gifts aside from their fangs are their eyes! They are as red as the blood they crave with a golden ring around the edges. They use these eyes to compel their victim. They simply tell their victims what to do and they do it. Fortunately we as witches have a slight defense against this IF we are aware. If we throw our power of the elements at them, it can distract them long enough to stake them. Something else that all Moon Witches must be aware of, there are good vampires! They only want to help rid the world of these abominations, you will recognize them by their eyes. They are a shade of green only seen on the Emerald Isle, herself! These eyes are ringed in gold. When the wards are in place they are the ONLY vampires that can cross them. Blessed Be to all the daughters and sons of the Moons.

Everything started clicking in my head all at once, Mason is so fast and strong. The memory of the night that he sent Mark through the crowd with such force and speed was replaying in my mind. His eyes, those green eyes, emerald green eyes, that I felt I couldn't look away from. That night he held my gaze until I felt my body's desire to perform just for him. I only felt comfortable while he was with me, as soon as he walked away the doubt came back. He had compelled me. And Oh My Goddess the ring! I saw him with that ring on his hand at the coffee shop! I felt like I couldn't breathe. I let the book fall out of my hands and whispered, "Son of a Bitch."

CHAPTER NINE

I heard a car pull up and Liam said very excitedly, "Lily, Masons' here!" I came out of my daze quickly! Everyone was in a mad dash to put our Wiccan books away but me. I got to the door, and flung it open grabbing the oak broom from the porch. I stomped my foot where the handle and bristles met and heard the crack of the wood. I walked with purpose down the steps and stood face to face with him. I watched him search my face.

"Angel, what's wrong?" I saw realization light up his eyes, he understood.

"Did you think that I was too stupid or to naive to figure it out Mason?" I spit my words at him. I heard my family trying to come through the front door and join us outside at one time. I turned to the group yelling, "Stay inside! I'll deal with the vampire!" They didn't have the information that I now possessed. The plethora of voices behind me was that of confusion and shock. Masons' eyes held mine. I had just a second to react. I held my left hand in front of me and called for my element, "Fire!" The flame narrowly missed his handsome face. That distracted him for just a moment. It was long enough for me to thrust the oak stick in the air and shout, "Goddess, come to your daughter and bless this wood with your power!" I felt the electricity course through the oak, and then into my body, the wind started blowing and I felt the Goddess' favor in me. I pointed the stick at Masons' fallen face.

"Get off of my property vampire! If you ever come around any of them again I…WILL…KILL…YOU!" Mason tried to speak but I spun on my heel and ran up the steps going back into my house and slammed the door!

When I turned around it was Braden who walked with me into the kitchen. He studied me for a moment and then asked, "Lily, are you okay?" I fought back the tears. I didn't want my cousin to know just how broken I felt. He hugged my quivering form.

I whispered to him, "Is the fact that I'm a witch the only reason that he got close to me, Bray?" My cousin couldn't answer my question, and the one person who could I never wanted to see again! "He's known all along what I am, hell he knew what I was before I did." I croaked out.

"Just remember Lil, he's a good vampire. He wants to help." Braden spoke from the heart. It didn't matter, we had a lot work to do and not much time to do it in. I straightened up from the hug and with the broken broomstick still in my hand and my broken heart now lodged in my throat I walked back into the living room and explained to my bewildered family what they had just witnessed. After I had finished speaking to the coven, they remained quiet. They didn't bombard me with a litany of questions. I needed a minute to myself so I grabbed the Book of Shadows and headed upstairs to my bedroom. I shut the door and immediately fell to the floor and sobbed.

I started berating myself silently: Did you really believe that you were going to have a fairy tale happy ending? How many times had I told friends of mine that I would never be that girl! The one that fell for a man too fast! Yet here I am on the floor devastated after less than a month. I didn't have the desire or the energy to get off of the floor so there I laid, crying myself to sleep.

Over the next few days my mind would play over and over again everything that had happened with Mason, without my permission I might add. Cam had tried to talk to me about it several times to no avail. The chaos in my head was just made worse with each successive phone call my voicemail received from him. During the afternoon of Thursday October 6th, I received another one of these messages.

"Lily, please give me a chance to explain! I'm glad that you know. I wanted to tell you myself. I don't want to do this over the phone or through voicemail. Please call me. I miss you…I love you." That was the message that cleaved my heart in two, and caused my element to have a mind of its own. As soon as I laid my phone back on the counter it burst into flames! My emotions were obviously all over the place but I really was trying to keep my magick under control. I was afraid of the personal gain rule that I had read about in the Book of Shadows. If we used our powers for something frivolous for ourselves, such as increasing our financial status, using a spell or potion for love or to hurt someone, we would have our powers stripped for forty nine years. The thought of not having my magick now made my head hurt. Declan walked in and saw my burned cell phone on the counter.

"Goddess Lily, did it try to eat your ear?" I looked at him like he had three heads.

"What are you talking about D?" He just pointed to my destroyed phone. "Yeah, well it pissed me off and my powers…none of our powers are under control yet!" I screamed. Shit! Now I needed a new phone. Riona walked in with Cassie, Braden and Cormac and spotted my charred cell, but Declan cut them off.

"Don't ask! She must have gotten another phone call from you know who." I just walked away before something started burning!

The next morning Ciaran went to the mall with me. Watching the expressions of the salesmen as I explained that I accidentally threw my phone into the fireplace was comical! I replaced my phone but didn't change my number. What can I say, I'm a masochist. On the way back from the mall Ciar and I started discussing the Wiccan rules that we needed to learn to live by as we stopped to get coffee and bagels for everyone.

"Lily you've read the BoS more than the rest of us. What are all the rules?" I started telling him almost all of the Wiccan laws, I saved the most important four till the end.

"And finally no personal gain, the threefold rule, no burning Rowan wood and last but not least an it harm none, do what ye will." When we got home the entire coven jumped in the conversation.

Seamus asked, with a look of deep concentration on his face, "So does the three fold law mean anything we do with our magick will come back to us three times or three times the effect?" I explained if we curse someone just for fun than the curse comes back to us three times more powerful. After our discussion all the boys were headed out to the barn to set up target practice for our training. They had just gotten to the front door as Riona was walking down the stairs with her hand on her forehead.

Liam asked our cousin, "Ri what's wrong? Do you need some aspirin?" All I heard was her moan and cough before I watched her fall forward. Seamus and Declan caught her before she hit the floor.

Aidan screamed, "Damn it! Ri talk to me sweetie what is it?" Aidan and Ciaran got to their sister before me. I sat myself on the floor next to her head. She started speaking.

"Lily, there are three that are coming for us!" Riona pressed both hands against her temples and howled like a wounded animal, "Ow!" She began speaking again in a distant voice, "One is a woman and two are men, they will bring a horde of vampires to kill us on Halloween. But the woman is not here, she will not come here for the fight. She waits until the rest of the coven is defeated. She wants only your blood, Lily." Everyone was looking at her. Braden grabbed the book, but Shannon spoke.

"Remember Lily, remember what Granny wrote to her about paying attention to what she saw? I read it in the Book. Each coven of witches has a seer." I must have looked very lost because Shan went on. "A seer...like a fortune teller only real!" That registered. Ri had been able to tell us little things without knowing how she did it but nothing like this before. Declan asked the question that I was thinking.

"Wait, is she having a vision?" Cormac handed her a cup of mistletoe and lavender tea. Riona took a sip sitting up, looking like her natural happy self.

"Damn Skippy! It wasn't like a movie. It was like I was there, like it was happening to us just now. Trust me, if we don't nail this stuff, we're in deep horse shit!" Great!

After Riona's vision we were in even more dire straits to learn how to hit our intended marks. We went outside and split into two groups.

The first group went over by the water well, and worked on directing their elements. While the second group was in front of the barn, with an old bull's eye paper attached to a bale of hay. That was the group that I was in, working with my grandmothers' crossbows, and I sucked!

I stomped my foot. "What am I doing wrong? I just cannot get this." Declan and Braden, the two hunters of our group, tried walking me through it again.

"Lily, grip the bow in your dominant hand. Now I want you to relax, focus on your target, and breathe before you pull the trigger." My brother instructed. I listened to his advice, but the next two times were not any better. As a matter of fact the last time I shot that thing I almost hit my favorite horse, a white Arabian named Winter. I handed the crossbow to Liam.

"Lily maybe the bow just isn't your weapon. Don't get mad! None of us can control our magick better than you." My youngest cousin tried comforting me as I walked over to the group working on their elements. I nailed throwing fire and hitting my intended target every time. That made me feel a little better. At least I didn't suck at everything! I still needed to figure out what was going to be my weapon of choice. I mean obviously it had to be blessed wood, but my method of delivery still needed to be discovered. We left all of the targets in place for tomorrows practice and headed inside to start working on other aspects of the craft we needed to hone.

Ciaran, Shannon and I were working on a potion to physically strengthen ourselves. "Lily, you're adding wormwood again, you're going to blow us up!" I looked up to find Shan and Ciaran were ducked down behind the breakfast nook. I looked abashed.

"I'm sorry guys! I don't know where my head is?" They looked at each other and I thought I heard one of them whisper, "Her head is still with Mason." But I let it go, and finished the mixture adding the correct herb, White Willow Bark. With a little pop and fizz my potion was ready! We had found twelve vials to hold the strengthening potion in until the day before Halloween. According to the BoS the potion would continue to strengthen in the vial, after we took the concoction it would mature in our systems until it was at its height of potency on Halloween night! My cell rang and I looked at the caller ID. Unknown. I was still pissed! One vampire was just as good as another, right!

"Hello?" I could feel his voice before I could hear him.

"Lily, I am so waiting to taste you. I see that you are keeping your little coven together as of late." I started giggling and answered him.

"Well, vampire, I'm making sure that we have plenty of very sharp, blessed stakes to stick in your chest. So you see I need a little help cutting all of the skewers to shish ka bob you guys. Its hard work and I would hate to break a nail." I was enjoying this so much! So I continued. "Oh and no need to bring any kind of lighter fluid to our little campfire on Halloween, you see I am the fire starter. Bye Fang face." I hung up on him and really laughed, I mean let loose at the seams laughed! My family laughed a little. They must have thought that I was crazy! It was the first time in a week that I hadn't thought of Mason and it felt good not to hurt... Declan looked at me and smiled.

"Well at least it's the fangers she's aiming her firepower at now and not harmless electronic devices." The whole kitchen filled with laughter then.

It was getting late on Saturday night but we were all still going. Caffeine infused night owls. Ciaran and I were working independently, trying to find any information we could about Riona's extra power. We went through every book, on every subject, absorbing as much as possible. If only we had Granny here to ask. She would know whether or not Ri could call a vision up at will. She would have the spell to get into that secret library and she would be able to tell me about this prophecy that I am supposed to live up to. But right now, the most important information she could give me was about Mason. I've tried to keep him out of my head but that wasn't going very well. My grandmother knew him, and regarded him highly. I knew that she really knew him though since they had talked about Masons' past. She would be able to answer questions for me and lead me in the right direction. But I would never have that opportunity ever again. I was still looking through my great grandmother Rose Moon's Grimoire when Ciaran spoke.

"Lily I don't want to pry..." I knew where Ciaran was going so I shook my head.

"He keeps leaving voice mails and texts but I can't Ciar." He nodded his understanding at me. I knew that if I wanted to talk about my broken heart, I had a literal army of amateur psycho-analysts at my disposal. We kept reading that evening until Ciaran found what we were looking for in the Book of Shadows. He relayed the information to us all at once.

According to the BoS, Ri could call her visions up at will but it took a great deal of concentration and practice. He also told us something else he found in his reading.

"The Book also talks about the spirit user. I'm not sure what it means or whom it's referring to but I have a theory that I want to test out. Lily?" I looked up at him searching his eyes, but didn't find any answers there. So I nodded my head and he asked everyone to step outside and we all obliged. When we got out by the barn Ciaran started.

"Lily when you were yelling at Mason, I noticed something." My heart sank with the mention of his name. I put my stone face on and nodded. "Well...your element is fire, but you conjured the air as well. So I'm wondering if you can also call the other elements. Water and Earth.

Try it Lily." I thought back to that encounter again and I remember that the wind did start going crazy but I thought that Shannon, Liam or Jessie our air users had done that! I nodded again. I turned myself so that my body was facing east, and concentrated on the wind. I raised my left hand to the sky and called to that element, "Air!"

It's response to my plea was instantaneous. A gentle swirling breeze had soon turned into a mighty wind that whipped my hair around my face. I laughed at the feeling of electricity running through my body. I felt part of myself stay with the element of air while another part of my power was ready for my next command. I turned clockwise, which I found out while reading my family's' Grimoire, was called deosil. I faced the south and called my element, "Fire!"

Again the element replied it assurances that it was listening, the fire pit sprang to life. The flames threw themselves out into the night crackling ever higher and harsher than I had produced before, to do my bidding. The warmth that caressed my skin was that of a returning friend. I thought of my mind, how it was compartmentalizing for me. Opening like a filing cabinet, and retaining information that I may need at a later date, but leaving the files open that I needed to work with now. I turned my body clockwise once more raising my hand to the western sky, "Water!"

As soon as I spoke its name, the clear fluid shot up out of the well like a fountain spraying everything in its reach. My body pulsed with current of electricity from so much power. I shifted my body to the right one last time calling on the final element that derived is power from the north, "Earth!"

Immediately the ground started to rumble and shake. All four elements had joined forces at my command. I twirled around like I was a little girl again and laughed jubilantly! I heard the squeals of delight, and wonder from my family. I felt an abundance of power coursing through my body. I threw both arms up to the sky and shouted, "Thank you Goddess for your love and power!" The entire coven started wielding their power over their elements and it was amazing! We danced and laughed under the moon as the water soaked us, the wind blew through our wet hair, the ground danced beneath our feet, and the fire warmed us to the core! We were Moon witches, and with our coven's power anything was possible.

CHAPTER TEN

The next couple of days went smoothly. I tried to keep my thoughts of Mason to a minimum. Liam and Jessie went to school while the rest of the coven worked tirelessly at learning the skills of our craft. Halloween was creeping closer each day and we still were not ready, but we were getting there. Riona worked on her visions, trying to call them at will. She read every book that related to divination in any way. Cassie, Aidan and Cormac were working on crystals, herbs and runes. I have to say that those three made a perfect team. Each witch let a category pick them and started studying everything from the correct phase of the moon to harvest a certain herb, the best crystal to work in conjunction with a certain spell and exactly which rune worked best with particular types of magick. There was a passage in the BoS that told us that each member of the coven would excel at something different but it didn't offer any specifics on who would be best at what. We had all been working for a couple of hours when Seamus went into the kitchen to grab something to snack on and came up empty.

He walked back into the living room with his stomach grumbling angrily at him and asked, "Uh…Lily, I just need to know are we aloud to eat today?" I looked up at him questioningly.

"Oh crap it's Monday! We need food! The parents are coming over for dinner tonight too!" Ciaran and I made a grocery store run. With twelve witches living under one roof we were going to have to make a regular habit of it. Ciaran and I stayed together combing the racks for everyone's favorite junk food. We also needed to replenish the cabinets of regular daily foods. Now that fall was here we were in need of fresh fruits and vegetables. The bill was $470.23 so I swiped my debit card and we headed to the Jeep with our bounty.

I looked up and I swear I thought that I saw Mason across the parking lot. It had to be my imagination or subconscious playing tricks on me because when I looked back at the spot he wasn't there. Part of me wanted to see him and tell him that I was sorry and the other part of me wanted to shove a stake into his chest for lying and deceiving me. It was no longer the fact that he was a vampire. I had plenty of time to work this much out in my head. If he wanted to kill me or the others he had plenty of opportunities. We were untrained, uninitiated witches with no idea of how to use our powers to fight him off. Braden's words echoed in my head, 'He's a good vampire, he just wants to help.' I had to stop this now! Mason had my heart, but I had to keep my head.

When Jessie and Liam got home from school with their escorts, Declan and Shannon, they announced to the room at large, "Well our Homecoming court was announced today." Jessie curtsied while big brother Declan smiled on in appreciation.

Aidan piped up, "Well Jessie will make the fifth Homecoming Queen in our family. Wait…what about Liam?" We all looked at Liam who was smiling also and replied in a very girlish tone, "Yes cousin, I was nominated for Homecoming Queen too! What color should my dress be?" We all cracked up laughing. Liam had gone on to tell us that he had been nominated for Homecoming King and that the dance was being held on Friday October 21st and the game was the following day. So if my math was right we had twelve days to find something for everyone to wear and arm ourselves against a possible attack!

"Well welcome to the chaperoning committee guys!" I looked at everyone as we were all cooking. We were preparing dinner together. We were also trying not to burn anything during this conversation.

"You're right Lily. We can't let them go there without us!" Seamus added while tasting the spaghetti sauce. We all needed a totally supernaturally free night! We had prepared one of everyone's favorite dinners.

The parents arrived to the smell of homemade Italian cuisine, including spaghetti and meatballs, bruschetta, tomato caprese, and for dessert Tiramisu. By the time that everyone was finished eating I noticed a few people loosening their belts. Everyone was talking about Jessie and Liam and making plans for this epic event.

"We are all volunteering as chaperones for Homecoming. Do you think that we have to dress up?" Declan asked everyone. Aunt Rae and Aunt Brig giggled to each other and answered in unison, "Yep!" I laughed at the worried look on Declan and Braden's faces. They barely dressed up for their own proms. I may have to pick their attire for the evening and take pictures! Jessie had settled on an iced baby blue color that would make her eyes pop! I started clearing the table as everyone else mingled and talked more about the dance. My dad and Aunt Rae found me in the kitchen as I was putting the last of the dishes in the sink to soak. My grandmother didn't believe in dishwashers, and it was my night to wash. I was counting on a ruined manicure in just under an hour!

My aunt started, "Lilybug, how are you doing?" I smiled at her, it wasn't hard to see why she was my mom's best friend.

"I'm good Aunt Rae, just tired. Who knew having a horde of hungry vampires wanting to feast on your blood would be so draining. Get it?" I laughed and Aunt Rae joined me. My dad however, did not find my little spout of humor very funny. Aunt Rae looked between the both of us, hugged me, and excused herself with the promise of coming back later this week to help with Jessie's dress.

My father moved in closer to me and asked, "Have you gotten any more calls from the vampires?" I just looked at him and nodded. As a group the coven decided honesty with our parents was the best policy. We needed them to be on their guard, we didn't know why they weren't getting the phone calls but thank the Goddess they weren't. My father went on.

"Lily, have you kids gotten any closer to strengthening the wards?" I didn't want to outright lie so I came up with the best compromise I could.

"Well, you see Dad it's not that simple. Some of the elements we need, we have but there are still a few things that we need to purchase. Don't worry though. We've got it under control." Yep that was a bigger lie than I had wanted to tell today. We had no clue where to find what we needed! My dad changed the subject on me and I was not prepared.

"So where is this Mason that I've heard so much about? I was hoping to meet him soon." My heart started doing somersaults in my chest and I was saved from answering by Riona.

"Hey Uncle Lochlan, there you are. My dad is looking for you." My dad hugged Riona and I telling us that he came over with uncle Donal and Aunt Rae, so he had to go.

"Ri, thank you. Was your Dad really looking for him?" She shook her head and proceeded to tell me that she could see that I didn't look happy so she concentrated and hoped to get a vision and she did. A vision that her father was going to look for my father! I laughed out loud, the first vision she's able to have at will is to help me out of having to talk about Mason. Classic!

The next day Riona was walking around looking sort of morose or concentrating but whenever any of us tried to talk to her, she would nearly bite our heads off. Everyone noticed Ri's bad mood and tried to avoid contact with her. I was working with Cormac and Ciaran on the initiation ritual spell and hand movements again. And thankfully I was remembering it! Now I was trying to picture myself doing this in the cold, at night with a slit clear up to my upper thigh! That was not a pretty picture. We had just gone through it for the third time when the doorbell rang.

Shannon answered the door and yelled, "Uh Lily it's for you!" I walked over and joined her by the door and my mouth dropped open. There was a delivery driver at the door and two more men bringing what had to have been ten to twelve vases full of Lilies! I couldn't speak. The delivery driver had me sign for them and I obeyed. Declan came downstairs.

"Oh my goddess! It smells like a funeral home in…..where the hell did they all come from?" He joined everyone staring at me. I grabbed a card from the closest vase it read, 'Lily, I didn't want you to find out from anyone but me Angel. I'm so sorry that I hurt you. I would run through

73

a blessed stake if I thought it would take away a moment of the pain you have suffered. I love you, Mason.' Was it possible that he truly did love me for me and not because I am Leeny Moon's granddaughter? I'm not sure if it was the pungent aroma of the Lilies or my overwhelming feelings for Mason, but I fainted.

I came to with my family all around me calling my name and someone saying they were going to slap me. I felt the couch under me but the whole right side of my body was sore. I looked at the window and it was dark outside now! I sat up, waving everyone off who was trying to help me.

"I'm fine. What happened and why am I sore?" I searched the faces of my family and my brother answered.

"Sis you fell out! And none of us were close enough to catch you. Sorry." He gave a whimpering smile, I laughed. I have never fainted in my life. But this was just another reason that I could not be an all-powerful witch. What powerful witch faints? I looked around the room and remembered the flowers, I tried to stand but still felt wobbly. Riona, knowing me as well as she did, had called Cam. She walked in right when Ri handed me all of the cards. She smiled. I guess she was feeling better?

"They're numbered. But I didn't read them or let anyone else read them." I smiled at Riona and mouthed thank you. Cassie brought in a glass of apple juice and handed it to me. I took a sip from the glass and thanked her as well. Cam sat down next to me and nudged my good side.

"Ok Lily, time to listen to what Mason has to say. Read the notes." I looked down and let my heart win out. I started reading. Mason told me he loved my grandmother as his grandmother, and that she was there for him when no one else was except the inspector. He told me that the moment he saw me he knew I was the only person that he would ever love. How he had been miserable without me and how he would stay away from me if that's what I really wanted, but only after he was able to speak to me in person. I looked back up and Shannon had a box of tissues ready for me. I had started crying without knowing it.

I grabbed the tissues and really let the floodgate of tears loose. I was crying, sobbing and trying to speak at the same time. Fabulous! All of the guys were looking at anything but me. The strong leader of the Moon witches was a huge snot baby! After about thirty minutes my eyes were, for all intents and purposes, swollen shut, my nose and throat were raw, and my right side still hurt. Cam asked Ciaran to make me some of that special tea that Granny always made. Ciaran knew exactly what Cam was talking about, 'The heartbreak tea' and the guys all disappeared following him into the kitchen, glad to be away from the crying girl. Cassie spoke up.

"Lily just call him. We really like Mason. We don't care that he's a vampire." She put her hand in mine and squeezed. I wanted to so bad!

My stupid pride told me no! I just looked at my sisters, cousins and best friend and stood up from the couch shaking my head. I started rambling again, terrified by my own raw emotion being shown in front of those that I loved. All of these people that looked at me like I was a woman of steel when in reality I was a bundle loose livewires.

"How can I tell him I'm sorry, he lied to me! I want nothing more than to lay my head against his chest again with him telling me that he'll protect me! Instead everyone thinks that I am this super witch. I'm not! I have no clue what the hell I'm doing, I just keep doing something trying to keep us all alive! Oh Goddess! Help Me!" I sobbed. The boys came running in with the tea to find me in a heap on the floor. Riona surprised us all.

She jumped up and said, "You're just going to let love go right out of the window because of your damn pride!" She turned and ran out the front door. For the second time today my mouth hung open. Cassie assured me that Riona just needed to cool off. I wanted to run after my cousin and let her feel how ripped apart my heart was. But most of all I wanted her back in the house where I knew that she was safe.

After forty-five minutes or so, Cam left and told me she would check on me later. The tea that Ciaran had made me had worked like a charm. My head and body felt normal again. I went out into the night with the boys to look for Riona, keeping the notes from Mason in my pocket. We all kept together. We still weren't sure how far on the property the wards were still strong. I was berating myself aloud for not running out of the house after Ri!

"Damn it! Why didn't I run after her? This is just another reason you guys should not trust me with leadership of the coven!"

Cormac was right next to me and responded, "Lily none of us knew that she would take off so far from the house." I just shook my head in the dark, trying to listen to the night. Trying to hear Riona. Nothing but the sounds of the animals burrowing in for the night. I started telling myself off in my head 'How could I have let her go charging out of the house mad and not have gone after her?' We were venturing further out onto the property when my cell phone started beeping that I had a new text message. I grabbed my phone and read the text: Sorry Lily, I'm at the New Town movie theatre. Be home later luv u Ri.

"Holy Shit!"

I turned and started running toward the house shouting what Riona had text me! "She's alone! They'll kill her!" Damn it, my lungs felt like they were on fire but I didn't care! I pushed myself even harder and faster. Liam was able to call the girls while running. Somehow we had walked out about a mile and a half! Seriously did we have this much property? I kept up with the guys only by thinking of my cousin. The girls had all the cars started by the time we got back. I have never driven like a crazy person before tonight, Mason had! But he wasn't here to help me! Shit! I can call Mason! He'll help us get to Riona! Screw my pride! I threw my phone to Braden who was sitting in my passenger seat and screamed, "Call Mason!"

He grabbed my phone and hit speed dial for Mason. I could hear the phone ringing and going to his voice mail. I was still driving like I lived in Hazard County and my name was Daisy Duke and not Lily Moon! I took a hard left and almost rolled my jeep! By the grace of the goddess I was able to steady myself and kept hauling ass down the dark country road with three sets of headlights in my rearview mirror! I kept sending up prayers to the Goddess, 'Please don't let me be late. I can't lose her. Please!'

"Keep trying Mason!" I yelled at Braden.

Everything was starting to go in slow motion. I felt like no matter how fast I drove that I was only going five miles an hour. I heard Braden continue calling Mason, get his voice mail, hang up and try again! Where was my vampire when I needed him? That's right MY vampire! I am in love with Mason but that is seriously not going to matter if I don't get to Riona in time! We were still five minutes away, but we were making up time by speeding! I shot up more prayers.

"Goddess please let there be no one in our way! Please keep Riona safe until we get there!" I hollered over the back seat at Jessie, "Call the others and see if anybody grabbed stakes!"

Jessie answered me. "Lily when Liam called we each grabbed a dozen and put them in each vehicle." I nodded my acknowledgment to her. We were coming down route 27 and there was the New Town Mall to our left that housed the movie theatre. Thankfully the lights were green and we were the only cars on the road, I hit the brake coming around the turn to take us into the parking lot, still praying to my Goddess! We came around the turn by the entrance of the movies just in time to see Riona walking to her car and two coming up on her fast! I started crying and screaming, "God damn it! We're not going to make it! RIONA!!"

CHAPTER ELEVEN

Everyone in the Jeep was screaming! The two men were right behind Riona, she must have heard them because she ducked down. She ducked down? I saw Mason coming from across the parking lot. I hit the gas and then slammed on the brakes ten feet from them. He had two stakes already moving so fast that it was a blur. I threw my Jeep in to park as Jessie tossed two stakes up to me! I jumped out of the Jeep and ran toward the fight. Mason had already hit one of his targets and started talking to us, readjusting his position. Keeping himself in front of us never taking his eyes off of the remaining threat.

"Riona get to the Jeep. Angel I want you to go with her." Riona obeyed running towards the vehicles of our group into the arms of the coven. I stayed watching the vampire with the red glowing eyes stare at me licking his lips. I suddenly felt a cone of power welling up inside of me, building until I thought I would burst. Instead of trying to hold it in I released it out into the night. Letting the power guide my actions and words. I smiled at the handsome creature that wanted my blood and began to taunt him.

"I'm Lilyann Moon, leader of the Moon witches. If you want me beast come and get me. I will not run." I moved from behind Mason tilting my head to the side exposing my carotid artery and continued, "This is what you seek, is it not?"

The vampire and I were in a dance of sorts to which I took the lead. I tightened the grasp on the stake in my left hand and saw Mason start to maneuver himself behind the vampire as he began to rush forward to claim his prize, my blood. The red eyed fiend was only three feet away from me when I lunged, forward shoving my stake through the front of his chest and saw the protruding end of Masons' stake that he had plunged through the vampires' back. I took a step to the side and saw firsthand what happens to a vampire after being staked. I watched this handsome vampire turn first to what looked like a stone sarcophagus. In the blink of an eye this once handsome evil creature began a transformation into something that resembled a piece of leather that twisted, and turned in on itself becoming smaller and smaller in front of my eyes. A moment later it was ash. I raised my hand to call air to blow the remnants away but Jessie, Shannon and Liam beat me to it.

I felt their combined power rush past me and the wind removed the reminder of my first vampire kill. My eyes met Masons' for a moment, my pride had picked this point in time to resurface. I turned from him searching for Riona. I found her with my family, the coven ran over to us. I wrapped Ri inside my arms.

"Oh my goddess, are you ok! Riona Moon I thought that I lost you!" I looked her over, not a scratch. I turned to face Mason and timidly spoke. "Mason, I don't know how to thank you. Uh...we have to go."

His smile didn't touch his eyes as my rejection reached his ears. I began fighting with my pride internally. I need to be with him. My pride answered, 'No he lied to you, he deceived you.' I was still facing Mason when I felt a push in my lower back, which sent me flying closer to Mason. I steadied myself looking defiantly into his eyes and my mouth opened letting the babbling begin.

"Mason I don't know what to...say or do. Or how to fix...I...I..." I ran to Mason, hugging him around the neck and cried. He held me so tight, rubbing comforting little circles in my back.

"Angel I'm so sorry you found out the way you did. I wanted to tell you. But it's in your hands now. I will go if that's what you want" I heard him whisper. I hugged him tighter, not trusting my speech yet. He just continued to hold me. I heard my family making sure Riona was ok. I knew what I wanted to say but how do I get the right words out? Again something inside of me took over. I lifted my head and looked into Mason's glassy eyes.

"You belong with me and I belong with you." I kissed Mason hard and passionately, not caring that my family was watching. When we started to break apart Mason held me around my waist. We heard all the cheers from my family. I looked at my vampire and told him what was on my mind. "No secrets. No lies." He smiled and reached for the hand I had my keys in and took them from me, tossing them to my brother.

"D, can you drive the jeep back to the farm, I'm not ready to part with my reason to breathe." Declan slapped Masons back and winked.

"It's good to have you back brother! Maybe now Lily will smile again." D jumped out of my reach before I could slap him. Mason herded us all into vehicles and we headed back to the farm with my heart intact again.

We got back to the house and started talking, Mason not venturing very far from me. He and I needed to talk a lot more about our relationship, but privately. The car ride back he had told me that he had been watching us, to keep us safe. He had anticipated an attack on one of us like this. I needed a glass of something stronger than tea so I went to the kitchen to open a bottle of Elderberry wine. My cell rang and I answered it thinking it was Cam, but I was wrong! I hit the speaker button.

"Hello Lily, I'd like to say that I was sorry that your cousin...my, my, my, what was her name again? Oh yes, Riona. She was as alive and vibrant as you. But she's not. I'm going to save you until last." I couldn't find my voice to combat with this animal. My mouth just hung open.

Mason ran into the kitchen, grabbed the phone and spoke up, "Sorry to disappoint you but all of the Moons' are alive and well. Although, the two thugs that you sent after Riona, they are very much dead. One by my hand and the other by my girlfriend Lily's, and my hand, combined! Good-Bye Dax! " Mason closed my cell and faced me. "Lily, how long have these phone calls been going on?" My brain wasn't working very well I so I just stuttered.

"I...I don't know, that night. The day that you came here and met everyone. That night after I spoke with you was the first time he called. Mase who is Dax?"

Mason had everyone get what they wanted to eat or drink and come into the living room. I grabbed a glass, filled it with vodka and found a spot next to Riona on the couch. Mason paced the floor, stopping in front of me and looked me in the eyes.

"No lies, right?" I nodded my head to him taking a very generous drink of my chosen poison. Mason snarled the next words. "Dax and Victor are my brothers. I also have a sister Maylee and as far as I know she's still in Ireland. But my brothers are here." I thought that I was going to choke and apparently I was not the only one that had put this information together with Riona's vision. Mason watched us with a quizzical look on his handsome face. "What don't I know Lily?" He asked me. I fiddled with my fingers. "Remember Love, no secrets." He knelt in front of me placing his hand on mine.

I launched into everything that had happened from the beginning. When I had first found out we were witches right up until we got to Riona tonight, with the help of everyone else. It took the coven two hours to fill him in and when we were finished, Mason threw back his head laughing! What the hell was so funny? He saw our crestfallen faces and so he answered.

"You told Dax that you were going to shish ka bob him?" I nodded my now tipsy head and defended myself.

"Well, I was really mad at you and I thought taking it out on him would make me feel better! And it did!" Mason pulled me off of the couch onto his lap and hugged me and whispered so only I could hear.

"One of the many reasons that I love you Lily. You are infinitely brave." I giggled.

Through the rest of the night we came up with a game plan. Mason was going to teach us all how to fight using many different aspects of Martial Arts. No one was going anywhere alone again. And Mason was going to stay here to help us with whatever we needed. Mason also asked me to be his date for Homecoming. I agreed, of course.

"I'll have the hottest date there!" He announced. We also talked about Riona's little outing and she confessed to forcing a vision that showed her Mason would be there to protect her. I was outraged.

"Wait Ri so you knew that going there would put you in danger? Why the hell would you do that?" She giggled and smiled at Mason, then me and answered.

"When I had the vision, Mason was there to make sure I was safe! I saw that he had been keeping his eye on us. But Lily in my vision I saw that you would get your soul mate back. You and Mason belong together!" She skipped over and kissed both Mason and I on the cheek and headed upstairs. I just looked at Mason and smiled.

"That one better find a man with lots of energy!" I told him pointing to the stairs where Ri had just disappeared. I laid my head on his chest just enjoying the moment. Everything between us happened so fast with so many deep emotions that I wasn't accustomed to these feelings. Mason ran his hand up and down my arm. I felt safe in that moment in his arms, so safe in fact I started to fall asleep. He cradled me in his arms and stood. I woke up. He spoke softly to me.

"Angel go back to sleep." My eyelids were now wide open. I didn't want him to leave me alone. I had put on a good front with my family about my fear but I admitted to him that I was terrified of his brother. Mason sat me back down on the couch and I snuggled back into him.

"Mase, how long did you stay here with my grandmother?" He answered my question immediately.

"Angel your grandmother allowed me to stay here as long as I wanted. We killed many vampires together. However, I do own a few homes in the tri state area. I do have other places to stay if that's what has you worried." I smacked his arm jokingly but that brought something else to the front of my already chaotic mind. I asked Mason about the secret room. We both went into the kitchen, next to the fireplace that had a wonderful fire burning, and he instructed me to place my hand on the wall and then told me what to say.

I repeated, " Ni mor a adnhail," and to my amazement a door appeared and swung open. "How do you know the spell?" I blurted out. Mason laughed quietly not wanting to wake the others.

"Lily I watched your granny say this spell a thousand times or more over the years. Only a Moon witch can open the door." The translation, Mason told me, was 'It has to be admitted.' We walked down the stairs, Mason leading the way of course because it was completely dark and he was the only one that could see without light. He told me that there were some candles on top of the bookshelves and tables but no matches. For me that was no problem. I lifted my hand, flicked my wrist and spoke, "Fire!" I felt the familiar feeling of power inside of me. Immediately my element answered, lighting all of the candles and setting a magnificent fire blazing in the fireplace. Mason stared at me in wonderment. I let go of his hand and started to walk around looking at everything, trying to take it all in. Mason came up behind me and spoke.

"Angel did you know that Granny was a fire user also? She told me that it took her years to hone her power enough to be able to do what you just did." I didn't turn around but I felt my breath catch. I've only had my powers for a couple of weeks. I had told him earlier about being able to call all four elements, but I wasn't sure if he had heard me, with all twelve of us witches trying to speak at the same time. I finally turned into him.

"Mase, did you hear me earlier about the elements?" He nodded at me and pulled me into his arms.

"Angel, I heard every word that my love said. Your special, Granny always said that you were, but I knew that the moment I looked into your eyes. You're special to so many people but especially to me." I laid my head on his shoulder, sighing now ready to ask the question that has haunted my dreams and all of my waking moments.

"Mason, did you know that you would love me back then?" I stayed there for a few minutes, drinking his smell in and waiting for his answer. He lifted my head so that we were face to face, looking into each other's eyes and replied, "Lily I knew that I loved you with every fiber of my immortal being when you looked me in the eyes at the mall. You are everything to me." My heart didn't try to beat out of my chest like I thought that it would, it was whole. I leaned in and kissed the only man that I would ever love this way. I wrapped my arms loosely around his neck while he moaned his happiness to me. I wanted to stay in this moment forever but it was time to start looking around and taking stock on what was in this room. So I reluctantly pulled away but held his hand in mine as we walked around. The first thing that caught my eye was a cabinet with herbs marked according to the phases of the moon. Underneath of that sat drawers that held crystals of all kinds. I got excited remembering we still needed a stone for the initiation ritual.

"Mason we still need a Selenite, help me look to see if we have one here!" Both of us started going through the little marked bags in the drawers. Granny had everything in here so I let myself believe that we would find it. But after twenty minutes of going through every bag in every drawer twice, we came up empty. Damn it! We split up in the room and really started searching for anything to help us. I started at the desk next to the fireplace. My grandmother had papers on top of the desk so I started leafing through those first. The first sheet of paper was a letter to the feed store with her order. I put that in my pocket. I would need to make that order soon. The next sheet of paper was a receipt for a store in Laurel, Maryland called The Crystal Fox. I read down her purchase and bingo!

"Mase, I found it! We can get the crystal here." I showed him the receipt and he agreed we would go together in the morning. I looked at my watch and holy crap it was four thirty in the morning. My body seemed to understand this fact as well because I yawned. That was all it took for Mason to insist on taking me upstairs, but I insisted that we stay in the secret room and work. So we compromised. We stayed in the secret room, and Mason pulled out the old cot that he used to sleep on and he made me lay down. I only agreed if he would lay with me. He could see that he couldn't win with my new found assertiveness, so we got comfortable on his old make shift bed. I rested my head on his awesome chest and listened to him breathe. While we lay there I thought of something.

"Mase, if you're a vampire how are you breathing? I hear your heartbeat, how is that possible?" I felt him nuzzle his mouth into my hair and laugh, "Angel I still breathe and I'm not dead just immortal." Huh. I snuggled in closer and felt my eyes getting heavy but again I heard him whispering the poem to me about a bird.

"On the wind that she has conjured, he soars with his crimson and gold feather. From the earth that she has conjured, he feasts on his bounty of heather. From the water that she has conjured, he frolics his body in the loch with a splash. From the fire that she has conjured, after 500 years he becomes naught but ash. From the spirit that she has conjured, he is reborn of the ash, new and whole again."

I was just drifting off when I heard Ciaran calling, "Guys come here! There's an open door next to the fireplace! I think Lily and Mason figured out how to get into the secret library! Lily and Mase are you guys down there?" Before we could answer I heard them barreling down the stairs. Declan spotted Mason and I on the cot and grinned. By six-thirty the whole house was up and in the secret room. I gave my cousin a kiss on the cheek, Seamus made coffee for everyone while Mason and I told the coven how to open the door to the secret room and that we had found out where we could get our hands on the Selenite. Everyone's spirits were lifted now, the atmosphere went from this heavy almost choking environment to being light and airy. Almost whimsical, magickal!

After I got cleaned up, Mason and I left the coven at the farm and headed to Laurel. The drive to The Crystal Fox was peaceful. Mason asked me all sorts of questions about my high school years.

"Lily, the last thing I want to know is, were you a cheerleader?" I stared at him and started laughing.

"Yes I was and I'll go you one better I was Homecoming Queen too." I continued my fit of the giggles. The conversation just flowed and we were both laughing when we pulled up to the shop.

Mason came around to my side of his car and opened the door for me, taking my hand. We walked into the most delightful aromas and were greeted by a young woman with cat like eyes.

"Merry Meet and welcome to The Crystal Fox. I'm the fox on duty." She was looking at the pendant that I had inherited and recognition lit her beautiful eyes. "You're Leeny Moon's granddaughter!" I held my head high at the mention of my grandmother and responded to her.

"Merry Meet. Yep, you caught me. I am Lilyann and this is Mason." Mason squeezed my hand and I just smiled. I answered her unspoken question. "My granny died a couple of weeks ago and I found a receipt of hers from here. So I thought maybe you guys could help me." I shot up a silent prayer to the goddess.

The sweet woman smiled warmly at me and replied, "Anything. Just name it." So I told her about the crystal we came to find and she led us over to a case housing all sorts of stones. She found the bin labeled Selenite and told me to pick one, to let my soul feel the vibration of the stone. My fingertip found the stone meant for me and I let it rest in my hand while she showed us other things in this incredible establishment. She talked to me about her talks with my granny.

"Leeny is in the bosom of our Goddess now, Blessed Be. Your grandmother was a very powerful and knowledgeable witch, with the most loving and pure heart." I felt a tear trekking down my cheek. The sweet woman placed her hand on my face and spoke again. "I know that this must seem like a great burden to take on at your young age but please know that Goddess will never abandon her daughter and your grandmother is always with you in spirit." I felt a sudden surge of kinship for this woman.

"Thank you," I said as I hugged her. We toured more of the store. Mason insisted on buying fall scented candles, smudges and teas. We made our purchase and as we were leaving the store I turned around, "Merry Part and Merry Meet again." She repeated the witch's goodbye. We walked out of the door and back into the sunny fall afternoon and began our trip back to Hampstead.

CHAPTER TWELVE

After returning to the farm to a home cooked lunch of chili that Cormac and Seamus had started right after Mason and I had left, we got down to work again. Mason took everyone but Ciaran and Jessie with him outside for target practice. I needed my sister to help me get into the shift, so that I could run through the initiation ritual with Ciaran in full dress so I would get used to the feeling of my attire. I admit I was too embarrassed to practice in front of Mason. After getting changed I walked down the stairs, and into the living room. I heard Ciaran and my father's sharp intake of air.

"Dad, what the hell are you doing here?" I tried to pull the slit together but it wouldn't budge. Damn it! Ciaran tried to weasel out of the front door. "No way Ciaran! Stay put. Jess come and help me change again. Dad I'll be right back down."

I stomped back up the stairs yelling over my shoulder. Jessie and I did THE fastest change job of clothes ever! I threw on my favorite jeans and my Towson State University sweatshirt, ran back down the stairs with Jessie at my heels, to find that Mason had now joined my father and Ciaran in the living room. For shit's sake!

"Well I finally met Mason," my dad said, smiling at me. What father smiles about meeting a guy his daughter is into?

I returned the smile and whispered in Masons' ear, "Did you compel my father?" I looked at his face as he smiled. Then he mouthed No! My sister broke the silence.

"Hey Daddy isn't Mason like totally great!" My father suddenly noticed that his youngest daughter was in the room. He broke his gaze from me and turned to her.

"Jessie, I brought my credit card over for you to go shopping for your Homecoming dress and accoutrements. You know I'm not very good at these girly things. Your Aunt Rae will be helping you, as well as your sisters." Jessie grabbed the card like any normal teenage witch would and promised not to spend too much.

"I've worked all of my life to give you kids whatever you need and want, so have fun. Just not too much fun and promise me you will not show a lot of skin. Please," my father responded.

Ciaran and Jessie excused themselves leaving my father, my boyfriend and I alone in the house. This is a fine little pixy fix I'm in. Izzy pranced into the room and leapt lithely into Masons' lap purring.

Mason responded by petting her gently, something that did not go unnoticed by my dad.

"Mason, you must really have a way with animals, that's my moms' old cat Isadora. She's a mean old thing and doesn't usually take too kindly to strangers but she seems to like you." Mason smiled at my dad, still petting Izzy, replying to his comment.

"Yes sir Mr. Moon, I adore them and they seem to like me. It's really all about not showing aggression or fear towards them. My father taught me that when I was a kid." My father nodded his approval at Masons' respect. It was starting to get dark outside and Mason spoke again.

"Well Mr. Moon, I really have to be going but it was wonderful to finally meet you. Lily always speaks so highly of her dad." Internally, I rolled my eyes as Izzy jumped off of his lap on cue, Mason and my father stood and shook hands. I sat there trying to figure out what was going on, Mason was up to something and I needed to know what it was!

"I'll walk Mason out and be right back." I said a little sadly. I got up from the couch and followed Mason out to his car and started to have a little bit of a fit. "Mason what the hell! You're supposed to stay here remember!" He stopped my little temper tantrum with a kiss. A very small kiss at that, but it was effective.

He looked into my eyes laughing, "Angel I'm coming right back as soon as your father leaves but I want to check on a few things and go pick something up for dinner for all of us. Just breathe." Whew! That brought a small smile to my face and a skip back into my step, as I turned around to go back into the house Mason smacked my rear end and said, "We'll have to watch one of my other favorite actors when all of this is over. John Wayne. You'll love the movie McLintock!" He was still laughing as he pulled away.

I went back into the house filled with my family saying their goodbyes to my dad. He saw me walk in the door and started speaking with a grin on his face, "Lilyann I really like Mason. I think that he's a keeper!" Will you still like him when you find out he's a vampire? I asked myself and nodded to father. He kissed me on the forehead and left. Goddess! When he pulled away I was pounced on by the coven

"Lil where's Mason?" Liam asked me loudly. I put up my hand walking to the kitchen to grab my phone. I hit the speed dial and Mason answered on the first ring.

"Miss me already?" I laughed as the entire coven tried to talk to him through the phone I raised my hand and pointed to the fireplace flicking my wrist and called, "Fire!" That had absolutely no effect on anyone! So I did the next best thing I could think of and I screamed, "SHUT UP!" Finally it was quiet.

"Mason left so that my father wouldn't know that he's staying here just yet and he went for dinner since none of us cooked." Cormac spoke up immediately and a little bitterly.

"Lily, Seamus and I made lunch!" I swear it was like having a kindergarten in my house at all times. She did that, he did this, that one took my mascara, I want that power! Goddess...I am never having kids!

"Are you hearing all of this love of my life?" I asked Mason. It was totally silent now not a peep from anyone including my vampire. That made me a little nervous so I called for him, "Mason, are you ok? Damn it, answer me!" He started to make little coughing sounds answering me.

"Lily...uh...uh...Angel did you hear what you just called me?" I went scarlet! Oh Hell! Who cares everyone already knows how I feel about Mason and I better start getting used to expressing emotions of happiness now. When my mom died I shut down inside never letting anyone truly see my feelings for them. I lifted my head proudly and said, "Yes babe. Mason I know exactly what I said and I meant it!" I heard gasps of shock from all directions especially from the phone. Mason recovered his normal confident demeanor and spoke normally to me.

"Well Angel, just before you called Inspector MacQuarie phoned me and wanted to meet tonight and I wondered if you would like to see him again?" I was actually excited to see Duncan this time without the fear of jail hanging over Masons' head. I asked him to please invite the Inspector over and we ended our conversation conservatively.

I was in the kitchen going through the BoS looking for a stunning potion to help us slow the vampires down during an attack when two arms came around me sitting two coffees in front of me, one cold and one hot. I smiled to myself wondering what I ever did to deserve the affection that this man always offered to me. I slowly turned around putting my arms around his perfect neck and asked a different question.

"So what did I do to deserve my special order of coffee? Hmm?" He bent down and kissed me.

"Because you are mine," he said, in between little kisses. I giggled, nuzzling into his neck and heard a voice that I hadn't been ready for yet.

"Ay lassie wait until he puts a ring around that pretty little finger of yours. Mason." Inspector MacQuarie was standing in the kitchen with a coven of witches around him. I untangled myself from Mason and walked over to Duncan and shook his hand.

"It's really good to see you again Inspec...Duncan." He cleared his throat at the mention of his formal title. I started introducing everyone as Mason brought in the Chinese food that he had picked up. As he was bringing this feast in all of us started unpacking bags, even Duncan helped. Everyone started grabbing for different boxes and filling their plates, I on the other hand had grabbed some pork lo mein and was playing with it while talking to Duncan.

"Is it hard, I mean the work that you do?" He smiled at me and then popped another dumpling into his mouth and chewed. Mason interrupted.

"Duncan I should probably fill you in on another little secret." I turned to look at my boyfriend trying to figure out WHAT piece of unknown information he was going to tell Duncan. Surely not the Covens' secret, my secret. I searched Masons' face again while my family sat eating oblivious to my fears. When Mason spoke I held my breath.

"Duncan you've met everyone here and they all know about my little condition, that I'm a vampire." I blew out my breath and sent up a silent thank you to the Goddess. What was I thinking? Of course Mason wouldn't reveal something so personal about my family and me without our consent. Duncan almost choked on a bite of a spring roll. I stood up trying to remember the Heimlich maneuver. Duncan waved me down as he coughed the roll down the correct pipe in his throat. Duncan's face was very red and menacing in that moment.

"Laddie, we talked about this, didn't we. The less people that know the better!" Mason got up from the table picking a small box up off the counter that I hadn't noticed before and placed it in front of the older man.

"Duncan I told them because they need to know. My brothers are here after them. Look at what my beloved brother left on her front porch," Mason said, nodding his head in my direction. The Inspector took the box and opened it. The look on his round face was that of horror! I grabbed the box before anyone could stop me and regretted it immediately as I peered inside.

A Lily lay next to a dead mouse, with what was obviously Dax's fang marks, and a note that read, 'I can't wait to play with you next Lily. I'll deflower you before I devour you. Your predator, Dax' Goddess help me!

"Saints preserve us!" Duncan yelled as the candles and fireplace all lit themselves again but this time my power went completely wonky and started lighting things outside! "Shit!" I ran out of the back door and tried to calm myself. I took two very deep breath's, in and out, raising my hand and called, "Water!" Instantly the element did my bidding for me, extinguishing the outside fires. I turned around to see Duncan's' face contorted in confusion. I was having a nervous breakdown!

I started screaming, "Come on Dax! Don't be a coward!" I was crying as I screamed and felt my throat getting raw. Mason had his arms around me in an instant trying to calm me down.

"Angel he will NOT touch you! I will kill him before he gets that close to you." All the same Mason scanned the landscape. We were joined by Duncan who was ushering me into the house.

"Lassie, come inside now! Mason go and check things out. I'll stay with them," he finished. I resisted being pulled by Duncan so he grabbed me and threw me over his shoulder and he ran back into the house. I needed to think. Dax had already been here! He had been on the front porch so close to my family.

"We'll get him Lily! He's not going to hurt you." Declan had his arms around me tightly trying to reassure me but he was wrong. My fear was for them, each of them. I hugged my brother back and stepped away from him shaking my head. I turned and faced them just as Mason came back in the door. I opened my mouth to speak but failed so I tried again and this time my voice was timid.

"You're wrong D. I'm not afraid for myself. I would happily die in any one of your places. He was here already which means, he'll be back. And now he wants me to suffer." I finished, looking at Mason hoping that he would tell me that my theory of his evil brother was not correct, but my love just looked into my eyes that held the wisdom of the truth. I couldn't look at them so I walked into the kitchen and grabbed the bottle of vodka and a glass.

"Do you mind making that two lass?" I hadn't seen Duncan sitting at the table. I nodded at him and grabbed another glass, poured two very large vodka's and walked to the table placing his in front of him. I needed to say something but first I needed a drink! I took a large gulp of the alcohol and let the burn make its way down my aching throat and into my stomach before I spoke.

"Duncan I'm so sorry that I made you nervous. This is all new to us, to me and I don't completely have a handle on my powers all of the time." I laid my hand on the table and he covered it with his own. He made me feel like he was my favorite uncle and I didn't have to pretend to be anything but who I actually was with him.

"Lily everything will be ok. My concern is Masons' brothers. Those two and that sister of his are real pieces of work. I want you to promise me, lass, that you'll be extra cautious," he said, giving me a look of concern as he took another large drink of vodka. After a few minutes the coven and Mason started trickling back in. Duncan shook everyone's hand and Mason and I walked him out. Duncan got in his car, starting it and rolled down his window.

"Lily, I'll not be a stranger. Saints preserve us! The friends that I keep witches and vampires!" He smiled warmly at us as he pulled away. I started back for the house, shivering and looking in every direction waiting for his abomination of a brother to jump out at me. Mason wrapped his arms around me on high alert. We walked in the front door to the coven heading upstairs. Ciaran was the last one walking out of the room.

"Lily we cleaned up the kitchen and locked the house down. Love you. Night Mase." Mason told Ciaran goodnight and looked at me. I grabbed his hand turning to lock the door but he did it for me. I just wanted to lie down in my bed, in my room, in real pajamas and talk to Mason. I led him up the stairs to my bedroom closing the door behind us. I went over to my dresser grabbing a set of thermal pajamas and headed to the bathroom to change. I asked him to light a candle for me, afraid to just flick my wrist at this point. I was so upset I could inadvertently set the house on fire.

I hurried and changed clothes, tossing my hair into a ponytail and brushing my teeth. When I finished I flicked the light off and crawled into my bed, under the blankets, next to the man that I knew held my heart. I felt him wrap himself protectively around me. That's where I stayed all night awake waiting for evil to show up at my doorstep and try to hurt one of the people that I loved. It was a nightmare that I couldn't wake up from until Dax was dead.

Mason and I, having laid silently in bed next to each other all night, were dressed and downstairs at the crack of dawn ready to take Jessie and Liam to school ourselves. After giving Ciaran instructions to keep everyone inside until we returned, Mason and I took my sister and cousin to school. The drive there took only a few minutes but everyone one of those minutes I feared for my family. We dropped them off watching them walk into the school and started to pull out onto the main road when my cell phone rang. The caller ID told me it was Aidan and so I answered on speaker.

"Hey Aidan are you guys ok?" He sounded excited when he answered me.

"Lily we went into the secret library and found another note from Granny! Get home you have to read this! And we're fine! Bye." I didn't have to tell Mason to get home fast. He had us back at the farm in a minute. We rushed through the front door. My family was in the living room waiting for us. Cormac walked over and handed a piece of parchment to me and an envelope to Mason. We both read the notes that we were handed. The note handed to me was again from my grandmother and addressed to the Moon Coven. I quickly read my grandmothers' words.

She was letting whoever received this letter (if we hadn't found out that we were witches) know that she had crafted a potion that would cloak her family as long as we never touched our magick inside. She also had a suspicion that someone was helping the trio of vampires related to her friend Mason. When I looked up Mason was now watching me with the envelope handed to him opened and a tear falling down his cheek. I didn't know yet what he had read that upset him but I was getting ready to find out. I touched his face erasing the moisture that had seeped from his eye and received the letter that he offered me. My love sat on the couch with Shannon as I began to read aloud.

'Mason, I fear that this note will not find you in time. I have scryed again and now know that you are correct, your family is hunting you, and therefore, me. You have become part of my family and I will do my best to protect you as well. If I fail please promise me that you will look after my children and grandchildren. I have created a way to keep them safe but you will need to see that the attached envelope reaches my sister Colleen, in Galway, she will know what to do. I'm not certain yet of their identity but I am positive that your siblings have a witch working with them here. Please know, Mason, that you are loved by me child. I should let you know also that I saw something else while I was scrying. Your love for her will be true and I very much approve! Take care of my family, watch over my Lilybug. Help her to love again and mend the broken heart that we have caused by leaving her. Blessed Be~Leeny'

When I lifted my eyes Cormac was the first thing that I spotted comforting Mason. I let the letter fall through my fingers walking over and knelt in front of him. I forcefully made him look at me by gently pulling his face to me. I felt more confident and certain of myself than I had in days. I searched his troubled eyes and let my heart speak for me.

"Mason my grandmother loved you, my family loves you…I love you." He looked directly into my eyes and my gaze never wavered. He was searching my soul for the truth and he must have found what he sought because he finally spoke to me.

"Lily it's my fault. They killed her because of me. I'm so sorry!" I fell backwards. "Oof!" I landed on my rear end at least. Mason reached out to make sure that I was ok and then pulled his hand back like it was poison and he was afraid that he would infect me. I regained my composure after being stung by his actions and words. I sat myself back up and got to my feet feeling truth and power course through me as I spoke.

"Mason stop it now! Dax killed my grandmother, not you and not because of you. Your sister wants me!" Mason stood at the mention of his sister. He paced back and forth cracking his knuckles menacingly. Can vampires have a nervous breakdown? I blocked his path standing in front of him. "Mason we have work to do. I need you." I watched as my words washed over his soul, returning his determination to stop his family once and for all. He pulled me into his muscular arms and spoke calmly.

"Lily I will kill them. Dax is going to suffer for taking Granny's life, that I promise." He finished, resting his head against mine.

Ciaran called for everyone to come downstairs. I hadn't realized that he wasn't still upstairs with us. I took off flying down the stairs behind Mason but in front of everyone else. Mason scanned the room for danger. Ciaran put his hand on Masons' shoulder.

"Calm down big guy. Look at what I found!" Mason took the book handed to him by my cousin. It was my grandmother's Grimoire. Mason read intently and then laughed loudly smiling at all of us. Ciaran answered our confused looks.

"Granny spelled the house! Mason is the only vampire that can cross the threshold! She puts watch sigils all over the place." Cormac smiled, grabbing the Grimoire, and spoke.

"Lily I've got this! I've been studying the runic symbols and how to protect with the sigils!" Cormac to the book and walked away. He sat at the desk intensely reading what ancient Runes my grandmother had used. I sent up a silent thank you to the Goddess! My loved ones are safe in this house. I would definitely sleep tonight, a little anyway. I was distracted at how every one of the people in this room had been hit by blow after blow but kept going, never giving up! I was so proud to be a part of my family. I suddenly felt Masons' hand in mine and turned toward him. He inclined his head in

the direction of the stairs. A silent plea for me to follow him, and I did. When we reached the living room we didn't stay. We walked out of the front door down the steps stopping on the front lawn before he spoke.

"Lily. I love you so much. Please forgive me." What the hell? He kissed my hand and walked about thirty feet away from me. He turned back around to face me, only it wasn't my Mason! This one had fangs and looked at me like I was the other white meat. For shit's sake!

CHAPTER THIRTEEN

Mason was going to attack me! I froze. I had never seen his teeth protrude from his mouth that way. He actually looked like a vampire. Damn it! He was almost on top of me when my mind started working again. He's a vampire! I flung my hand up at him screaming, "Fire!" and the element flew at him like a flamethrower. I spun around running for the porch, and almost tripped on the step. I caught myself on the railing and saw him, now out of the corner of my eye, coming at me again! What the hell is wrong with him! I threw my other hand up crying for all of the elements. "Air, Fire, Water and Earth!" The elements came from all four directions like a vortex. Unbearably strong wind spun around him, fire raced around the next layer of my protection, followed by water that enclosed the flames and lastly the ground started to break open shaking horrifically inside of the cyclone of power that was holding him there. He was fighting my power.

"Goddess Help me!" I screamed as I frantically searched for a piece of wood, nothing! I could hear that my family now realized something was not right and were coming to help! Mason had broken free of the elements and had forcefully grabbed me from the porch throwing me on the ground. I didn't hit as hard as I should have. I heard the terror in my covens' voices as they ran from the house toward us and knew that my life would end right here and now on the already too warm grass. I looked into the merciless eyes of this vampire as he smiled at me bringing those fangs to my neck. I waited to feel the pain of his sharp teeth puncturing my flesh, hearing my family screaming at Mason to stop!

They didn't know how to fight him off of me. Instead of agony, I felt his lips brush against my neck kissing me. What the hell is going on around here? Is he playing with me the way that his brother was? I opened my eyes to see my Mason again! I almost cried in relief. My family stood there in shock, none of them able to move. He was off of the ground in one swift fluid movement reaching down to help me up. I timidly took his hand and got to my feet, trying to pull away from him, but he wouldn't let my wrist go. He had a look on his face that was serious and dangerous yet caring. There were hints of the monster inside straining his carved facial features as he spoke to all of us.

"That's how fast and frightening Dax, or any other vampire, could have gotten to any of you. And to me that's unacceptable! We start training as soon as Jessie and Liam are home from school." I was in shock! This had been a demonstration to show me how weak I was. I honestly didn't know how to react. For the first time since meeting this man, and opening my heart to him, I was afraid of Mason.

I walked around trying to physically and mentally cool off. It was only early afternoon and it had to be eighty degrees already. Welcome to Maryland's crazy weather! Ciaran walked over to me concern written all over his face.

"Lily, did you know that he was going to do that? Are you hurt?" I shrugged out of my hoodie and answered him.

"No! I had no idea. I just thought he wanted to talk. I'm fine, physically." I smiled at him as Mason approached us. He stood there until I made eye contact with him then I unleashed my anger.

"Mason what is wrong with you? I thought that you were trying to kill me!" I glanced at him only to find him smiling with that cocky little grin that I loved.

"Angel I needed you to think that I was honestly going to hurt you. I had to see what you could do to defend yourself when caught off guard. The other night you held your own, but on sheer adrenalin. I was there to keep you safe. But what if I wouldn't have been there?" Everything that he was saying was true, but it still pissed me off. My heart was still beating out of my chest, but I gave him a tentative smile.

"Ok, I get it, and I forgive you…a little," I said winking at him.

After Mason and Seamus got back to the farm that afternoon, with Liam and Jessie, we all changed into workout clothes, and of course I was the last one outside. I wanted to get Masons' attention. I let the new found confidence that occasionally showed itself in me have its way now. I walked down the steps of the porch wearing my black spandex capris, black tank top that showed off my silver belly button ring, and my white sketchers. I knew that I was not gorgeous, but I have been able to turn a head or two in my lifetime. I watched as Masons' jaw dropped.

Aidan playfully punched his arm saying, "Liam let's put some music on and get started." I walked over and stood by Ri and the girls, pulling my hair in a ponytail, Mason never taking his eyes off of me. I responded with a coy little smile then turned to talk to my cousin. Liam chose a hip-hop CD and put it into the player. The music started as Mason stepped into the center of the circle the coven had made around him, and started our training.

"The first thing that I'm going to start you on is a few different types of kicks. Watch me and then you try." Mason lifted his left leg in front of him and snapped it forward at the knee with lightning speed. It landed in front of him then he brought his right leg up bending at the hip aiming his knee to where his intended target's head would be and snapped his foot out as quickly as the original kick. I was totally impressed, however I couldn't think about the kicks.

My mind was stuck on how hot he looked when he was performing these stunts! I started fantasizing about his rock hard chest again. What it would look like with that shirt off. I came back to reality with Mason standing in front of me smiling and my family laughing. He leaned down to my ear.

"See something that you like?" I started biting my lower lip and looked away blushing. He spoke again. "Because I certainly do. And she's all mine." He stole a quick kiss, and turned back around having us imitate his movements. Goddess! He is seriously yummy! Mason walked around the group cheering us on when we had it right, and correcting us if we weren't doing the kicks properly. I was shocked at how hard of a workout it actually was to just kick for an hour! My legs felt like Jell-O. Mason called us all back to attention.

"Very good! Those kicks are going to help keep your attacker further away from you during a physical fight but we need to work on your stake maneuvers while implementing your magick as well." We followed my vampire over to the barn. He had set up an obstacle course of sorts for us. There were hay bales for us to practice on with our stakes, old grain bags filled with saw dust for us to kick, and different objects for us to direct our power at. It was so sunny and warm outside for the middle of October that everyone's skin was glistening with sweat. I finally had the opportunity to marvel at Mason's chest as he took off his shirt with the other guys, and I nearly tripped over my own feet being so caught up in my view. My boyfriend caught me before I hit the ground, laughing.

"What am I going to do with you?" I gave a little nervous laugh as I straightened myself back up, thinking I have a few suggestions for that little query. That thought would have to be filed away until later because just then he broke us off into groups of two's and three's instructing us on how to move while kicking, and to focus our minds so that we could also incorporate our magick at the same time.

We were improving rapidly under my boyfriend's tutelage. Mason had each one of us hitting our targets on the move. Stakes, legs, and magick were landing exactly where they were supposed to. It was amazing. An hour later, we had all gone through the drill a dozen times or more so he had us stop.

"Better! All of you are without question Leeny's grandkids. She would be proud." We were all beaming. We had never seen our grandmother fight. We didn't know her as a powerful witch, but Mason had. He called for me to join him letting the rest of my family go inside and get cleaned up. Mason walked me through a few more drills.

"Lily, I want you to try calling fire as you lunge with the stake." I did as he instructed. I positioned myself in front of him, stake in my dominate left hand. I waited to see what direction he would come at me from. He didn't keep me in suspense long. He advanced on my left side, reaching for my tool. I spun into his attack, landing a perfect roundhouse kick to his side calling my element, "Fire!" The flame sprang to life in front of his face making him step back, and I saw my opportunity. I threw a front kick and hit my target in the middle of his chest, throwing him off balance enough for me to fling my body against his, knocking us both to the ground. He landed on his back with me straddled on top of him, and my stake raised inches above his heart. He looked up at me smiling from ear to ear. Pride written all over that God like face.

"If this were a real fight I would have won and you'd be dead. Right?" He tried to move my weapon but I resisted as he spoke.

"Yes Angel. I would be dead." Now I smiled proudly! I was not a weak little girl who couldn't fight. I was becoming a strong witch that was deadly. "I'm quite enjoying my view."

I looked down at him as he spoke, and realized that I was still sitting straddled over top of him, and he was staring at my chest with his playfully evil little grin. Faster than a cobra strikes he had the stake out of my hand tossing it over his head out of my reach, and flipped me over so that now he was lying on top of me. I felt the sweaty skin of his bared chest against the flimsy material of my tank top. Our eyes locked on each other. The magnetism between our bodies was palpable. He lowered his head, gently brushing his lips up my jaw line, then up to my mouth, kissing me passionately while I lay in the grass. My entire body tingled in response to each of his touches. My attraction to him was overwhelming. I brought both of my hands up to his face holding his lips to mine and allowing the passion to work its own magick between us. His answer to my touch was primal. He pressed his lips, and body, harder against mine letting them meld together. I wanted Mason so badly but knew that this was not the right time or place. I wanted our first time to be something that was enchanted. I pulled my face back slightly letting my tongue run across his lower lip. I felt his body quiver above mine.

"We should probably go inside." I said this reluctantly and a little breathlessly. It was dark now and a chill was setting in this October evening. He agreed that it was time to go back to the house. Mason got to his feet first helping me up into his arms. I would never tire of his smell or the feel of full lips against mine. I brushed myself off on the way back home and something popped into my mind so I blurted it out.

"Mase I want to go on a hunt with you, like Granny did." I heard the snarl that echoed from the back of his throat.

"Angel I am not taking you on a hunt! I will not dangle you in front of Dax like a piece of steak held in front of a hungry lion!" He pulled me closer to his body as we got to the porch. I could feel the pure hatred of his brother radiating from him. I let the subject drop for now, but only for the moment, because my phone was ringing. I let Mason get cleaned up, in my bathroom, while I answered my cell. It was Cam.

"Hey Lily, I need to talk to you about my journal. Can I swing by tomorrow?" I didn't like the way she sounded. It was like a forced calm screening her terror. I answered my best friend.

"Cam you can come over anytime, you know that. Do you want to come over now?" She hesitated as if she was contemplating the idea, and then answered.

"No. Tomorrow would be better. I need to do some research about this issue tonight."

I responded to her with, "Ok Cam, but if you need me before then I'm going to keep my cell with me all night so just call ok?"

She agreed, we said our goodbyes, and hung up. I was just standing in the middle of my bedroom when Mason walked out of my bathroom, freshly showered, wearing another pair of sweatpants, and a plain white tee shirt. He saw my worried face and approached.

"What's wrong?" he asked. I walked over to the dresser putting my phone on top, and reached inside my top drawer for pajamas. He was now standing right next me. "Lily what's wrong? Talk to me. I am sorry about what I did earlier." I shook my head at him and answered.

"It's not that Mase. Although I should let you know if I see your fangs coming at me like that again I will not hesitate to stake you!" He laughed at me, and then took my hand over to the cedar chest and pulled me onto his lap as he sat down. I looked into his concerned face, and told him about Cam. I told him everything about the ghosts, the voices in her head, and the phone call I had just received. Mason took a moment before he gave me his opinion.

"Angel I'll help you look for answers but I want you to get a shower and something to eat. You need your strength." He kissed me on my forehead, and I got up heading back over to my dresser to get my pajamas. My cell rang again. I answered immediately, afraid that Cam needed me. I hit the speaker button.

"There's my lovely Lily. Did you get the package that I left for you beautiful?" Dax said playfully to me. I looked at Mason. He held his hand out for the phone, but I wanted to set his brother straight so instead I spoke into the phone.

"Dax, I received your disgusting box. You do realize that you can't hurt me, don't you?"

He laughed menacingly, "Lily I can have you whenever I am ready. My pathetic little brother can't stop me and he knows that. That's why he came here to find your grandmother. He thought she could help him and look where it got her!" He laughed again. My stomach churned thinking about what he had done to her. Mason grabbed the phone out of my hand. He was beyond livid and growled at his brother.

"I am going to find a way to kill you Dax! I will protect Lily and the rest of the coven. It must suck to watch your little brother have what you want so badly and know that she loves me! I read the note Dax. You don't want to give her to Maylee anymore you want her to desire you." I grabbed the phone out of Masons' hand and laughed hysterically.

"I want you to hear this Dax! Mason, I love you with all of my heart and soul. You are the only man that I will ever love." I hung the phone up on his evil brother! I looked at my boyfriend again letting the words in my head rush out.

"Mase I think that we need to find out about the prophecy! Granny mentioned it a lot in her Grimoire, how I was the only one able to stop this. Tonight we hit the books, and we start as soon as I get out of the shower. Tell the others." I kissed him softly then grabbed my clothes, and headed to the shower to wash the feeling of dirt from my body and mind.

After my shower, and a quick turkey and tomato sandwich, I grabbed the Book of Shadows joining my coven and Mason in our quest to find out about the prophecy. I asked Cassie to look for anything on ghosts to help with Cam's problem. At around midnight Jessie and Liam were ready to fall over from physical and mental exhaustion with the rest of the coven so I sent them all off to bed. Riona told me that her mom had called, and we were going shopping for Jessie's Homecoming dress the following evening, and we were starting at the mall. The scene of the last attack. Wonderful! Mason refused to let us go without him so my vampire was going to go to the mall with the girls. I already felt bad for the poor guy.

Mason and I went up to my room and I crawled from the bottom of the bed to the top, and struggled to get under the blankets until he helped me. I was going to pay tomorrow for the workout today. He lay next to me letting my head rest in its favorite place, his chest. I was drained, no sleep last night and tonight my legs are aching. I remember Mason reciting that poem again, I needed to ask him about that, but this was not the time for that it was the time for sleep.

"Go to sleep my Angel. Let nothing haunt your dreams tonight. I am here...I love you." Mason whispered to me. I burrowed my head further into his chest whispering back to him.

"I love you more." Then I gave into my body's command, falling asleep almost immediately.

I blinked my eyes a few times rolling over to the nightstand that held my alarm clock and yawned. As I moved I felt every muscle in my body protest. I reached for my clock sure that the little bell that usually woke me up would start ringing. I looked at the time and sat bolt upright in my bed. It was nine o'clock!

"Shit! Ow!" I needed to get downstairs to make sure that Jessie and Liam were at school and the rest of us needed to resume our search for the prophecy. Mason walked into my room with a tray of food, and placed it on the cedar chest. I was frantic.

"Mase the prophecy, and Liam and Jessie! I have to get them to school and then Cam...the ghosts I have to..." He cut me off.

"Angel calm down. Ciaran and I took them to school, Cassie has made progress on Cam's little condition and the rest of us have been working on the prophecy. You needed your sleep. We all voted!" He said smiling at me. I rested my head in my hands and yawned again.

"I don't know why I am so tired. I have pulled all-nighters before and have never felt like this!" I yawned again looking at my vampire. He was smiling weirdly at me "Mason what do you know that I don't?" He continued to smile as he spoke.

"Come downstairs and see for yourself." He grabbed the tray and we went downstairs together. I got to the bottom of the stairs just in time to see Ciaran say aloud, "Candlestick!" and watched in disbelief as the one that he had spoken to levitated in the air and began zooming through the room landing in his outstretched hand.

"What the hell kind of freaky stuff are you doing Ciaran?" I asked him still not truly understanding what I had just seen. I walked over to the couch and sat down. I looked to the room at large waiting for someone to explain what this craziness was or to wake me up from a dream! Mason answered my question.

"Love, this morning Ciaran came to me because his powers are growing and he needed to talk to someone." I looked at Ciaran as Mason continued. "We took Liam and Jessie to school and came right back here to hit the BoS and found a passage about all of your powers. Angel you called all four elements at one time yesterday. All of your powers are growing. That's why you're so exhausted. You're expending an incredible amount of energy wielding all of that power." I didn't know what to say. Mason handed me the Book of Shadows, and I read where he pointed in the book. Goddess! What else are we going to be able to do? I looked up to everyone waiting on my reaction so I said, "Stake!" sure enough one of the stakes I had in my room came flying down the stairs and I caught it!

"Wicked!" I said grinning

We had all agreed to talk about the prophecy tonight after we returned from the mall. Aunt Rae pulled up while I was hammering out plans with Cam. She was going to come over after dinner and our little shopping adventure. Mason, Cassie and I drove in my Jeep leaving Riona, Shannon and Jessie to ride with Aunt Rae. The drive to the mall was uneventful, we only spoke of dresses, shoes, and accessories. We pulled up next to Aunt Rae and we all went into the mall together, Mason holding my hand and talking to Riona's mom.

"Now Mason you call me Aunt Rae too, ok?" My boyfriend nodded his head. Jessie walked into the shop first and started going through the racks of formal attire. Mason kept his eyes on us at all times, close to the entrance of the shop, sort of like he was the Secret Service. My sister gathered a few dresses, taking them into the changing room. The other girls did the same. We were the only customers in the shop at the moment so we had the salesclerk all to ourselves. Jessie walked out of the changing room with a little strapless number on, a soft baby blue with a bubble skirt. The only problem was there was hardly any fabric! Aunt Rae almost had a heart attack. Jessie went back into the room at our expressions, to try a different dress on. While she was changing I checked the rack closest to me. I found a beautiful iridescent pink strapless dress with a fluffy skirt. Perfect for me to hide weapons under in case I needed them. Mason spotted me and winked his approval. Jessie came out of the dressing room, this time in a beautiful iced blue gown. It was a halter top with clingy, shimmering material. My baby sister looked amazing in it! Cassie, Shan and Ri had already purchased their dresses. I was taking mine and Jessie's up to the counter while she looked around for earrings to match when Riona screamed, "Ow!!!" Then she fell to the floor holding her head, Mason got to her first, and he was whispering in her ear when I got there.

"Stay with her Angel. She's having a vision, I'll go deal with everything else." He said as he started to turn but Ri whimpered, "Mason. Please!" My boyfriend turned back around kneeling in front of my cousin.

"Ri sweetie what is it?" His voice was very calming, but Riona continued to whimper as Shannon and Aunt Rae ran over to us.

"What's wrong Riona honey?" I turned to my aunt and cousin.

"Oh she tripped. Mason and I will help her. Will you take my credit card Aunt Rae and pay for mine and Jessie's things?" Aunt Rae looked at her daughter, waiting for reassurance that her child was okay. I looked at Riona and there was no way she was in any condition to help so I then whispered to Mason. "Compel my aunt!" He looked at me to see if I was serious, I nodded my head! He rose from the floor and, stood in front of my aunt staring deeply into her eyes. I watched as her pupils slid in and out of focus as he spoke to her.

"Aunt Rae, Riona tripped and fell. Lilyann and I are going to help her up. She's fine, right." Aunt Rae nodded to him then turned to go to the counter to finish my transaction. I just watched my vampire successfully perform what he had failed to do on me, Compulsion. I waited for Mason to come back to the floor where I sat rubbing Riona's shoulder trying to comfort her. Mason encouraged her.

"It's ok to finish the vision, go ahead Ri." Riona began whimpering again.

"Mason your brother...he...he wants to make you suffer. He came here on Maylee's orders, but he has seen Lily now and, he wants her to be his. He says he will take her from the light turning her into his dark love. He's planning to...Goddess he's going to bite her, making her his mate forever on Halloween after he kills you in front of her, with a weird sword!"

CHAPTER FOURTEEN

I felt like the all of the air had been sucked from the room. Riona came out of her vision crying.

"Lily, Mason what are we going to do? How are we going to stop Dax?!" Mason stood up calmly reaching down to help Ri up off of the floor. He surveyed my face, but I gave nothing away. He took my hands pulling me to my feet. I kept my expression neutral, I had plenty of experience in this department. The conversation in my head began as soon as we were led from the store by my boyfriend. 'What the hell am I going to do now? I can't fight Dax yet! I'm not strong enough. I need to find the prophecy. I will never allow him to take me alive'

"Angel, let's go inside." Masons' voice brought me out of my internal struggle. We had gotten back to the farm without me remembering any part of the drive home! "Oh," I took the hand that he offered me, and headed into the house.

"Lilyann, we need to talk about this." Mason said. Cam stood up as I entered the kitchen. Shit! I had completely forgotten that she was coming over. I needed to put my problems away until later. My best friend needed me now.

"How are you feeling honey?" I asked her as I hugged her. She was trembling. I pulled away from her looking into those hazel eyes. "What's happened Cam?"

Mason went to the fridge and grabbed a bottle of orange juice, and handed it to her. She sat down at the table, and played with the label on the bottle. This was going to be a long night.

"Lily your grandmother wants you to open spirit because you're in danger!" She blurted out. I just looked at her as comprehension finally dawned on me!

"Wait...did you say spirit?" I said excitedly! This was the second time that this spirit thing has been mentioned and now by my dead grandmother! She just looked at me like I hadn't heard her.

"Lily did you hear me. You're in danger! She told me that someone wanted to REALLY hurt you! This is serious!" I felt it in my soul this was the answer. Spirit whatever it is, was my ticket to defeating Dax! I hugged her.

"Cam yes I heard every word." I said smiling at her. "Now tell me everything. I want you to tell us about all of the ghosts that you have seen and heard. Start with my grandmother though please. How did she look?"

After forty five minutes of Cam telling us how my grandmother was adamant that somehow I had to open 'spirit', Mason was trustworthy, the witch that had betrayed my grandmother was now in fact keeping tabs on me but she didn't know who it was, and that I did have the power to defeat Dax, Cam sighed.

"Okay now you know everything. Lily I'm scared for you!" She said to me in a partially calm voice. The kitchen was full with the coven and Mason listening to her talk to me. Ciaran spoke up.

"But what IS Spirit? We still haven't figured that out? The danger that Granny is talking about has to be Dax and Victor." I watched as my family all nodded their heads in agreement. We filled those in that had not been around for Ri's vision at the mall. Their faces fell, and Mason, who had barely taken a few steps away from me since our return spoke.

"Lily I'm taking you away from here, away from Dax's reach!" He said with confidence. My eyes found his, and he read my answer there.

"I'm sorry. I will not run. I will fight. My grandmother says that I AM strong enough to win this battle, so I fight." Mason stared through me. I leaned into him, and whispered, "We'll talk about this later in private. I love you." I kissed his beautiful lips quickly and turned back to the room directing my attention to my sister.

"Cassie what did you find out for Cam?" Cassie knew me well, so instead of voicing her fears for me she cleared her throat and proceeded.

"Well everything that I have read makes it sound like Cam has a connection to the other world, the spirit world, and her pregnancy triggered it." My sister turned to my best friend and asked, "Cam could anyone in your family see ghosts?" She thought about it for a moment and started laughing. It took another few minutes for her to be able to speak.

"Lily, I can't believe that we didn't think of this! Remember my grandmother always talked about 'her ghosts' coming to see her. We just thought she was batty! But your grandmother was a witch and they were best friends. Maybe she really did see ghosts." She smiled so brightly that is transformed her entire being back into the happy, carefree person that I had known most of my life. I returned her smile.

"You're not crazy sweetie, just supernatural like the rest of us." We all laughed at my statement except for Mason. His face showed just how worried he was, and it cut my heart like a knife. I had to turn to Cam as she grabbed, and started hugging me, laughter coming from her beautiful mouth that I hadn't heard in a little while. That made my burden a little easier to bear. My best friend was feeling better than she had in a while and, decided that it was time to go. Cam needed to spend time with Luke that didn't involve her crying inconsolably. She told me that she would call me tomorrow, she was going to be fine now. After Cam left, the coven wanted to talk about 'my' situation now. Mason stood quietly against the stair railing in the living room staring at me as Ciaran spoke.

"Lily so what's the plan to stop Dax? He's not touching you! We're a coven, we fight for each other." Mason continued watching me, biding his time before he spoke. The worry etched in the lines of his chiseled face. I couldn't look at him any longer. I turned to the coven and voiced the only thing that made sense.

"We look in the Book of Shadows. There has to be something in there about what spirit is and, how I touch it. Someone turn on the coffee pot please, I'm going to change." I heard them all start scurrying. I headed for the dress bag that was draped over the back of the chair where Mason must have put it, but before I could touch the bag he had it in his arm ushering me up the stairs.

He closed the door behind himself, and laid the dress on the cedar chest. I walked to my dresser knowing that it was only a matter of minutes before he exploded. He had stayed silent too long, but I was not ready to talk to him yet so I went into the bathroom to change, and brush my teeth. When I came out he waited for me to give him my undivided attention. I turned to face the man I loved.

He began, "Lily...I don't know how, but we are going to stop him! I was serious downstairs, let me hide you and your family until we figure this out." I couldn't look him in the eyes. What I was getting ready to say to him was already ripping me apart inside.

"Mason I want you to leave. At least until after Halloween, I will not let Dax hurt you because of me." Shock was written all over his face, which promptly turned to anger.

"Lilyann Moon! Damn it! I am NOT leaving you! I will protect you! Do you understand me! Look at me Angel!" He placed both of his hands on either side of my face and made me look at him. The tears left little trails of moisture as they weaved their way down my cheek. Mason caught a teardrop on his fingertip, and looked at it, mesmerized. He looked back into my eyes.

"This tear is precious, it's part of you my love, and you will not waste another on fear for me or anyone. We are together, and we will fight this battle head on, hand in hand." I wanted to protect him, and he desperately felt the same way about me. I looked back up into his emerald green eyes losing any and all determination to keep him away from me. I was such a coward!

"Mason, I love you. I need you to be safe. If I can defeat Dax, I want to have a life with you. Remember I am the one able to stop all of this craziness!" He pulled me into his arms holding me protectively. Goddess! I sent up a silent plea 'Help me keep the coven safe. Help me keep Mason safe.' He pulled back a little to look at me.

"So together, right love? We fight like we will live, as one. Let's go find out about spirit and the prophecy." I kissed him gently, so euphoric yet pained for his decision to stay with me. Somehow I was going to keep my love safe! I put my arms around his neck laying my head on his shoulder.

"Angel...I will take you on a hunt with me but only if Ciaran comes along as well." I raised my head sure that I had heard wrong. I searched his face for any sign of deception, nothing.

"Mason do you mean it?" I asked. He shook his head yes.

"You are right, you need to learn quickly, but I want Ciaran there as well because his powers are growing as rapidly as yours. I like our chances of you not being killed with him around. Your combined power will help." I hugged him again, tightly this time. I would learn how to hunt the vampires. What it felt like killing them on my own, which would put me one step closer to killing Dax. That made me think of Ri's vision.

"Mase, what is the sword that Riona saw in her vision?" I asked him. Mason's jawed tightened along with every muscle that I could feel.

"Lily, it's the death blade. That is how a vampire kills another of our kind. I have my fathers' here in your closet." He said in a forced voice. So many things have happened lately that were beyond weird, this being one of the lesser ones, I just nodded my head. I would talk to him later about when he had brought it here, I knew the why. The fight would be on the farm so it needed to be here with him. I wanted his mind off of everything, for him and I just to have the time a relationship needed to flourish, but that wouldn't happen until after Halloween...if we survived.

Everyone was changed, working throughout the house on different things all leading back to two topics, the prophecy and spirit. Ciaran was stretched out on the couch when I came downstairs followed by Mason. We both went over to him, he moved his legs when he saw me. I sat down next to him, and Mason sat on the chair on the other side. I spoke.

"Ciar, I need to ask you a question and it's pretty heavy." Ciaran sat up when Cassie and Seamus walked in to the living room.

"I am going to take Lilyann out with myself hunting and I would like you to join us," Mason said to my cousin as if he were inviting him out to the club. I was even more shocked when Cassie spoke up.

"No way Mason! You said it earlier, your brother wants my sister. Taking her out there would be suicide!" she said, fear written all over her beautiful face.

"Cassie thank you for loving me, but I have to do this. I need to learn to REALLY fight if I'm going to kill Dax! We all do." I replied to my sister as Riona walked into the room looking worn out.

"We will all learn, Lily. By the way Mason she will be fine. Ciaran needs to go with you this time, and the parking lot across from the mall is where you'll find them. I'm not going to go into detail. Ciaran and Lily need to fight on their own. Tomorrow night after ten." She said sitting in the fluffy arm chair. I looked at Ciaran, he nodded, then to Mason, who stood up.

"Well I need to talk to you and Ciaran about our game plan, and everyone else needs to find out EVERYTHING they can about the prophecy and spirit. Let's go you two."

The three of us went up to my bedroom. Mason went to my closet as I sat on my bed and Ciaran sat on the cedar chest. He turned from the closet with a long sword that was curved at the end, its handle made of bone.

"Mason what the hell is the curved part for?" I asked but regretted it immediately as Ciaran and my boyfriend looked at me with raised eyebrows. I understood. That curved portion would take a vampires head off with one swing. I physically shivered at the thought of Dax having something like that around Mason's neck.

"Angel, I have to fight with this. Especially against my brother, I was able to use the blessed stakes because a very powerful witch blessed them. But this is my weapon of choice. The proper name is a Falcata." He said as he handled the sword lovingly. He put it back in its sheath at the site of my horrified expression. I don't know much about swords but I do know that that one is serious! Mason turned to us as he began talking.

"Tomorrow night is going to be rough, mentally and physically, on both of you. Your grandmother used to reserve using her power for a few days before we would go out to make sure her power was fully ready. So, no magick for you two until our hunt. I'm going to work with you outside in the morning so I want both of you in bed now!" Ciaran hugged me, and patted Mason on the back as he left. My hot vampire looked sternly at me.

"I mean it Angel. I will not take you unless you rest now!" I knew he was right, again.

"I will, I promise. I'm not trying to make you angry with me. Will you make sure the rest of them are still researching my little issues, and then will you lay with me?" Mason walked over to where I was on the bed, and sat down next to me. He placed his hand on my cheek, and I placed mine over his.

"Oh God, or Goddess, whoever is listening. I love you Angel, so much I am in physical pain at the thought of anything happening to you." I moved my hand making it easier to lean into him. He wrapped me into his arms. I was exhausted again, and my body responded with a yawn. He helped me under the blankets, and lay with me. I started drifting off to sleep as he recited his poem, which prompted me.

"Mason where did you learn that poem you keep saying to me?" He giggled a little when he replied.

"Funny enough Granny taught it to me. She made me memorize it. She said it was her favorite poem. Didn't you know that?" I was so tired I couldn't remember a lot of things right now. I nuzzled into him and whispered, "Maybe. Mason." I felt his head move toward mine. When his lips were close enough, I kissed him slowly, wanting to savor this before falling asleep. All too soon he pulled his mouth from mine and whispered, "Sleep, my love." I reached my head up again.

"Mason...I love you." I snuggled back into him, allowing the warmth of his body to transfer to mine.

"I still can't believe that you are mine and that you love me as I do you. I love you Lilyann Moon, my Angel. Now sleep." I did as I was instructed without hesitation in the arms of my love.

I was running from him but getting nowhere. Where was MY vampire?

"Mason, help me!" I cried. As I ran I glanced down at myself. I was wearing my grandmothers' shift that I had inherited. When had I put that on? I heard him behind me.

"Lily, you are mine now! My sniveling brother can't help you." I flicked my wrist in the direction of his voice and called, "Air, Fire, Water, Earth help me!" Nothing, not even a hint of my magick! I continued to run as fast, and as hard, as I could. It was no use! Dax grabbed my arm keeping me steady so that I didn't fall. His grip on my wrist hurt, not that he cared. The wickedly handsome vampire yelled at me.

"Tell my pathetic brother that you choose me! Tell him that it's me that you want! Tell him NOW!" The pressure on my wrist was starting to become unbearable, but I would never give in to this monster.

"NO!! I hate you! Mason is the only man that I have, or will, ever love!" I tried desperately to pull away from him. I had no magick anymore. He sat my thrashing form on a log and tied me to it. When he moved Mason was suddenly in front of me bent over an old tree stump with his wrists bound together. His crying whispers were carried to me on the wind.

"I love you Lilyann. I'm so sorry." Dax grabbed his sword, and I knew what was to come next. He stood over my love, his own brother and raised his weapon over Masons' head and whack! "NOOOOO!!! MASON!!"

Something was stopping me from getting to him! I could feel somebody holding me...no they were trying to help me?

"Angel it was just a dream. Calm down, and let me untangle you from the sheets and blankets." Mason. I stayed very still afraid that this was the dream, I was crying so hard my eyes were burning, and cloudy. He moved carefully sensing my hesitation. I rubbed at my eyes trying to clear them. Finally I saw my salvation from that horrid place in my dream. I looked up into the worried face of my love. I threw my arms around him sobbing.

"Mason...Dax he...I couldn't...my magick!" He held me tighter to his chest, letting me cry. After a good five minutes of crying, and squeezing Mason as hard as I could to make sure he was alive and intact, I sat back up and launched into telling him what happened in my dream. I was calming down with the wonderful way that he cradled me to himself.

He reassured me, "Angel I am here. I will destroy Dax for haunting your dreams this way!" I shivered at his menacing voice, for a moment he sounded like his brother. He laid me back down, pulling me protectively into him. I felt like nothing could hurt me right now except to be away from him. We were like two pieces of a puzzle fitting only to each other. He spoke soothingly to me.

"Angel I've got you. I only went downstairs for an hour, I checked on Ciaran and came back up. How could I have left you alone? I'm sorry, my love." I just wanted to be held.

"You have nothing to apologize for. You were doing what you needed to do. Just don't leave me alone right now, okay?" He held me even closer, if that was possible. I tried to let myself fall asleep, but every time my eyelids would close the horrific scene in my head would play, and I was scared awake again.

It was finally time to get out of bed, and get ready for the day. Mason stayed outside the door of the bathroom while I got dressed. Ciaran was sitting at the breakfast nook eating a bowl of cereal as we walked in. I looked on the counter and thank the Goddess! He had started the coffee pot. I kissed my cousins' cheek.

"Thank you Ciar!" I grabbed a mug and poured my source of energy for the day. Ciaran looked at my face, and said, "No sleep for you either, huh?" I guess we were up shit's creek without a paddle. None of us had gotten any sleep, and we only had one week till the Homecoming dance for which we were all anticipating trouble. If that wasn't enough on our toppling plates, Halloween was only two weeks away!

"I know that you two are not going to back out, so as soon as you're finished let's go outside and start working." Ciaran and I finished and headed outside to a chilly fall morning. All traces of the warmth gone. Mason had us run five miles around the property telling us it was for endurance. Like that made it any better. I kept looking all around me, just waiting to see Dax run at Mason with his death blade. We made it back to the barn, and started our kicks to which Mason would throw in a punch or a thrust from our stake. We worked for four hours on our techniques, not utilizing our magick. Mason started working with his sword while my cousin and I tried to attack each other using any means necessary.

At first we had each landed a kick or a punch on the other, but now it was serious. I continued to look for any opening, but we were too evenly matched now. Ciaran tried to lunge at me to the left of my body, but I spun out of his grasp. I tried a roundhouse kick to his head, he ducked out, and so we just stopped. Sweat dripping off of us, we turned and saw that Mason and the rest of the coven had been watching us.

"That was a fight! Ciaran and Lily I am positive that you can handle this now!" I was so hot and tired I just wanted a shower, until I spotted the sword again. I couldn't explain it, I just needed to hold it.

"Mason I want to try something with the sword, may I?" He searched my face and nodded. I walked over to where it lay on the ground, and knelt in front of it. How many vampire lives had this death blade taken? I wrapped my fingers around the bone hilt. I stood up, raising the sword from the ground. It was heavier than I had imagined, it took a great deal of effort to lift it above my head, but I finally managed it. I sent up silent prayers. 'Goddess, come to your daughter and bless this metal with your power.' I stood there with this weapon of death positioned over me when all of a sudden it became too heavy for my arms to keep above my head. In an instant it came slashing down in front of me cleaving the wooden post of the birdhouse in two. Great! The sword landed in front of me on the grass. Mason was already at my side.

"Lily, are you hurt?" Crap!

"Mason I'm so sorry that I touched it, I was trying to bless it." I said to him shamefully. He smiled at me a look of pure relief washing over his handsome face.

"Okay warrior princess, thank you for trying to bless the death blade Angel. I love you." I leaned forward to kiss him when Declan starting making a little whimpering noise.

"Eh...eh Lilyann! I built that birdhouse, now look at it! First you destroy phones and now my birdhouse." My brother stood there with a look of utter loss on his face. If he hadn't been so upset it would have been hilarious. Mason walked to D.

"What if tomorrow just you and I come out here and work on it together? We haven't had much time to hang out, and I would like to know more about you." My brother's eyes lit up, and he smiled at Mason and answered.

"Brother that would be awesome!" I gave him a little smile, mouthing thank you to him as Ciaran and I headed in to grab a shower, food and arm ourselves for tonight's fight.

We left the house at ten on the button that evening, sending prayers to the goddess for our safe return from our family. The drive to our date with destiny was quiet. I was double checking my stakes, I had one strapped on the outside of my left thigh, one strapped across my back, and one on the seat next to me so I could check the laces on my sneakers. I didn't want to trip tonight! I made sure they were double knotted, and grabbed my stake. I watched as Ciaran made the same adjustments. We were troops going into battle…but would we be victorious?

"Ciaran if something happens and we need each other remember what we talked about." He nodded his head, and reached his hand behind his head and we bumped fists. Mason shot me a concerned look in the rearview mirror. I smiled at him and spoke. "We've got this Mase. No worries, babe. I love you." We pulled into the parking lot, and my vampire turned my jeep off. We all slipped out, going in different directions. No sign of them yet, it was now or never. Mason had me staying to the shadows, but I deviated from his plan and sure enough as soon as I walked out into the glow of the parking lot lights two vampires were coming at me with blinding speed. They were almost on top of me when Mason screamed, "LILYANN!!"

I was prepared to end this right here, and now.

CHAPTER FIFTEEN

I spotted Ciaran coming from the direction I needed him to, yelling, "Now Lily!" I threw my hand in the air in front of me and called to the night.

"Ciaran's power, Air, Fire, Water, and Earth!" Our power flew at the two advancing vampires, causing an even bigger vortex than the one I had produced to stop my boyfriend. They were stuck, but I had no clue for how long. "Ciaran send the stake!" I hollered over the roar of the wind. Ciaran called his power back to him and sent the stake zooming straight for the chest of the vampire in front of me. When it was only a few inches from the monster's heart I spun around, lifting my leg up, performing a perfect spinning back kick shoving the wood deep into the vampire's heart. He fell. Dead before he had hit the ground. My vortex was starting to wane.

Mason and Ciaran were running across the parking lot from different directions. They were not going to help me, I needed to fight this vampire myself! I pulled my power back into me, feeling it fill my entire body. I grabbed the stakes from my thigh, and back, simultaneously as I yelled, "No! Stay back! He's mine!" The beast in front of me ran his tongue over his top lip as he swept his red eyes up, and down my body.

"This is gonna be fun sweetheart." His voice made my skin crawl, but I didn't allow the disgust for him to cross my face. I wanted to draw him closer to me so I put on my sweetest, most innocent smile, and let the honey drip from my voice.

"If you think that you're Vampire enough to take me, than do it. Wait what's your name? I want to know who I'm getting ready to kill." This crazy confidence was going to get me killed! He curled his lip at me.

"The name's Erik princess, and I'm gonna rip your pretty little neck apart!" I heard Mason behind me snarling. I began moving to my right, making him adjust his footing, he moved to the left. I never took my eyes from his. That was a trick Mason had taught me. In a fight you can see what someone's next move will be in their eyes. He was close enough for me to smell his odor, but I wanted him closer. I called, "Fire!" My element went straight for the face of the animal to my left, but he jumped to the right with blinding speed. Little pieces of hair fell from my French braid landing around my face. I kept my focus on my target as I heard Ciaran yell, "Mason move, Fire!"

There was trouble behind me, and I couldn't help them. I was here locked in a fight of my choosing. Erik and I circled each other. I caught a glimpse in my peripheral vision of Mason swinging his sword, I felt my heart stop beating for a minute then felt a sharp pain in my side. Damn it! The vampire had spotted my moment of distraction, and landed a perfect kick to my side knocking me on my butt. He tried to jump on top of me, but I rolled left scrambling back to my feet. I had lost a stake in my fall so I held onto my remaining weapon tighter as we circled each other in a dance to the death. I feigned right, and snapped back to my left, nailing him in the chest with a round house kick sending him stumbling back a few feet. I came at him again with my power. The fire singed his hair this time. I smelled the stench of it burning in my nose. From behind Erik another vampire was heading toward me.

"Hello Lily. Dax will be so pleased." It had to be Victor. The family resemblance was obvious. What the hell had I gotten myself into! I was too close. He lunged, forward punching me on the side of my head. I tried to recover, but I was falling backwards, and he was on top of me. Shit!

I screamed, "Goddess help me! AIR, FIRE, WATER, EARTH!" I felt the blast of power leave me throwing him backwards! Mason and Ciaran were on either side of me, poised for the fight. My head was throbbing.

"Angel are you okay?" Mason asked. I rushed to my feet. Ciaran had never looked as calm as he did now. His gaze stayed focused on the vampire directly across from him. "I'm fine Mase." I whispered. Three vampires stood ten feet in front of me.

"Mason you know that Dax will have her. Be a good brother and give her to him. He just might forgive you," Victor said looking smug. I kept my eyes on Erik. I had no clue when this little pow-wow would finally resolve itself into the battle that was brewing, but he was positively bouncing with anticipation.

"I see that you're still our big brothers whipping boy. Lily is off limits to you, Dax or Maylee." Victor's face physically changed with the mention of their sisters' name. Mason whispered to Ciaran and me, "When I say go throw your power at them."

I continued to stare at Erik waiting for my queue as Victor replied to his brother, "Maylee...she's not here and Dax wants Lily. Don't force my hand Mason! I will kill you. Just hand the girl over..." My boyfriend shouted, "Now!" Ciaran and I didn't hesitate, we threw everything we had at their little group. Our powers united, and did something completely unexpected! It created a barrier, all three vampires tried to run towards us, but when they reached the spot our magick had coalesced they were zapped with bolts of magickal electricity. Mason grabbed my hand.

"Let's go!" Ciaran started to head in the direction of the Jeep. I refused to let him drag me away.

"Mason we have to kill them!" I said trying to desperately to break free.

"Lily, damn it stop trying to get yourself killed! This is not a fight you're ready for!" He didn't fool around this time. He picked me up and tossed me over his shoulder. Ciaran ran beside him. I had a perfect view of the vampires trying to get past our shield. It didn't work, they continued to get zapped as they tried to get past it.

Victor screamed, "He's going to have her Mason! See you tomorrow night, brother!" Mason threw me in the back seat. He took off like a bat out of hell!

"What the hell was that? Mason what do you mean I'm not ready? I held my own back there!" I stared at the back of his head while mine pounded!

"I am not going to let you get yourself killed because you want to play Super Witch! You're not ready," Mason said, losing his cool with me for the first time. I hate fighting with anyone, but this was different! He was treating me like a little kid that was having a temper tantrum over a toy that their parents wouldn't let them have. I sat there incensed as he drove like a maniac back to the farm. He pulled onto the property, and became visibly calmer as we passed the unseen wards. Mason parked my jeep, and we all started getting out.

"Ciaran are you alright?" Ciaran nodded at me with a grim expression on his face. "The reality of our life now is a little overwhelming." I knew the feeling. I put my hand on his shoulder as Mason came around the Jeep to meet us.

"We'll be fine bud, okay," I said looking at his face. It had changed in the past hour. Ciaran had always been handsome, but now his features held something else. Wisdom. The front door swung open.

"Lily, are you all okay?" Cassie asked. The three of us nodded in unison to my sister. "Thank the Goddess!" She stayed in the door way as both guys turned to go into the house.

"Uh...Mase can I have a word with you out here please?" I said keeping the emotion from my voice. They exchanged a glance, and Ciaran headed up the porch steps giving Mason and me time alone.

"I am not sorry for dragging you out of there. Lily, I would die if I lost you. Don't you understand that yet?" He said unapologetically. I stood there brooding with my arms crossed in front of my chest trying NOT to zap him!

"Mason I am a witch damn it! I have to at least try to fight! I am not on a suicide mission, but you're family wants me, and my family, dead! What exactly do you propose that I do?" I slung my words at him. I have heard of the typical 'my boyfriends' family hates me' business but his took it to a whole new level! He tried to put his arms around me, but I shrugged him off of me.

"No! You have to accept the fact that this is my life. It was Granny's and now it's mine. I could get hurt Mason, hell I might even die, but if I do it will be protecting them!" I pointed to my house. He didn't give me an opportunity to fight him off this time.

He wrapped me up completely in his muscular arms and whispered gently into my ear, "And I will gladly lay down my life protecting yours." He kissed my hair softly continuing to speak. "Seeing you in action tonight, I was both proud and frightened Angel." I wasn't mad at him anymore, I couldn't be. He was only trying to keep me alive. I wrapped my arms around his waist. I felt the tears welling up in my eyes, but I fought them back. "You fight with the same tenacity as Granny did. She would have been so proud of you." I raised my head.

"Mason, the dance is tomorrow. You and I both know that I have to fight again."

He sighed. "I knew that you were going to say that. Yes we protect the school, but this time I want Cormac, and Declan with us." He kissed my forehead as I nodded my agreement. Dax would definitely come for me again. This time my fear was for the town. Dax's plan to have me had been thwarted, and he would surely seek his revenge. The school's gym would be packed with innocent teenagers, and teachers who were oblivious to the evil that was lurking in its own backyard. It made a perfect hunting ground, and a sure way to settle his vendetta. Mason took my hand and we went inside to work on a plan to protect the town. I needed to see if Riona could call a vision. We were going to need all of the help we could get our little Wiccan hands on. This was going to be a long night.

The next morning everyone knew what part they were going to play. We had decided it was safer to keep Liam and Jessie home from school. I had called my dad, filling him in on the previous nights' events. Of course I omitted the part about Mason being a vampire. I wasn't sure if my father was ready for that kind of information yet. He promised that he would call the school and take care of that end of our plan.

Last night while reading the BoS Cassie found something we had been looking for from the beginning of this journey, defensive spells. We had picked a few that were relatively easy to understand and perform. I so could have used a particular one last night. 'Stopadh in'ait na mbonn' it was a spell to stop an attacker dead in their tracks! Goddess we have been going about this all wrong! It was my fault really. I didn't know what we needed to learn. Granny had been a witch all of her life. She was raised in a family that openly practiced the craft.

"Hey Lil, can I talk to you for a minute?" Ciaran asked, bringing me back to reality. I looked up into his troubled face.

113

"Yeah. What's up?" He got right to his point not bothering with preamble.

"You and I faced real death last night. We both fought, and killed people. I don't think that they're ready for that." He looked like a returning combat veteran. He was strong, resolute but altered from the mental wounds he had obtained by dealing out death. I understood what he was feeling. These were our family members, brother, sisters, and cousins that we were talking about. Ciaran and I had always been the most similar. We had always protected the younger ones. Now we were arming them for a paranormal war that could conceivably cost them their lives, and that was an unacceptable outcome.

"I feel the same way Ciar, but we both know that they have to fight. Goddess! Why can't I be the only one! I hate this, I hate the fact that all of your lives, your futures are at stake! Maybe I should just hand myself over to Dax now." I screamed at the fireplace. My cousin walked over to me and forcefully turned me to face him. He searched my face as Mason, who had apparently overheard, came through the back door.

"Lilyann Moon! Yes, we are in all kinds of hell right now! And yes I am scared shitless that I could lose one of you guys, but NEVER, ever say that again!" I looked into his eyes, and saw a fire that had never been there before. "What's going on Ciaran?" Mason looked between the pair of us, waiting for an explanation, which my cousin offered.

"She's ready to sacrifice herself!" I just stood there staring at the flames that were licking the top of the brick in the kitchen. I could feel them both staring at my back. After a few moments he spoke.

"Angel, they'll be fine, but if you walk away from them I promise you Dax will kill the rest of us." He stood behind me, so close that I could hear every one of his steady breaths. "I want you to come outside with us. Duncan pulled up just before you began yelling, he has some helpful information about my brother." I spun around to face him so quickly that I felt dizzy for a minute.

"What information Mason?" I demanded. He beckoned me to follow him, and I did.

"Duncan how exactly did you find this out? I mean your source, how does he know this?" The inspector had just finished telling us about his undercover work with the police department. Duncan was a hunter. He had taken the position to gather the location of vampires in the area. Through his little façade he had overheard the rumblings of a huge vampire war that was being recruited for. The witches that this army was being prepared for were up for grabs. Their blood was allowed to be consumed. All but one, mine. Dax wanted me alive, and unharmed. Mason however was another story altogether. He was to be destroyed by any means necessary, and by any vampire that could get their hands on him.

"That lunatic brother of yours isn't messing around this time, boy-o. He wants her something fierce!" I started pacing. "Lily from what I've heard, the magick that protects your property comes down on Halloween. Is that right?" I nodded my head at Duncan while answering.

"Halloween night, but we know how to reinforce the wards. It's just staying alive until then. Tonight's the Homecoming dance, if he goes there a lot of innocent people could get hurt, maybe even killed." Duncan scanned the covens' faces then turned to Mason.

"Saints preserve us! Looks like I'm going to a dance laddy."

All of our parents had showed up at the farm to take pictures, of course. I walked down the stairs as gracefully as I could. Mason met me at the bottom. I took his outstretched hand.

"You are absolutely stunning Miss Moon." I raised my eyebrow at him. My dad smiled at me, and gave me the thumbs up. He was such a dork, but a cute one. Duncan was standing next to him talking. I leaned over and asked, "Mason who does my father think that Duncan is?"

He bent down to my ear, and whispered, "My uncle, Love. Here comes your sister." We were all waiting for Jessie to appear. A moment later she didn't disappoint. She floated down the stairs with dark curls gently bouncing as she moved. She was the picture of poise, elegance, and beauty. The blinding light of the cameras' flashing began in earnest. It took about thirty minutes for us to leave the farm.

We arrived at the school early, as we had been instructed. Jessie and Liam stayed close to Duncan until their dates arrived, and then they walked around the gym. The chaperones had been given our instructions by Mrs. Jennings, the assistant principal.

"Lilyann, the school wants to thank your family for doing this tonight. You know how young kids are. They never want their parents around," she said smiling. Mrs. Jennings had been here for years. She was really nice, but a bit jumpy.

"It's our pleasure plus we get to see the school again," I lied quickly. She walked away to check on the refreshments as the students began arriving. The music started as the lights were dimmed. The school gym had been transformed into a glittering fairyland. If I was just a student it would have been amazing, but I knew all too well what magic was almost certainly getting ready to unfold. I checked for the umpteenth time to make sure that the doors were covered. Riona and Aidan were standing at the doors on the far wall, and this time instead of nodding Ri nodded towards the door closest to Mason and me. I whipped my head around just in time to see Victor walking in the door. Mason snarled. He really needed to stop doing that!

Declan, Cormac, and Ciaran were at my side in an instant. Mason took the lead as we headed towards Victor. I started taking long cleansing breaths. I needed my wits right now. Before we reached him, Masons' brother was out of the door and lost in the darkness of the night. Mason held all of us back as he surveyed the school grounds.

"They're out there. Get ready!" Mason shouted. I sent up a prayer to the Goddess, "Keep us safe!" I grabbed the stake Cormac offered me. The vampires started slinking toward us from every direction. Mason grabbed at the middle of my dress and pulled. It revealed the stakes strapped to my thighs. I threw my hand into the night and let my voice be carried on the wind, "Fire!"

My element directed its ferocity at the predator running straight for me. The blast of power that came from me stopped him dead in his tracks three feet in front of me. I jumped on top of him sending both of us flying backwards. I landed on top of him and, using all of my weight, I shoved the stake deep into his heart. My days of being a cheerleader were useful tonight. I back flipped off of him plunging myself into a new fight with Declan.

"Hey sis! Nice of you to join us." I laughed. Leave it my brother to make jokes at a time like this.

"Dekko use the defensive spells!" He laughed. He waved his hand at the vampire on his right while he said, "Stopadh in'ait na mbonn!" The spell caused the creature to stop dead. Declan raised his crossbow, aiming straight for the heart, and pulled the trigger. He had hit his target. There were spells, stakes, and bodies flying all over the place. I caught a glimpse of Mason. He had his sword slicing through the air against Victor. I heard Cormac scream my name a second too late. I felt the hot breath of the beast that now perched himself on top of me.

"Oooh I get the Queen!" I had totally had enough of these creeps thinking that one of them was going to have their way with me!

"Goddess, send me the power!" I screamed. The vampire on top of me was no longer smiling with victory. He was crying in anguish as I felt the familiar electricity ebb and flow on the surface of my skin. I pushed him away from me with ease. I got to my feet in one fluid movement. I was able to see everyone. Declan and Cormac were fighting to my left. Ciaran was to my right, he had just staked another vampire, and Mason was in front of me in a deadly serious fight with his brother. Victor had just swung his sword at Masons' head. He ducked and came back up swinging his own death blade at his brother. Everything was happening in slow motion. It gave me an extra moment to make my move.

I turned my body to the east, and raised both of my hands over my head repeating the words that entered my head, "Nocht chosnaionn me," Air protects me. "Tri thine chosnaionn me," Fire protects me. "Uisce chosaionn me," Water protects me. "Talamh chosnaionn me," Earth protects me. I had turned in a full circle. I faced Mason and Victor, who were both in mid strike when they finally took notice of me. Masons' mouth hung open as he stared at me, Victor took off running. I felt strong, but his reaction to me was unwarranted. All eyes were now on me. The remaining vampires hissed and followed Victor. Cormac was the first to speak.

"Lily what the hell happened to you?" I looked down at myself. My pretty iridescent pink dress was now ripped and tattered and covered in blood, dirt, and the Goddess only knew what else. My hair was falling out of its bun, but other than that I was intact.

"Come on guys we don't have time for this! We need to check on the others." Mason grabbed my arm.

"Angel, you can't go in there like this, Cormac go get one of the girls!" Cormac took off through the door. He returned a moment later with Cassie in tow.

"What happened?" I heard my sister's panicked voice. Mason turned me around again to face her. Cassie literally jumped back at the sight of me.

"Okay, seriously do I have vampire goo on me or something?" I said sarcastically. Cassie opened her purse and grabbed something inside, and handed it to me. It was a compact mirror. I opened it and looked at my reflection. "What's wrong with my eyes?" I cried. They were glowing, like neon glow stick blue! I watched my family as they pulled away from me. Mason wrapped me up in his arms.

"All of you get back in there, and act normal. Lily and I will wait out here to make sure that there is no more trouble." Mason ordered them. "It's fine Angel. It's the magick, it's getting stronger. You're getting stronger, Love." He whispered in my ear as I continued to cry. The door of the school opened again and I heard Duncan's' voice.

"Is she hurt bad lady? Here let me take a look." He pulled my face towards his. I kept my eyes tightly closed. "Well she's banged up a wee bit, and her dress is ready for the trash bin, but I don't see anything too bad." I had settled myself down. I had never been a vain person, hell I didn't even think that I was pretty. I opened my eyes and looked Duncan directly into his. "Saints preserve us!" the Inspector said. I think hearing him say that again made me giggle. Mason looked at me smiling. He ran over to his car and retrieved a pair of sunglasses. I put them on and Mason draped his jacket over my shoulders as the first students began making their way out of the dance. Mrs. Jennings found me.

"Lilyann, are you alright?" She hadn't even looked down to see my tattered dress. Mason stepped in front of me looking her in the eyes.

"Lily has a migraine headache but she stayed to fulfill her chaperone duties, right?" I observed the sweet woman's' eyes slid in and out of focus. Mrs. Jennings smiled at me.

"Thank you for staying Lilyann. I know you have a migraine." She patted my shoulder and walked away. The coven walked out of the school together, and by the looks on all of their faces everyone knew about my eyes. Great! I turned to Mason. "Let's go home."

CHAPTER SIXTEEN

I went right upstairs. I needed a shower, and I wanted to see if there had been any change with my eyes. Thank the Goddess Mason let me have my space. I undressed in my room and walked into my bathroom. The reflection in the mirror gave me the answer I needed, my eyes were back to normal. I turned the water on as hot as I could get it. I washed the vampire stink off of me, got out of the shower and dried myself off. I wrapped a towel around my naked body and walked back out to my room. Tap, tap.

"I'm getting dressed. Give me a minute." I had rushed over to my dresser grabbing the first things my hands touched and throwing them on. After I had buttoned my jeans, "Come in." Mason walked through the door with a cup of what smelled like chamomile in his hand.

"How are you Angel?" he asked as he handed me the steaming tea. I took a sip to busy myself an extra minute to gather my thoughts.

"I'm good Mase...really I am. I mean I wasn't earlier, but my eyes are back to normal and this is all part of the magick inside of me. Right?" Mason just nodded. I wanted to find out what this thing with my eyes meant. I needed the book, but first I had to talk to the coven. Mason took the mug from my hand and placed it on the vanity. He grabbed my face in his hands pulling my face to his with more eagerness than ever before. Our lips met causing an explosion of emotions to erupt. Every feeling that had been pent up inside of me had finally found an outlet to release themselves. I bit Masons' lower lip seductively.

"I need to ask you something?" I said in jagged breaths. Mason tried to keep our lips glued together. I was ready to take our physical relationship to the next level! The Goddess knew I was, but again this was part of my life that had to be sacrificed right now for the greater good. I pulled back. "Mason, I really need to ask you this." He looked deeply into my eyes.

"Lily what is it?" he asked almost apprehensively. I had been mulling this over in my head for a few days.

"Mason will my blood make you stronger?" Rage began overtaking the beautiful features of his face. I had to back pedal a little.

"I'm not saying here drink my blood. I'm asking a general question. If ANY vampire were to drink my blood would it make them invincible?" It was clear from the expression on his face that he knew that I was not being honest, but my deceit did calm him a little.

"Yes Lily, theoretically it would make that vampire indestructible for a short time." Hmm… that could be helpful! If Mason would drink from me, the upcoming fight would be easy. Plus it would tie Mason and I together in a way that most people couldn't understand. "Lilyann get it out of your head! I will not drink from you. Not even if you are offering it willingly." I stood my ground. I knew exactly what to say to make him change his mind.

"Not even if MY life depended on it?" I said calmly and with deliberate innocence. I watched the fight taking place within him. I knew that if it came down to my life or my death, he would drink from me. A small little part of me felt like I should have been branded with a scarlet M for master manipulator! Mason remained solemn as I lead him downstairs.

Jessie was showing off her Queenly wave for the game tomorrow by the time that we had made it to the living room. Duncan was laughing jubilantly until he caught sight of Mason.

"How're you feelin lass?" he asked casually. I allowed the relief I had begun to feel wash over my entire being.

"I'm better Duncan. Thank you for asking! Look, my eyes are normal again." The smile that he offered was forced as he continued to survey my boyfriend. "Congrats Jessie and Liam!" I walked over and hugged both of them. Cassie was the brave one, maybe because she had seen it firsthand.

"What was up with your neon eyes?" I rolled my eyes at her.

"If I knew the answer to that Cass I wouldn't have freaked out!" I elbowed her playfully "Remember you're the one who is always worried about her looks. Where's the Book of Shadows?" My family laughed at my witty retort. Ciaran pointed towards the kitchen. That's where I headed. I heard his distraught voice before I entered.

"Duncan, she wants me to bite her! She basically gave me no out!" I coughed as I walked into the kitchen. Both men looked in my direction.

"And that's not exactly what I said Mason. I asked you if you would still object to drinking my blood if my life depended on it. I'm not asking you to drain me! But if a tablespoon of my blood could end this fiasco with your family then why not?" I heard the sharp intake of air from Mason.

"There are other ways Lily! You don't know what I was like before, what if I couldn't stop. You have no idea how strong the bloodlust is! I could kill you Lily!" He yelled at me, and then rounded on his friend. "Duncan talk some sense into her!" Mason stormed out of the back door. I raised my hand in front of me halting his attempt to explain.

"Duncan, I don't understand because he hasn't explained it to me, but what I do know is that we are running out of time and I would do anything to save my family! That includes you and Mason!" My mind was made up!

"Lily I know that you love him, I also know that the pair of ya's would run off and get yourself killed to protect the other. But you have to trust him. Lord knows it took me long enough to figure that one out! He's only trying to..." I cut off the rest of his statement.

"Save me. Yeah I know Duncan." He gave me a coy little smile. The rest of the coven joined us in the kitchen.

"Hey, what's all this secretive talk about?" Declan asked in a joking voice. Mason walked in the back door at that exact moment.

"Another note, it was on your Jeeps windshield." Our eyes met as Mason handed it to me. He didn't have to say it out loud, it was written all over his handsome face. It was from his brother. As I read the letter I felt the familiar crackle of electrical current slide up and down my skin.

'My dearest Lilyann, I hope that you enjoyed the entertainment tonight. I truly believe that you are an intelligent woman, but when will you understand that I can have you whenever I want. And trust me my sweet, the time is drawing ever closer. If you fight me, I'll just have to start tasting the good townsfolk of Hampstead. Oh I hear that congratulations are in order, Little Jessie the Homecoming Queen, and macho Liam the Homecoming King. I wonder who will win the game tomorrow. See you there! All my love, Dax.'

I walked over to the fireplace as I folded the letter. I silently called for my element and flicked my wrist towards the logs. Flames shot up immediately, and I tossed the letter into them. The paper burned, becoming ash instantly.

"Lily what did it say?" Ciaran asked, but it was Rionas' eye that I caught. She knew, of course she knew.

"I need the book." I said as she handed it to me. "Riona, we need to talk. How much do you already know?" Riona held her head high with pride.

"I know enough. I haven't seen whether or not the plan your concocting is going to work." She lowered her chin just a hair and continued, "But I do know how he's getting that stuff on the property and through the wards." Masons' head jerked up.

"Wait, Riona you've seen how?" She nodded her head to him. "And how he was able to get to Granny." Mason cracked his knuckles menacingly.

"Ri, I need you and the book downstairs with me in the library." She eagerly nodded at me. "Liam and Jessie you guys have a big day tomorrow, get some sleep. The rest of you get changed and meet us downstairs!" I said sneakily.

"Hold it! Angel I want to know what you're up to." I felt almost giddy for the first time in weeks.

"Not yet. But..." I grabbed his hand and squeezed at the sight of his protest. "I promise that it will not get me killed, okay. I think that I'm onto something here, but I need to be sure before I fill you in. Every life in this town may depend on it!"

After countless pots of coffee and much reading I had found what I was looking for. My glow in the dark eyes were definitely the mark of the spirit user, however we were still working on just what I could do! We had also found the spells that were going to come in handy at the football game.

"I think...that I am exhausted. I'm going to have to rest my eyelids on toothpicks to keep them open." Cormac yawned. Mason handed Cormac a mug.

"Drink this, Lily made a wake you up potion." I hadn't stopped after reading the threatening letter that Dax had sent, there was far too much to prepare. I had a plan to save the town, but still no idea how to deal with hordes of hungry vampires that had already marked the farm with a big old bulls eye for Halloween night!

"Let's go. I want it set up before the game!" I said confidently.

Duncan had met us in the school parking lot. "Do you have everything ya need Lassy?" I had just chugged the remnants of my coffee.

"Got it! Duncan you will stay with our parents, right?" Duncan hugged me.

"Lass I know what my part is." He had no superhuman strength or any magickal powers, but it was reassuring none the less!

"Hey Lil?" I looked at my brother. "Yep Dekko!" He smiled as we gathered our things.

"I still can't believe that we can do all of this crazy stuff! I keep waiting for one of those stupid reality show cameras to jump out at us from behind a bush." He changed his voice, "So you idiots REALLY thought that you were witches! How thick are you people!" Every one of us stared at Declan.

"What? That would really mess up my game with the chicks!" I thought that I would choke from laughter.

"Dekko, A, you have no game and B, what chicks? You haven't been on a date in over a month!" Cassie said primly. I stopped dead, bent over and laughed until I thought that I would hurl!

"Cassandra Moon! You do have the smart ass gene! I'm proud of you!" Declan said smiling. It was good to know that we still had our sense of humor during potentially life threatening situations. We stood in a perfect circle on the fifty yard line. I faced the east end of the field and began calling the corners. "I call to the Guardians of the East. Hear my words, hear this witch's cry. Stand strong beside us, and let no human die." I repeated the same verse in each direction. When I had finished each of us in turn took the garden spade that we had brought with and dug a small hole. Each member of the coven had cast a glamour spell on twelve clear quartz crystals. I placed my crystal in the hole that I had dug for it.

"I offer my power to aid in this spell. Blessed be." Around the circle, eleven times, that same plea was said. Mason caught my eye and smiled warmly at me.

"Hey, Lily what's happening? Look!" It was VERY obvious what Aidan was talking about. All of our moonstones were glowing, casting the most amazing rainbows everywhere!

"Wait, are my eyes glowing again?" I asked a little nervously.

"Nope, no neon glow eyes Lily!" Seamus laughed.

"Thank the Goddess!" I said happily. I got up off of the ground, followed by the rest of my family. Mason came a little closer to us.

"I hope that this works!" I knew exactly how he felt.

"Our great-grandmother Rose had to do this once to protect her village back in Ireland. We followed her instructions to the tee, so I think that we're good." This spell would ensure the people of Hampstead stayed safe until Halloween, after that I had no clue. But I was sure as hell going to try!

We met our parents in front of the bleachers. "Mason I'm so glad that you and your uncle were able to come out to support our team." My dad clapped Mason on the back, happily, then shook Duncan's hand. "Lily I REALLY like him, good son-in-law material." My father whispered enthusiastically. Goddess help me! We made our way to the top row of the risers. The referees called for both teams' captains to join him on the field for the simulated coin toss.

"The home team North Carroll has won the toss and had deferred to the away team. The home team will kick." The crowd exploded! Liam was in his glory, he had already scored once and now he was running again to the end zone. "Go Liam!!!" That was the only thing that was completely audible over the roar of the crowd.

"Angel I had no idea that you knew so much about football." Mason said excitedly. We didn't let our guard down, but it felt normal.

"Mase did you forget how many male relatives I have?" Twenty yards, ten, five "Touchdown!" The announcer screamed. North Carroll was up fourteen to zero at halftime. I had missed all the usual ceremonial hoopla last night so I was totally excited to be able to witness my sister and cousin on the field. The cheerleaders came out first and made two lines facing each other. They were fluttering their pom-poms.

"And with no further delay here are your Homecoming King, and Queen, cousins Liam Moon and Jessica Moon!" The announcer relayed to the crowd. Everyone in the stands were on their feet again. My fathers' camera never left his eye, he must have taken over a hundred pictures.

She made the perfect queen. Liam's co-captain handed my sister the most beautiful bouquet of roses, and she lit up!

With the half time spectacle over I kept thinking that maybe he wouldn't show up, but I was completely wrong. Mason whipped his head to the left end of the field. There were two figures walking directly towards the uprights. Damn! "Daddy you stay here. Do you understand me?" He examined my face.

"Lily what is going on?" I didn't have time to explain. The coven knew it was time. They all started slinking off to their predetermined positions.

"I don't have time Dad! There are vampires here, stay put!" I took off so fast that I nearly fell down the bleachers, but Mason caught me.

"Angel, calm down. I have faith in you. This is going to work!" Hand in hand we made our way to the other side of goal posts.

"Finally up close, and personal. Hello little brother," Dax said with a malicious grin on his face. He was handsome, the same physical build as Mason. They could have been twins except for the eyes. The glowing red eyes that called attention to Dax's face. "Lilyann, you're even more beautiful up close. Hmm...I wonder?" He reached his hand out toward me, Mason growled. I wasn't afraid of him anymore. I knew something that he didn't.

"I wouldn't if I were you," I laughed. His hand was three inches from my face, and ZAP! I didn't do anything, my amulet did. "Oh you didn't realize that my grandmother had put that little spell into place, huh?" I glared mischievously at him. Those crimson eyes tried to hold mine.

"Cuiro' Dhoras!" My deflection spell worked. "Let us be invisible to the humans Goddess! Te'igh I Bhfolach!" I yelled as Mason raised his arm, giving the signal to the others. I pushed him behind me as his brothers growled.

"Where are all of the people? You little witch! What have you done?" Dax screamed as Victor lunged for Mason. I threw my hand out in front of me, "Cosain!" Victor was knocked off of his feet. I put my hand on my hip smirking.

"Well Dax, like you said this is a game to you right? I'm playing for keeps. I plan on upping my game, so bring yours. You have no idea how many tricks this witch has up her sleeve." I turned on my heel and put my hand on Masons' muscled chest. His jaw was set, and both fists were clenched. His fangs were out, so that when he would breathe in and out it would make a hissing sound.

"This isn't over Lily! I will have you, and there's not a damn thing that you or my baby brother can do about it. Maylee sent me armed, your little parlor tricks will not help you for long, my sweet!" I turned my head and watched as he ran his tongue across his lip. Ewww! I turned away from him and stared straight into those green eyes that had stolen my heart.

"I love you Mason. Please calm down, for me." His breathing began to regulate, and his fangs had retreated.

"Fourth quarter, and it's third and a long twenty two yards to the end zone. The score is fourteen to twenty one. North Carroll needs a touchdown to win it. Six seconds on the clock." The announcer was screaming. "And number twenty-four has the ball, can Liam Moon pull out a victory! Fifteen yards, ten, five oh no he almost had...wait, Touchdown! Liam Moon has done it!" I wanted to jump up and down or run over to him, but I stood rooted to the spot as Masons' family left and my father showed up.

"Lilyann Moon...he had...those boys were... What in the name of all that is holy is going on?" I had never seen my dad this flustered before.

"Dad this isn't the place to have this discussion. We will talk about this rationally, like adults, back at the farm." I let the authority ring from my voice. I hated pulling that card on him, but this situation was getting ready to get hairier than a werewolf during a full moon!

Riona, Cormac, Mason and I were the first ones back to the farm. Now that the people in the town were safe for the time being, it was time to prepare for an even bigger threat, my dad. He came through the front door pointing at Mason.

"I saw him Lily, at the game, he had fangs! He's one of them creatures that killed my mother!" My father actually looked like he was going to attack Mason.

"Cosain!" I had to put up a shield to keep my dad from killing my boyfriend! "Dad, listen to me! He is NOT one of the creatures that killed Granny! He knew her. He stayed in this very house with her." He started protesting immediately.

"I saw his...those...he has fangs!" The others had finally started to matriculate into the house.

"Oh crap! Dad knows about Mason," I heard Declan whisper to our sisters and cousins. I put my hand in Masons, and laced our fingers together.

"Dad please sit down, and calm down! The rest of you parentals too. Mason and I will explain everything to you all together, including why, how, and who killed Granny." I said totally exhausted and completely famished. Between Mason and I, we told the story, the whole story. Different members of the coven jumped in at different points to help explain certain events, even Duncan who had showed up shortly after my aunts and uncles' interjected information that he was privy to. I had even let my father read his mothers' Grimoire. I watched as his tired eyes reached the bit about him and my mom telling Granny that they were expecting me. He actually smiled.

"Dad, now you know as much as we do. Granny loved Mason. He is a vampire. He is a good, honorable, and decent man, and…I am madly and deeply in love with him." The entire family gawked at me with their jaws on the floor. Goddess! I leaned into Mason.

"Angel, you and the rest of the coven need to eat. All of you exerted lots of power and energy earlier. I'll go grab takeout." I held onto him. I wanted him to stay with me I wanted to hear him say…my poem.

"Mase didn't you tell me the other night that Granny taught you that poem? You said that it was her favorite, right?" He nodded slowly.

"Lily, we can talk about that later you need your rest, and food." But I shook my head at him.

"No… Dad do you remember what Granny used to tell me about my being afraid of the dark?" It was right on the tip of my tongue. Why couldn't I remember… "Lily bug when you're afraid of the dark, picture a mighty phoenix not a meadowlark. And, my bug, if its love that you desire find the emerald eyed Mason and he'll start the fire. No worries, No fears, no not for my Lily with the eyes so blue. The secret of spirit is hidden inside of you!" I finished and almost fell to the ground. Mason scooped me up then placed me next to my dad on the couch.

"Mr. Moon, they all have to eat. I'll go get something quick. Please don't leave her side," he said not taking his eyes off of me. My father stood up facing the love of my life.

"No. Mason it's clear that she needs both of us. We'll take care of them together. I'll order food. Stay with Lily. Donal, Rae, Cath, Duncan let's get them settled and comfortable. We're taking care of the young ones tonight!" I caught my dads' eye as he started for the kitchen. We understood each other for the first time in a long while. We both smiled.

CHAPTER SEVENTEEN

I woke up Sunday morning to the most beautiful set of emeralds watching me, Mason's eyes. "Good morning Angel," he said as he gently lowered his lips, softly brushing them against mine. My entire body tingled with pleasure and desire. He raised his face just a fraction.

"So...what's on the agenda for today? Are we going to fight more supernatural creatures?" I asked a little miffed at him for ending that kiss too soon. Mason gave me a genuinely loving smile.

"No my love, today is a day for us. They only supernatural creature you will be battling is me...and that's only if you want to keep me from kissing you. I know that you have questions about my past. I want you to know everything about me. So I have taken the liberty of planning a day that only consists of you and me. We'll worry about everything else later." He kissed me once more before he left me to get dressed. I began to feel like I was floating on a cloud until I remembered the previous days' events and the fight that was awaiting us in eight short days.

Mason met me at the foot of the steps holding a blanket and basket. "Where are we going?" I asked a little concerned. He took my hand smiling, grabbed my coat and we walked out of the front door.

"We are staying here on the farm." I gave him a quizzical look. "I'm taking you on a picnic lunch which I have prepared with my own two hands." I laughed hysterically at the thought of Mason in the kitchen with an apron on...As if!

"So...we're having sandwiches?" He smiled sheepishly and nodded. We had walked out to the gazebo by the pond. He placed his burden on the bench. I stood next to the pond enjoying the crispness of the October air. I never understood what my mom meant when she used to say that she could smell fall. I did now. I smelled the leaves, cinnamon, pumpkins, and magick. I felt Mason standing behind me. He slid his arms around me as I stared out at the water. I'm not sure that I would ever get used to how incredibly fast he was.

"How did it start? I mean...how did you become a vampire, were you bitten?" He laughed jovially as he tightened his embrace.

"No. I have never been human. I was born a vampire. My mother was human. My father was a vampire, and a good one at that." I leaned my head back a little, snuggling into him and he kissed my temple.

"Lily, my dad was a good man until the clan war that claimed my mothers' life. They loved each other with the same fervor that you and I do." He intertwined our fingers as his hand found mine. "I guess I should start this story at the very beginning. How vampires came into existence. I know it by heart now.

A beautiful young witch named Ana was bound and forced to watch as her human lover, Landon, was slain by a rival coven. He was killed to teach Ana's coven where they stood in the pecking order. But the rival coven didn't realize what they had actually accomplished by killing Landon. The agony that she felt brought Ana's true power to the surface. After the killers left, she wept on the ground, a broken woman. She cried her grief to the stars, 'Goddess help me, I will have my revenge!' Ana dragged herself over to Landon. She sat on the earth next to her dead love, grabbing his dagger. She held it high in the air above with one hand, and with the other she wiped the tears that fell from her eyes. 'With this witch's blood a new life I give to my love' Ana brought the dagger to her wrist and sliced it open. Blood dripped from her wound into Landon's mouth. At first she thought that her dark spell hadn't worked, but after a few moments she noticed the movement in his throat. Landon was regaining color to his pallor skin with every drop of Ana's blood. 'Yes, my love, drink.' She beamed sending prayers to her Goddess as he began moving with more tenacity. But something wasn't right when her love opened his eyes. They were no longer the beautiful brown that she adored, but a piercing red, as crimson as the blood that he was still ingesting. Ana pulled her arm from him, but she had already cursed the world with the creation of this abomination."

I turned to face my own love with tears racing down my cheeks. "Mason…what happened to Ana?" He gently wiped my tears away and took my hand.

"I will finish the story only after you eat something." I nodded. I wasn't hungry, but if this is what it took to hear the rest of the story, then eat is what I would do. Something kept scratching at the surface of my brain about this story. Had I heard it before? Maybe Granny told me about it when I was a little girl or something. We walked back over to the gazebo. Mason had spread the blanket on the wooden surface. I sat down on the hard floor. Mason joined me with the basket he had prepared. He opened it and pulled out a thermos.

"What, no wine?" I joked. He gave me a mischievous little grin.

"Nope. No alcohol for anyone right now. We'll save that for the celebration that Riona is cooking up for after our victory." I couldn't look him in the eyes. I wasn't at all confident enough to say that we would win.

"Oh Goddess! Wait…where is the coven? I didn't see them as we left." I started to get nervous.

"Angel, they're all fine. They were in the library with Duncan, and your dad." Hold up! His statement took me by surprise.

"My dad…in a place surrounded by magick? Mason he wouldn't…" My boyfriend laughed at me.

"Lily, he is. He wanted to help in any way that he could. He's your father, have a little faith in him. He loves you and wants to protect his family as much as I do." I rested my head on his shoulder pondering his words. The fall air had a bite to it.

Mason handed me a thermos with the lid popped open. The aroma of rose hips, and cinnamon hit my nose, suddenly making me very thirsty. I drank deeply from the container. After I finished I had to ask, "You made this? It's just like Granny's with just a hint of..."

He finished my statement, "Cinnamon, and honey. She used to make it for her and me when we were hunting." Hearing her name brought a smile to my face. She was all around me, which reminded me of something else.

"So...the prophecy. It's been me all along, I'm the spirit user. I still don't understand what that truly means or how that's going to help us survive this." I looked away toward the trees and finished telling him what was on my mind. "Mason, I think that you're a bigger part of this than we originally thought. I don't think that it was by chance that you were sent here for Granny's help. Someone, even back then, knew that you were a part of this. My grandmother gave you and I separate pieces of the puzzle, but I think that it's obvious that it's about you and I. Now we need to put them together." He turned away from me and took a drink from his own thermos.

"Mason is that...blood?" I moved closer to him, curious. I hadn't seen him drink his necessary sustenance in our time together, but I had assumed that he received his nutrition during his time away from me. A trickle of red ran down his lower lip. I used my thumb to wipe it away. I should have been completely grossed out, but instead I was intrigued. I put my thumb to his lips. Mason's lips were parted slightly, but the look on his face was a mixture of fear, confusion and longing. His tongue slowly flicked out, taking the blood into his mouth, and then he kissed my thumb.

"Every day you surprise me Lily." I gave him a questioning look in response. "I never drink this around you," he held up the container with blood, "because I was afraid if you saw the beast inside that you would run away. But instead you just come closer." He held my eyes with his.

"Mason its part of you, and I love you. Let me ask you something. Are you going to run away from me because my eyes glow like a neon bar sign? Of course you're not."

I leaned forward and used my tongue to trace his upper lip. I could taste the remnants of blood on his lip. It didn't bother me, that surprised me.

We didn't break our gaze until I felt his lips pressed against mine. Our lips moved like a perfectly choreographed dance. As he pulled his mouth from mine slowly, he gently bit my lower lip. That little gesture made my entire body sizzle with delight, a feeling that I had started to yearn for every time that he touched me. "Well…at least I know that you're not afraid to bite me somewhere." I joked. He stared at me with an expression of distain on his face. He still hadn't come to terms with the fact that he may have to drink from me. He was still banking on me being able to use spirit to defeat his brothers, and I still had no idea how. I folded myself back down onto the floor and winked at him.

"Okay as much as I would love to have a full-fledged make out session with you right now, we really need to get back to the prophecy." Mason cocked his eyebrow at me.

"Would you really? Alright…if you insist. I think that we need to start by dissecting both of the pieces, line by line. The first line of your special song talks about picturing a phoenix. Those birds' wings were red and gold which correlates with the poem your grandmother taught me." He was on to something here. I started thinking about what he had just said, and then it hit me.

"And your ring has a phoenix on it. Where did you get it?" His face went even paler than it already was.

"For the love of all that is holy! Lily this ring was my father's. He gave it to me just before the war, just before my mother was killed and he became evil. This ring had been his fathers before him and so on…back to the beginning of our vampire line." Granny had to have known this. There was no way that this was a coincidence, I didn't believe in them, not anymore. My mind raced over both poems again, and then it hit me. There was still a piece of the puzzle that was missing, but I knew where to find it.

"Mason I need you to finish Ana's story." He pointed to the basket.

"First you eat something, remember?" I finally realized why Ana was affecting me the way that she was.

"Mase listen to me, Ana and Landon have something to do with all of this. I know it! I couldn't understand why this story was getting to me, but I just remembered. The day that I figured out you were a vampire, I read my family's Grimoires. In my great-grandmother Rose Moons' book she wrote about her ancestor Ana. The witch that had created a race of beings that drained every witch that they could get their hands on." His eyes opened wider than ever.

"Lily…are you trying to tell me that Ana is…" I nodded to him.

"A Moon witch. She's my family. Do you see now why we have to know the whole story? Not just the story that you were told." He quickly got to his feet and reached down to help me up.

"Let's go get the Grimoire then." In the blink of an eye Mason had the basket packed up and the blanket draped over his arm. I took his hand into mine and squeezed.

"I think this is it Mason. We'll be able to figure out what the prophecy is and how we can use it to our advantage on Halloween." I said smiling brightly, finally feeling like there was hope that my entire family wouldn't be slaughtered. He returned my smile and we were off. We headed back to the house, and the book that held the clues that I so desperately needed.

We walked still hand in hand through the front door. Riona and Declan were in the living room with the Book of Shadows. They both looked up. "Uh…Mason you were supposed to take her out for a romantic day. Keep her away from the house, remember?" Declan checked his watch. "Dude, if an hour is the best that you got, then we seriously need to work on your skills," he said laughing. My father and Duncan walked in talking.

"Dekko shut up, you dork. We think that we've figured out where to find the last piece of the prophecy puzzle. Where is Rose Moons' Grimoire?" My brother gave a mock offended face as he jumped up from the couch and left the room.

"Wait…what other part? I thought that my mother gave each of you half of it." My father looked completely confused. I tried to explain to him and the others what we had discovered. Duncan turned his head away when I mentioned Landon's name.

"Duncan…what do you know about this?" I asked. Duncan didn't turn around nor did he answer me. Mason started to move, but I rested my hand on his shoulder. "Let me," I whispered.

"Duncan what is it, what's wrong?" I saw the tears welling up in his chocolate brown eyes. I wrapped my arms tightly around him. He squeezed me in return.

"Lilyann, he's my ancestor." Duncan lifted his head and even though I was standing in front of him, it was Mason that he was looking at. "Mason and I both are descendants of Landon, the first vampire."

What exactly was Duncan saying?

"Duncan, you and Mason can't be related. He's like five hundred years old and you're like forty, right?" Liam joked. They looked at each other. I turned to face Mason.

"It's true, isn't it?" He sighed.

"Yes. Duncan comes from my father's brother's line, which makes him my great nephew to the twentieth degree." Huh. I had to stop hearing about these things like this! I had forgotten that my father was in the house.

"Mason…but…Duncan is…how in the world?" Riona walked over to my father. It was clear that I was not the only one that had been sideswiped by this news. She helped him over to the couch where he sat down. The rest of the gang had filtered in from different areas of the house. Shannon caught my attention.

"Hey Lily...oh no." She scanned the room. "What the hell's happened now?" I was peeved at Mason again for withholding information, but this time my anger was also directed at Duncan.

"Oh you know, the usual. I have to search a book for an answer, angry vampires want to kill us...oh and Mason is Duncan's uncle, which is something either of them could have easily told us at any time...so that we could have avoided this awkward moment." Declan was walking back in with a few Grimoires in hand, but stopped dead in his tracks at my little rant, and his head snapped up.

"Wait a minute. Did you just say...?" My derisive laughter landed all eyes on me.

"Yep, you heard it right Dekko. Can I have the books please?" I was so over finding things out like this. "Okay, we all know now. Big deal, of all of the supernatural things that have happened to us over the past few weeks this is what surprises you guys?" I turned around. "Duncan I told you this before, you are a part of my family, and as such you'll have to deal with the fact that I'm mad at you," I said as I mock punched his arm. I turned to face my father. "Daddy are you alright over there?" My father's face confused me.

"Is this...Is this, the kind of thing that happens in this house regularly?" I just smiled at him.

"Drink some tea, it helps. Mason let's go upstairs and start reading. We need to see just how it all fits together." He followed me up the stairs. I left the door open as we walked into my room, I didn't want my father to have a massive heart attack tonight if he happen to come upstairs. I kicked off my boots and plopped down on the bed. I immediately started thumbing through the first book until I found what I was looking for. Mason joined me on the bed, but stayed on the other side a couple of feet away. I continued to read as I scooted myself right up against him. I leaned my head on his chest. I heard his contented sigh.

"Sweetheart, I should have told you about Duncan and I being related, but in my defense, I just didn't know how much weird that you could handle. Forgive me?" I looked up at him trying to arrange my thoughts so that the words would come out properly.

"Mason...I love you, when are you going to see that I'm not going anywhere? Weird is my life now. Let's figure this out so that we can fight for our right to our supernatural lives." He took the book out of my hands and began to read the story of Ana and Landon from Rose Moons' Grimoire

The creation of the abominations that we now fight was started by one of our own, as a matter of fact, my very own great-great grandmother to the twenty-second degree, AnaRose Moon. I am documenting the story that has been passed down to each witch, so that we know the real

132

reason that we fight the vampires. Our kind created them, and now we must end them before they end every other being.

Ana, 17 and Landon, 23 were to be married at the end of the following month of October of the year 1512 in our motherland, the home of the emerald isle, Ireland. Ana's approach to learning her craft was ambitious to say the least. She spent most of her time honing her skills, perfecting her magick, and absorbing the knowledge the rest of the coven bestowed upon her. The rest of her time was devoted to learning how to become a proper wife for Landon McShaw.

Landon was human, and that's all that the coven needed to know to dislike him. He was a tall, strapping man with locks the color of sage bark and eyes that reminded one of chocolate. Ana had always known that she came from the most powerful line of witches in the world, but just as she knew this fact she had also always known that she would one day be Landons' wife.

On the morning of Samhain, Ana was being prepared for her hand fasting ceremony. There had been rumbles of a major coven war brewing for a fortnight, however none of the Moon coven dared to believe that the McKnight coven from Scotland would start a war during Ana's wedding, they were wrong. Apparently the Scottish coven had crossed the Giants' Causeway silently through the night, because just as Ana was about to say her vows the tree that the witch and her lover stood under suddenly burst into flames.

Ana positioned herself in front of Landon, shielding him from the spells that were flying through the air around them. The Moon coven was strong, Ana was strong, but the McKnight's were devious, and wanted to prove that they were the dominant coven by drawing first blood. Two male witches separated Ana and Landon from the rest of her coven and herded them into a thatch structure that was used to house sheep. Ana knew that they were in trouble when she couldn't see the rest of her coven. The taller of the two male witches threw a binding spell that hit her square in her chest, knocking her backwards. She hit her head and blacked out for a few minutes.

When she came to, her hands and legs were bound together with Elder rope, and Landon lay on the floor in front of her. An athame hovered over his heart for only a moment before it plunged itself into his chest, ending his life.

Ana had just become an initiated witch the previous weekend, during the full moon. She didn't know how to use all of her powers yet, she didn't even know what all of those powers were. But watching the life leave her beloved's eyes, anger began welling up inside of her causing her still unknown abilities to start manifesting themselves. The days of Ana's innocence were far behind her now…there was no going back. Ana broke free from the binds that held her. Landon's murderers watched as

Ana's eye began emanating the brightest blue light, which flashed at her enemies. The killers fled, knowing now what Ana truly was.

A spirit wielder.

She moved her body close to Landons. She wept loudly, attracting the attention of the rest of her coven. They had been searching for the pair to no avail, until they heard the dark spell that came from her soul. What Ana didn't know was that she was what they called a spirit user. Once the spirit user touches dark magick, he or she will no longer be in the favor of our Goddess. Ana took Landons' dagger from his lifeless hand and raised it high above her head, chanting the dark spell (which I will not recite here for obvious reasons) and brought the blade down, opening her wrist and allowing her witch blood to flow into her dead lovers' mouth.

The wind and dark clouds gathered as the abomination drank deeply from this once pure witch. The coven watched as it opened its eyes, no longer brown and endearing. Now they were scarlet and menacing. Ana pulled her wrist back from the beast, but he was much stronger than she was now. The only thing that made him waiver was Ana playing with the tartan cloth that he had wrapped around her wrist the night that he had proposed. He only hesitated for a moment before jumping up into the air with blinding speed. He grabbed Letty, Ana's cousin, an uninitiated witch on his way out of the window. Ana tried to run after the creature, but she was stopped by her father. There was no way to undo the magick that Ana had created, except to kill the creature and all that he would infect.

Ana was placed in Elder bindings until her death two short years later. She rambled on about her love, but her magick worked no more. Letty's drained body was found two days after she was taken. She was given a traditional witch's' pyre even though had not been a full-fledged witch. And as for Landon, the first creature of the night, he drank from many, until rumor has it that a powerful witch back in Ireland caught up with him and drove a blessed stake through his heart. Because of the dark magick that one powerful witch performed that fateful day, we the Moon coven, will always fight to eradicate these leaches.

I looked up at Mason. "Ana was a spirit user too. She gave in to the darkness." My love hadn't looked up yet, but I knew that he was ingesting what he had just read. I was already there. "Mason…what happens if I make the same choice? If something happened to you…to my family, I would have done the same thing!" I couldn't breathe. My entire body shook with fear. I knew myself better than anyone, and I would like to think that I would make a more sound and reasonable decision. But if it came to my family…could I just let them die?

"You're not Ana, you're nothing like her. Not in that respect Lily. You would never use dark magick. It's not who you are," he said looking me straight in the eyes. The only thing running through my mind was how carelessly I had offered Mason my blood. Could I do that now...if the lives of my coven depended on it? I would have thrust my wrist into his face just last week, but now I wasn't so sure. Granny would have known what to do. She would have known what path to choose. I caressed my pendant. It must have been obvious who was on my mind. Mason spun me around to face him.

"You remind me off her." He looked at my grandmothers' necklace that now rested against my chest. "She loved her family with an intensity that was rivaled by none other, until I met you." I gave him a sly little grin.

"Really? It doesn't seem weird to you that we've just met, and already we are literally trying to take the proverbial stake for each other? I mean...I know how I feel about you Mason. I've known from the moment that I looked into your eyes that I wanted you. That I had to make you mine, but you already know this." He smiled my favorite smile, the real one, the one that was reserved for only me. He tried to say something. I had to cut him off before he crossed a line that I could never recover from. "I guess it's time that the Moons' decorate for Halloween." I said with a completely fake smile plastered on my face. "You coming?" He knew me well enough to know that something else was on my mind. But not well enough to know what that was. He was already at the door, waiting on me now.

"I'm never going to get used to that, you know." Now it was his turn to give me a totally mischievous smile.

"Good, it'll keep you on your toes."

CHAPTER EIGHTEEN

I stood on my front porch admiring the work that my family had put into decorating our home. Wicker harvest wreaths adorned the windows, a broom made entirely of cinnamon was swaying from the porch's roof. The porch railings and doorway were lit with a fall colored garland and twinkle lights. And, yes as cliché as it was, we had even carved pumpkins and we were lighting them with bayberry candles. Which now shimmered in unison with the gentle autumn breeze that blew tonight. Aidan walked out of front door and down the stairs, joining me on the front lawn. I could hear the Halloween music still emanating from the living room. He handed me a mug of steaming liquid.

"Hot apple cider...you look like you could use this," he said in response to my questioning look. I took a sip and allowed the fluid to warm me from the inside out. "I never realized how beautiful she made all of this." He swept his arm in front of as much of the property as he could, I tried to answer him, but he spoke over top of me. "Lilyann, they're threatening to take it all away from us, our family, our friends, our lives. Granny believed that you could save it, that you could save us. Do you think that you can?" Wow. Talk about something coming out of left field. I had to be honest with my cousin.

"Aidan, I'm not sure what I can do alone. I know that all of us working together and fighting has to be better than us sitting here doing nothing, right?"

I looked past him as I fidgeted with my cup. I heard the door open again, but I only had eyes for my cousin right now. "Bud, I hope that you know that I am willing to give up my own life to save yours, all of our family's." Aidan began to nod his head when we both heard the cackling laughter that sent a shiver up my spine.

"Oh she'll try Aidan...what's that code for Lily? Hmm...maybe for 'If it comes down to you or me, then it's my rear-end that I'll save.' Right sis?" I wasn't sure if Cassie was trying to be an evil witch for Halloween, but with this attitude that's exactly what she was acting like. Mason had walked out with my sister to find me, and after her little explosion he protectively positioned himself between us. My sister didn't hesitate.

"See Aidan...how quickly he got in the middle to protect her." She spit he last words at all of us.

"Cassandra I swear that one of these days I am going to let you have it, but trust me sister it will not be until this is over and you are safe!" I threw my words back at her. I had no clue when this childish behavior between her and I would end, but Goddess please let it be soon. She whipped her hair from her shoulder as she turned on her heel and headed back into the house. We have one week before our family's Armageddon and she picks now to go off of the deep end?!

"Lily, don't pay any attention to Cassie, you know how she gets sometimes. And...well the vampires have us all stressed out. Cassie's just taking it out on you." My face must have said it all because Aidan piped back up. "And obviously she's wrong for it, but cut her a little slack. Okay?" I just nodded afraid to open my mouth. My sister had some nerve! I have spent every waking moment trying to figure out how to save them, not worrying about my own life. Couldn't she see that if something happened to one of them, my life would end as I know it?

Mason took my hand as my cousin walked back into the house. "Love, tensions are running high right now. Please, give no merit to what your sister says. She's afraid...we all are." Again I just nodded. Would this ever end? The fall chill had me shivering. Mason took off his jacket and wrapped me up in it.

"You should go with Cam tomorrow to her appointment, it'll take your mind off all this...at least for a few hours." I was able to manage an "uh huh" this time. I'm not sure how he always knew what I needed, but he just did.

I called Cam to let her know that I was going to go with her, and I needed the address. We spoke for a few minutes. "Lily just let her vent. You and Cassie have always had that crazy love/hate sister relationship, but in the end both of you have always been there for each other." I took a deep breath for the hundredth time that day. We exchanged a few more thoughts and made our plans to meet the next day.

When I laid my cell phone on the nightstand Mason was coming through my bedroom door. "Ready for bed, Angel?" I tried to argue that I wasn't sleepy, but my body gave me away with a yawn. He lay down next to me, and pulled my head to his chest. I knew that I wouldn't remain awake long in this position. I tilted my head up and was surprised to find his lips meeting mine. This was definitely what I needed right now. I let myself get lost inside of this kiss. Our mouths moved in unison never missing a beat. This must be what an intricately choreographed piece of classical music must feel like to a composer. His hand traced my hairline while his lips traced my jaw. I could feel my heart thundering in my ear as he pulled back and laughed his coy little way. "Time for sleep Love." I rolled onto my back and responded with a, "Hmph!"

In my head, logically I knew that we had mutually decided that now was not the time to take our physical relationship to the next level. But Goddess help me, it was getting harder and harder to abstain! "You and I will be together soon, my love." He whispered. My body curled back into his, until my head once again rested on his chest.

"I love you," I whispered to Mason.

"And I love you Angel, now sleep…sleep peacefully." He said and then he kissed my forehead.

I was running down a dirt road. My chest hurt so badly from the labored breathing. I needed to look behind me to see if I was making any head way, but I was afraid of what I would find. My feet continued to make purchase with the earth beneath me. I began hearing heavy, ragged, taunting laughter. It felt like it was coming from every direction. Where was Mason? If he could hear me, he would help me. "Mason, please I need you!" It hurt so much to perform this small task, but I kept calling for him, and then began calling for the rest of the coven. "Ciaran, Declan, Cassie, Braden, Shannon, Seamus, Cormac, Riona, Liam, Jessie, Aidan!" Nothing, no response. The tears stung my cheeks as the wind hit them. Come on Lily, think, where can you run? Nothing looked familiar. Where was I? There were no houses or lights that I could make out. I ran harder, and faster. I knew that my body would ache in the morning. I still couldn't see anyone, but in the distance I could hear a mixture of things. A man laughing coldly, the sound of an Irish setter howling, and a familiar female voice. I couldn't hear what she was saying though, but I knew that voice from somewhere.

"Wake up Lily! You're dreaming. You have to wake up. He can't hurt you Lilyann. WAKE UP!"

I was fighting with someone…actually with a lot of someone's. I felt so many arms around me. Oh my goddess! Think of a spell, think of something.

"Lilyann, stop fighting with us, so that we can get you untangled from the blanket. Mason stay back…I told you it was in her dream. The danger isn't here. It's somewhere with lots of hills and stones, big stones!" Riona was speaking.

"Ri?" I choked out.

"Yes, Lily it's me. Come out of there and I'll tell you what's happening. At least the part that I understand." My family helped me out of the blankets that were wrapped around me like tourniquets, cutting off blood flow to different parts of my body. I slowly poked my disheveled head out of the remaining sheet, like a little kitten, to find the coven staring back at me. Mason ran to my side, his head darting to every corner of the room so fast that it was like watching a cartoon character. I finally found my nerve.

"Will someone tell me what the hell is going on?" Everyone's eyes fell on Riona. I stood up feeling braver with each passing moment, "Well?"

Riona sat down on the bed. "Lil sit down, and I'll tell you what is going on." I obliged, desperate to know what had happened that had drawn everyone into my room, and had set Mason on edge.

"Okay like I said before I have to start from where I understand. I fell asleep normally and started dreaming about something random. It was my senior prom, I think. All of a sudden I felt you call for me. I looked all around and couldn't find you. I sat straight up in bed with Izzy on my chest swatting at me, I think that she was trying to wake me up. I could hear you now screaming at the top of your lungs, so I ran in here with everyone else. Mason was on guard with his death blade. It was Cassie who said that I should try to force a vision and get to you that way. We were trying to wake you up and nothing was working." I glanced up to meet my sisters' eyes. She had been scared and crying. She walked over and sat on my other side and took my hand. I squeezed hers in response, whatever had happened earlier, we were ok now. Riona continued.

"I kept trying to have a vision, but it wasn't working until you called for me again. Then I got sucked into your dream. I could see you running, I could hear the insane man laughing and I'm sure that I saw and heard Granny's old dog Brogue. Then I just kept telling you to wake up, but the really weird part was I felt someone or something was trying to push me out of your dream, like they wanted to keep you there. You finally woke up…and well you know what happened then," she finished abruptly.

I sat there dumbfounded, trying to ingest all of the information that I had just been given. Izzy jumped up into my lap, and rubbed her head against my hand. "Oh…sorry Izzy." I scratched behind her ear, and she purred her approval then jumped back down. One month ago my life was boring, but it was my life and I was in control. Now I was a witch along with my entire family, I had a vampire boyfriend, a best friend who was communicating with the dead and crazy blood thirsty vampires' hell bent on ending my life. Hmm…maybe Thanksgiving would be normal? Probably not. Mason kept glancing in my direction as he paced the room searching for danger. "Mase, come here." The look on his face could have killed. Note to self: do NOT get on his bad side.

"Well sleep is totally no longer on the agenda for tonight, so why don't we go downstairs and start the caffeine now." Cassie said as she elbowed Braden.

"Yeah…I'm hungry too." The coven took their cue and left Mason and I alone. I waited until after my brother left shutting the door behind him.

"Mason…please come here. I need you." He moved so quickly that if I would have blinked I would have missed his movements.

"My love, are you okay?" I smiled gently. He laid his sword on my bed, and pulled me closer to him.

"Mase, I don't know what's happening to me, or why. How could someone get into my dream? I felt…I felt like he wouldn't let me leave."

I buried my head into his chest. I needed to be as close to him as possible. He held me to him, saying the same thing over and over again.

"Lily I will not let my family hurt you, I will find a way to save the coven. I promise you this." I felt secure for the moment, but there was something that I hadn't told anyone yet about tonight's terror. I knew that I had to fill him in.

"Mason, I didn't tell the others the last thing that I remember before coming out of my dream, but I need to tell you. It could be a clue." His green eyes met mine and he nodded his head in encouragement. So I continued. "The mans' voice as I left said clearly that my vampire couldn't protect me forever and her blood would be my downfall. Who the hell is 'her'?" We sat there looking into the depths of one another's eyes for so long that the knock on the door made both of us jump.

"Coffee is ready Lily. Mason the boys' made breakfast." Shannon called through the door to us.

We had agreed before descending the stairs that for the moment, we would keep this piece of information to ourselves. My family's nerves were already frayed, and as we had learned earlier, emotions were running high. There was no need to burden them any more than absolutely necessary. Mason was behind me as we walked into a busy kitchen. The aroma of pork sausage, bacon, hash browns, eggs, and pancakes hit my nose only slightly after the smell of coffee. I grabbed a mug of coffee and drank it black. When I had finished my first cup, I poured more coffee and also reached for a plate filling it with a little bit of everything. Everyone's eyes fell on my plate as I shoveled a fork full of scrambled eggs into my mouth. I felt ravenous. I barely chewed my food before swallowing it. "What?" I said after taking another drink of my coffee to clear my throat. Everyone in the kitchen laughed at me. I couldn't remember the last time that I had eaten, but I was making up for it now!

I was perfectly groomed and out of the house by nine o'clock. The short drive to the medical center left my mind no time to wander which, for once, was a good thing. I spotted Cam standing at the entrance, waiting for me. I pulled my Jeep into the closest parking spot. I ran up to her shaking from excitement, and caffeine jitters.

"Lily I am so glad that you were able to be here today…Whoa! Are you going out on a date after we see the baby? I haven't seen you this dressed up since that date with Mason." We hugged each other as she whispered, "Especially with everything else going on. How're you and Cassie doing today?" I pulled back a little and smiled brightly at her.

"Cam, you were right. It was just nerves." I started filling her in on all of details from my 'nightmare'. She was completely engrossed in everything that I had to tell her on our walk into the doctor's office. She signed in, and we both sat down to wait and talk.

"So…wait, I'm confused. Was the mystery man in your dreams or in Riona's vision?" I leaned closer to her, we were the only ones in the waiting room, but you never know when a busy body secretary is eavesdropping.

"Shhh…he was in my dream, but Ri had to call a vision to get to me, and she heard him too. So I guess both really." I sat up straight when the door opened. "Camden Myers"

"Lily, come on," Cam called. I jumped up, not sure of the proper protocol when accompanying a friend to an obstetrician. I followed Cam, and the middle aged nurse down a long, cold hallway. The last door on the right was open, and we were ushered inside. The nurse had my friend go to the restroom to give a urine sample. Then she took her weight, blood pressure, and about ten tubes of blood. I was never having a baby! After all of that she asked Cam to change into a hospital gown.

"Just relax sweetie, hop up there on the table and the doctor will be in with you shortly." The nurse said softly. As soon as the door closed behind the nurse I began laughing hysterically. I wasn't even really sure what I was laughing about. Cam started giggling with me.

"Cam…oh…my…goddess! Do you have to go through that every time you come here?" I laughed out. My best friend was saved from responding when the doctor knocked twice on the door and entered.

The tall, silver haired physician was handsome, but a little old. He began asking her questions that she would answer very succinctly. An odd expression crossed Cam's face and I knew that something wasn't right. She tried mouthing something to me, but I didn't understand her. I shrugged my shoulders at her and mouthed, "What's wrong?" Her eyes darted from me to the doctor, who sat oblivious, back to me and then to the corner of the room. Oh goddess, not here…not now. I watched her mouth form the words, "Need a distraction, Granny's here."

I nodded my understanding to her. Okay super witch, what can you do here? A plan was taking shape in my mind, but I needed the doctor to move just a fraction of an inch to the left. I tried to whisper my words as I pictured what I wanted to happen.

"A distraction is what I need, to you the goddess this I plead. Electricity!" I said as I flicked my wrist in the direction of the ultrasound machine. Sparks began coming from the wall. "Um…Doctor your machine thingy is sparking like fourth of July fireworks." The doctor looked down to see little blue bolts of electricity popping from the plug.

"Oh…heavens! Alice! Alice get in here please." The older doctor grabbed a towel and pulled the cord from the socket. The nurse came running in to see the result of my little magick show.

"Cam please excuse us for a few minutes. We need to get this out of here and call our technician." The medical personnel rolled the machine from the room and closed the door.

"Cam why did I just short out that machine?" I said to my best friend. Her eyes were focused in the corner of the room. She nodded and then looked at me.

"Lily, Granny's here, and she has a message for you. It's very important that you understand, okay?" I nodded to her. I looked in the direction that she was, but I saw nothing.

"Lily-bug, evil is coming at you from many directions now. I'm not sure who all the players are. Some are keeping themselves cloaked, hidden from me. Are you ready for the Initiation ceremony?" I nodded. I wasn't sure if this was real, could my best friend really be talking to my dead grandmother? Cam spoke up again. "Lily, the entire family needs to be on the farm on Halloween, it's the only way to keep them all safe. The evil that is working against you will try to divide you, if your loved ones were not with you, you would be distracted. Keep them in the center of your circle and your mother and I in your heart. Touch spirit, open it and let it free. We'll be with you in spirit. I love you." With the rapid pace that the tears were falling from my eyes I was sure that I must look like a raccoon by now.

Cam looked at me. "I'm sorry Lil, she's gone."

Damn it!

CHAPTER NINETEEN

Cam and I had parted ways at her car. We had decided that she and Luke would come to stay at the farm on Sunday, October 30th. I drove home thinking about my grandmother and spirit. How do I touch spirit? I could really use her expertise here. I felt like I was going into battle practically naked. Sure, I knew a few things that I could throw at one or two vampires at a time, but hundreds? No way! Spirit was the key to winning this fight, to protecting the ones that I loved. Ana didn't know how to touch spirit and when she did look at the mess that she created. I scanned the trees as I passed. My vision was sharper, my senses on high alert. The spell that the coven had cast at the Homecoming game would keep the people of Hampstead safe for now, but I knew that the vampires were lurking around. That thought made my blood begin to boil.

"Oh Goddess...not now!" As I glanced in my rear view mirror I was shocked to see that my anger had somehow triggered my new freaky glow stick eyes. I fumbled around in my purse for a pair of sunglasses. As soon as my fingers found my shades I slung them into place, and raced home.

"What happened just before you became a set of Halloween twinkle lights, Lily?" My brother joked. I'd had to cover my eyes back up after showing the house at large. It wasn't that they were afraid of me. They said that the light coming from my eyes now hurt theirs if they looked directly into them. As if I didn't have enough to worry about.

"I told you already I was thinking about the vampires, and it pissed me off!" I narrowed my eyes in his direction. My body began quivering. What the hell was wrong with me? Mason finally spoke.

"Angel, I think that your eyes are tied to your emotions." He wrapped his arms around my waist as I took a few deep breaths to calm myself. A feeling of peace began spreading through my body. I felt like my grandmother was with me, and somehow I knew that I was okay. I removed my glasses, and sure enough I was back to normal.

"If you keep this up Lily we're not going to bother putting lights up anymore. We'll just stick you in the window." Braden was laughing with my brother. Mason glared at them, until I began laughing at myself.

"We need to figure out where the hell everyone is going to sleep. We have ten extra people staying here on Sunday," Riona reminded us. I had a few ideas, but I wanted everyone's input.

"What if all of the girls stay in my room with me? That would free up a couple of beds." Mason arched his eyebrow. I winked at him.

"Plus I doubt any of us are going to sleep," Jessie said innocently, but she was right. I knew that there was no way that I would sleep Sunday night. I would be too busy going over every step of the ritual in my head. We didn't have an Initiated witch to lead the ceremony. I had to perform the ritual flawlessly. Sunday night I would be the Moon coven's official leader. After an hour of reorganizing, we had a plan. It would be tight, but at least everyone would have somewhere to sleep. My family would be safe.

The next morning Mason had gathered everyone outside to work on our combat tactics. I was shocked when I saw Luke parking his car. "Hey Lily, can I talk to you for a minute?" Mason stopped what he was doing and followed me over to my friend.

"Hey sweetie! What's up?" I said as I hugged him. I distinctly heard a growl coming from behind me. I backed up a little, standing between Mason and Luke. "Duh, I totally forgot that you two haven't met yet. Mason Shaw this is Luke Myers, Cam's husband." I said beaming at them both. "Luke this is my boyfriend." Both men extended hands and shook. Mason slid his arm around my waist. He was jealous. It was the little moments like these that I looked forward to lately.

"It's nice to finally meet you Mason. Lily, what is going on? Cam came home yesterday hysterical." How do I explain this to a member of the military without him thinking that we're all crazy? I had no clue how much Cam had filled him in about "our" world, but I was getting ready to find out.

"Luke...what has Cam told you lately about me?" He was looking past Mason and I, to where the coven was still working. "She told me everything Lily, she's talking to dead people, you're a witch, and he...he's a vampire." He finished skeptically. I nodded my head, and knew that I was going to have to show him. I raised my left arm and spoke, "Book of Shadows!" The screen door leading from the kitchen popped open and the book came flying through the air, and landed in my outstretched hands. I chanced a glance at both men. Mason was smiling encouragingly while Luke had a look of confusion plastered on his face.

"It's...its true." Mason and I both nodded this time. Luke straightened his posture and instead of talking to me he addressed Mason. "Mason I'm not going to mix words, you scare me a little bit, but you're obviously perfect for Lily. I didn't believe in any of this supernatural stuff until this very moment. Cam said that there were bad people coming to hurt Lily. If this is really going down than I'm going to fight with you." Mason smiled.

"Luke it's obvious that you are a strong and caring man. I appreciate that you want to help protect her, but these "people" that are coming here are vampires, bad ones. I like Cam a lot, and I love Lily, she's my Angel. That's why you can't fight. These creatures would drain your blood in front of your wife, and Lily. Lily has to fight, she's a witch. She would be distracted, and that could get her killed. I will not allow that to happen." Lukes' face fell as reality enveloped him. I knew Luke, he would gladly lay down his life for me.

"I need to do something. Mason, you're a man. I mean you're a vampire, but you're also a man...one that loves Lily. You understand, don't you? How can I help?"

Mason gave him a slight nod. "I've got just the job for you."

After a little discussion, it was back to work. I allowed my anger and fear to lead my actions. Mason had made a fatal mistake and had gotten too close to me. I landed a kick to the side of his temple. He stumbled backwards and I continued my attack. "Fire!" I called and my element responded. The flames singed the sleeve of his shirt as I threw my practice stake at him. It had hit its mark.

"Lily, you've killed him!" Luke screamed. I forgot he had never seen this kind of training. Mason pulled the stake from his chest slowly.

"No, she didn't kill me Luke. This is not a blessed stake. It hurts and slows me down, but I need her to fight me as hard as she will my brothers. But thank you for your concern." Mason assured my friends husband. We spent the next several hours going over tactics, and how to handle multiple attackers. Duncan joined us later that afternoon. My boyfriend had given each of them a job for Halloween. Luke was going to be the guard of the inhabitants inside the circle, my family. He would keep our parents from jumping into the fray when we got hurt. Duncan, the vampire hunter, would be joining us in the fight.

The rest of the week Luke and Duncan were regular fixtures at our house. Duncan already had experience dealing with vampires, but this was all new territory for Luke. Mason had given him a crash course in supernatural 101. Tension and frazzled nerves were in abundance at my house. We were snapping at each other to the point that we had taken to avoiding each other. Duncan had become a peacemaker.

"You lot need to give it a rest already! We haven't even fought yet, and you're letting them win." Our parents had been notified about the upcoming events and they were all on board.

I had barely slept at all that week. The bags under my eyes had bags of their own. On Friday, Ciaran had found more information about spirit.

"Check this out Lil." I took the book that he offered me. He pointed to a specific hand written passage. Every witch in our family had added to the Book of Shadows from the beginning of our line. That line began with the author of this passage, Ana's mother Celia Moon.

The day that my daughter was born of me, I knew that she was different. She held power like no other witch. But today, her morality was tested and I am sad to say that she failed. Her Landon was taken from her and instead of allowing him to return to the Goddess' bosom, she used her special gift to bring him back from the dead. Spirit was too much for my sweet daughter to handle. She knew not that it would harm the balance of our world by performing this dark magick. Maybe if we had known how to harness this power before she touched it we could have saved so many. I doubt the Goddess would bestow this gift to another witch of our line, but in the event that she does, do not use this gift with malice, or hatred in your heart, the consequences could be dire. Touch it with the love our Goddess intended. Blessed be~Celia

"Great! So does this mean instead of shoving a blessed stake through their hearts I should bring them a fluffy bunny for lunch?" How the hell could I fight the vampires without hate in my heart? They're the reason that my grandmother was gone, and for that alone I wanted revenge! Ciaran laughed.

"I think that Celia means that you need to be careful. Not to make the same mistake that Ana did." I knew that Ciaran was right, but would I be stronger than Ana if it came down to it? I still didn't know the answer to that.

"It doesn't tell me how to touch spirit either," I said exhaustedly.

"I've been thinking a lot about that actually. I wonder if maybe Mason is right. Remember he said that he thought that your eyes were tied to your emotions. Well what if spirit is too?" Ciaran said timidly. I just gawked at him. Was he onto something here? "I mean almost every time that we have fought the vamps, your eyes glow. And then when you were upset the other day, they lit up again." He was definitely onto something. Mason appeared in the doorway with Luke and Duncan at his side.

"What are you three up to?" I said just before Mason reached me. He wrapped his arms around my waist, pulling me close to him.

"We were just working on a few moves outside." My eyes narrowed. He just smiled at me. Mason gave me a very sweet little peck on the lips.

"Don't worry so much Lily. I have to get home. Cam wants to run to the store to pick up a few things for our stay." Luke gave me a quick hug and turned to my boyfriend. "I'll stop tomorrow Brother," he said bumping Masons' fist. Luke said good bye to everyone else and left.

"I'm here until the day after Halloween Lass." Duncan pronounced. I hugged him appreciatively. I was exhausted. Sleep deprivation was obviously causing me to lose my mind. I thought that I just saw a shadow by the front door. Click, click, click. I heard someone outside. Apparently everyone else heard it too, their heads all jerked toward the noise.

"Stay here!" Mason ran toward the front door and I hightailed it after him. "Damn it Lily get back in the house," he screamed. It was so surreal. Even in the total darkness I could see perfectly. My powers were growing by leaps and bounds daily.

"Mason over there. Someone's at the edge of the property," I pointed. My foot hit something hard. "Ow! What the hell?" I looked down to find a package by my foot.

"Lily I mean it stay here!" He glared at me before running toward the stranger. I did as he asked. I picked up the package and examined it. I knew who it was from even though it was unmarked. Dax.

"He was gone, but it was definitely not a vampire." Mason had chased after the still unknown visitor to no avail. I was eyeballing the box. The living room now stood full of witches. Everyone wanted to know what was in the box, however no one wanted to touch it.

"Saints preserve us! Give me the damn thing!" Duncan grabbed the package and lifted the lid. He reached in and pulled out a phone. There was a yellow note stuck to it. 'Lily play the video files in order.' Duncan read the piece of paper then passed it to me. I didn't even look at it. I handed it to Mason.

"Should we even bother?" Duncan said aloud, but it was obvious the only opinion he was interested in was my boyfriends'.

"You might as well," Mason responded. I sat down on his lap as Duncan opened the file. I heard Dax speaking, "Lily this girl is going to die, and it's your fault. What was your name again?" His voice asked, taunting the girl.

"It's...its Lily." My head dropped. Oh Goddess! He's going to kill this girl because we shared the same name. I began trembling. Mason pulled me closer.

"I am going to end him Angel." He spoke his next words directly into my ear. "Remember what you asked me, I will. If your life depends on it, I will." I lowered my head to hide my face. The other Lily's screams only lasted a moment, but that was one minute too long.

"There's another one." Duncan announced. I nodded my head. Riona was sobbing. I owed it to Dax's victims, they died in my stead. I heard my grandmother.

"Of course we can take a walk Lenore. Let me get my sweater." I jumped off of Masons' lap and ran over to Duncan.

"Give me that." I took the phone. Ciaran and Mason gathered around me to watch my grandmother.

"It's such a beautiful day for a walk Leeny. I meant to ask you, how is Lily doing at that fancy school of hers?" Granny's demeanor changed for a split second before she responded.

"Lenore, she is doing great. As a matter of fact, she's involved with a young man. I introduced them." My grandmother's friend stopped dead in her tracks.

"Do I know him Leeny?" My Granny shook her head.

"No I don't think so. His name is Mason. He's a handsome thing." Shock was written all over the old woman's face. They walked down the driveway towards the mailbox. Without warning my stomach began doing flip flops. I continued to watch the little screen as both women reached the mailbox. The movement was sudden and the scream ripped my heart open. Dax bit my grandmother! The scream ended along with her life. More screams ripped the living room apart. The coven finally realized what they were listening to, our grandmothers murder. Dax looked into the camera after draining my grandmother and throwing her lifeless body to the ground.

"You should have stayed with her little brother. She sent you off to watch over Lily and now she's dead. She tasted good, sort of like chicken." He threw his head back and laughed maniacally. I had never seen Mason like this. His fangs were bared, and his eyes began rolling in his head as they changed colors from green to red and back again. "I will have Lily in the end," Dax finished. The screams and sobs wouldn't stop. "Goddess help me."

It took Duncan and me over two hours to get everyone calmed down and into bed. Mason had taken off after the video ended. I must have called his cell a hundred times just to hear his voicemail. I was worried sick. I went into the kitchen, and turned the kettle on.

"Ay Lass, why don't you sit down and let me take care of that for you. And don't you be worried about Mason. He'll be back." Duncan put his hand on my shoulder. "You stood strong back there after what you had just witnessed. She would have been proud of the way you took care of your family, your Granny." I slumped forward, and finally allowed the tears to fall. The backdoor opened and we turned to see Masons' solemn face.

"I'm sorry Angel. It really is my fault that she's gone." I felt a banshee like scream building up inside of me. My entire body shook with rage. I was wanted to shove my stake so far into Dax's heart for the pain that he had caused.

"Are you insane? He did that to her because of me Mason! He killed my grandmother on Maylee's orders, to get to my power. Now he wants me because he has some delusion that he's in love with me. This has nothing to do with you, except the fact that he got to torment his little brother." I said cracking my knuckles. I paced the length of my kitchen literally vibrating across the floor.

"The pair of you need to stop this now!" Duncan bellowed. "This is exactly what Dax wants." He stood facing Mason. "You did what Lily's grandmother asked you do to, right?" Mason looked past Duncan and me and nodded. The inspector spun on his heel looking me directly in the eye. "Have you ever met these people? No. They killed your grandmother because they're power hungry. It could have been Ciaran or Shannon that had been given the power of spirit. They would have killed

148

her to get to them, and he killed that girl to torment you Lily. He's a monster." I took a deep breath.

"You're right. But they're still going to be just as dead on Halloween, even if I have to die in the process." Unable to face either man right now, I walked out of the kitchen and headed to my bedroom.

I was lying on my side when Mason slid into bed behind me. "Angel...I need you." I turned around, ready to face anything.

"Are you hurt? What's wrong?" I hastily wiped my eyes.

"My heart hurts. I'm in physical pain knowing what that animal did to Granny. My soul hurts because he sent you that video, both of the videos." He fell into my arms and cried. We cried together.

CHAPTER TWENTY

"Lily. Lily, Mason wake up. Lily, your dad's downstairs." Cormac called. I didn't understand why he was screaming. "Lily it's Sunday!" I bolted out of bed. Holy hell. I had completely slept through Saturday. I tried to get my bearings. I scanned the room. Mason had also been asleep. Those videos had affected all of us, but we had to put that behind us for right now. Mason and I changed our clothes and went down to see who else had arrived for this gigantic sleepover.

When my boyfriend and I had reached the foot of the stairs everyone was here. Great Goddess this living room resembled a can of packed sardines. My dad walked over and hugged me.

"Were you able to get any sleep last night?" I nodded my head. "I called yesterday and Duncan said that you were all sleeping." Uncle Donal laughed. "Yeah we thought that maybe Mason had gotten hungry and turned you all into vampires too," my dad joked. My stomach twisted on itself, threatening to make me physically sick again. Ms. Lenore was going to pay for what she did to my grandmother. Riona knew that it was a friend of Granny's. She just couldn't get a good look at the culprit. I know now, and the coven will deal with her after we handled the current mess. The coven had decided to destroy the phone, and never tell the adults the horror that we had all witnessed.

"Mr.Lochlan what is all of this?" Mason asked pointing to the bags. My father grinned mischievously. He put his arm on my boyfriends' shoulder as if they were lifelong friends

"Those, Mason, are a few elder wood treats." Duncan bent down and opened the bag closest to him. He looked up smiling.

"Are those what I think they are?" My dad and uncles all nodded their heads happily. I knelt in front of the bag. There were little pieces of wood shaped like bullets.

"Dad, what the hell do you think that you're going to do with these?" I lifted my gaze to meet his. He smiled. "Oh the hell you are!" I yelled. I jumped to my feet. My father and uncles thought that they were going to fight with the coven. I quickly raised my arm, "Trashcan!" At my command the large wooden container whizzed through the air and landed about a foot in front of me. I held two of the wooden bullets in my right hand and called, "Fire!" They ignited just before I threw them into the trash. I had already lost too much. This was not up for negotiation.

"We have to take our potion," I said to the coven. I ignored the adults as I passed them.

"EW…now it looks like motor oil." Jessie cringed. I had to agree, this was going to be gross. However, we needed the extra strength. The next thirty-six hours were going to the most difficult of our young lives.

"Let's just guzzle it fast, but make sure you have something to chase it with to get the taste out of your mouth," Aidan said repulsed. I caught a glimpse of my dad glaring at me from across the room. Mason went over to talk to him as we tipped our vials up. Actually it wasn't that bad. It sort of reminded me of black licorice. I grabbed my coffee and cleared my throat.

"Well it's done. Anyone feel any different?" I looked around the room.

"I…think that I now have indigestion. Errrp," Braden belched. Lovely. The rest of the coven laughed. I guess we would see if the potion actually worked.

"Lily, may your father and I have a word with you outside?" Mason asked diplomatically. I nodded. I didn't look at either one of them as I walked past. They followed me outside. I stood on the front porch with my guard already up. My arms were crossed to my chest as I tapped my toe. Mason broke the silence.

"Lily, your dad is going to fight with us." His words felt like a sucker punch to the gut. I could feel the blood rising to my face. I was trying desperately to control my emotions.

"Mason, he is not fighting! Would you really let my father risk his life?" I started pacing uncontrollably. My dad grabbed my arm as I began another pass.

"Lilyann Kathleen Moon! My mother wanted me to fight. That's why she willed my dads' gun to me. There was a note stuffed into the chamber. She spelled this gun for the fight." He wiped a tear that had escaped his eye. "She knew…she knew that she was going to die. She explained everything in her note. Here." He handed me the little piece of paper. I read it to myself. She had told my dad about Mason. That he was good for me, and to not be difficult about our relationship. She had indeed told him that his gun was ready for supernatural action, and how it was to be used. She had told him how to make the wooden shrapnel for the gun. My grandmother had closed her note by telling her son how much she loved him.

I walked over to my father. "You do not leave the circle. Agreed? You can shoot that thing from inside of the circle." He nodded. He turned to Mason and hugged him. Wait…hell just froze over! I watched as the door opened and my family poured out.

"Okay guys get all of the grocery bags from my truck. I need to feed you all before the ceremony tonight. Quit being a bunch of lookey lou's, Mason is part of our family." Aunt Rae commanded.

"Yes ma'am," Declan said cheerily.

My aunts were all in the kitchen cleaning up. They had prepared a feast. After the boys had brought all of the bags of groceries, suitcases, and miscellaneous items in, they began taking the things needed for the initiation outside. They were going to start setting it up after dinner. Mason and my father had ganged up on me about what I had on my plate. I wasn't hungry, but they kept telling me how I would not be strong enough if I did not eat something. I ate a little bit of chicken simply to appease them.

"If this is how it's going to be from now on, I may have to find a new boyfriend." I said jokingly. They both glared in my direction.

"Are you sure that you want to deal with her for the rest of her life?" My Uncle Hugh laughed. Mason winked at me.

"Is forever long enough, because I'll settle for nothing less."

It was time for me to get ready. Cam went upstairs with me to get dressed. She sat on my bed as I went into my bathroom to change into the shift.

"Lily, are you scared?" Her voice was timid. I saw no need to lie.

"Yes, I am. I'm worried sick for all of you. I just want to protect everyone Cam." I said truthfully as I reappeared. The shift clung to my body as I walked over to the mirror. The electrical current was back and running along the surface of my skin. I felt power, and wondered if this is what Ana felt also.

"Lilyann, you're glowing." Cam sounded awestruck. I quickly assessed my eyes. They were fine. What was she talking about? Someone knocked at my door then opened it. Aunt Rae poked her head in.

"Need any more help?" She smiled warmly. I waved her in. "Oh my, Lily. You look just like your mom right now. You're a vision," Aunt Rae announced.

Cam had fastened the garter to my left thigh, while Aunt Rae slid the cuff onto my right bicep. As each magickal piece adorned my body I became more confident. My fear was ebbing away, and being replaced with the sense of belonging. My destiny was laid out before me. Now I just needed to accept it. I was ready. Five weeks ago, the supernatural world overwhelmed me. I had worked tirelessly to show myself that I could handle this new path. The entire coven had proved themselves more than worthy of this responsibility. It was our time to change the world, and it would all begin tonight. "I'm ready for the diadem," I proclaimed. Aunt Rae's eyes found mine in the mirror as Cam placed the moonstone and silver circlet on my head. She understood what was happening to her niece. I felt the change begin, my eyes were beacons. The glow came from inside of my soul.

"Oh...my...god!" My best friend stuttered.

I followed the two women from the backdoor. I was barely dressed, but I was warm. I had prepared myself by drinking rosehip tea. I held my head high as my bare feet touched the grass beneath them. My eyes lit the way. I heard the stunned gasps of family members who had not been introduced to my new appearance.

"She's become an angel," I heard one of my uncle's mutter. My father stepped forward amidst the, "OH's and AH's!" We were face to face.

"Your grandmother knew what she was doing sweetheart. Take your rightful place at the head of our family's coven, like my mother did before you." He kissed my forehead and went back to his spot. Mason held my athame out to me.

"You are stunning, my love." I smirked. I took my tool from him, and raised it above my head.

"Goddess, your daughter calls to you to bear witness to this evening's initiation of twelve Moon witches! I ask for your blessing." The moonstones that we all wore began glowing.

"Do you see that?" Ciaran asked. I nodded. A gentle loving web of light connected each of us. Our Goddess had sent her approval. I walked over to the cauldron, and called my element to light the fire for me. "Fire!" The beautiful flames danced in the light of the full moon. I walked the circumference of our circle tracing it on the ground with my athame. Only a witch that had been initiated could enter the circle. A small opening was left untraced for us to do just that, after we had taken our oath. First I needed to call the elements to protect us during our ritual.

I had purposely created the opening at the northern point of the circle. I began there. I bent down and grabbed a handful of dirt. "I call from the North, Earth. With this soil that leaves my hand, I beckon you with my command. Protect this circle." I turned clockwise. Shannon handed me the lit smudge stick made of sage. "I call from the East, Air. With the smoke that leaves this stick, I beckon you to unveil all tricks. Protect this circle." Again I turned to face a new direction. The cauldron stood in front of me. "I call from the South, Fire. With these flames that burn so bright, I call you here to stand with us this night. Protect this circle." I turned for the last time. Cassie held out a copper bowl filled with water. The Triple Goddess Moon had been etched on its side. "I call from the West, Water. With this sacred liquid that falls to the ground, with my oath you are bound. Protect this circle."

I stood at the little opening and began. "I, Lilyann Moon, stand before you Goddess in this sacred place with only perfect love and perfect trust in my heart. I give my blood oath to serve you willingly, to help keep the natural balance in order. I vow to protect those that cannot protect themselves." I spoke clearly and confidently. I poured one of the bottles of Elderberry wine that sat atop the makeshift altar into the cauldron, it bubbled. Hazy smoke rose from the potion. I retrieved the Selenite from the table and it went into the potion next. All that was needed now was my offering. I pricked my fingertip with my knife, and gave my blood to the cauldron. One of the twelve white candles on the altar lit itself as I entered the circle. I turned to face everyone. "As the Goddess wills it, so mote it be." The Goddess had accepted me. I was the first initiated witch of this coven.

Ciaran stepped up next. "I, Ciaran Moon, stand before you Goddess in this sacred place with only perfect love and perfect trust in my heart. I give my blood oath to serve you willingly, to help keep the natural balance in order. I vow to protect those that cannot protect themselves." He put one of the rose quartz into the black pot. Ciaran poked his finger with a pin allowing his blood to fall into the cauldron. Another white candle sprang to life. He entered the magickal circle as the next initiated witch. He and I exchanged a quick hug.

Next up was Riona. She took her oath perfectly. Our parents looked on as we took the same oath that so many years ago they walked away from. One after another my family took their oath and candles sprang to life revealing a new witch. After everyone was inside, I took my athame and closed the circle. Mason stood off to the side with my father. They were whispering to each other as they watched our progression. It had taken over an hour for all twelve of us to take our oaths, but not we were an actual coven. We needed to finish the ceremony.

On the ground, inside of our sacred space lay colored candles. We each grabbed one. We needed to pledge what character trait we were bringing to the table.

Jessie began. "I'll bring love to the circle."

Liam followed her. "I'll bring integrity to the circle."

Shannon spoke. "I'll bring morality to the circle."

Declan went next. "I'll bring loyalty to the circle."

Seamus piped up, "I'll bring dedication to the circle."

Aidan beamed. "I'll bring trust to the circle."

Riona went after her brother. "I'll bring communication to the circle."

Braden was ready. "I'll bring imagination to the circle."

Cassie raised her head. "I'll bring pride to the circle."

Cormac spoke. "I'll bring honesty to the circle."

Standing next to me Ciaran said softly, "I'll bring compassion to the circle."

I smiled in return. It was my turn. I took a deep breath. "I'll bring selflessness to the circle." When I had finished speaking, flames erupted from the candles that we were holding. I was smiling to myself as I looked down. Someone had found sparkly iridescent moonstone candles for our ritual. The pinks, purples, and blues danced from the candlelight inside of each candle. It was magickal. The new Moon coven gathered in the middle of our circle. We extinguished the flames together as one. I used my bare foot to open the circle. Single file we made our way to the onlookers.

The offering table was overflowing with food and drink. My aunts had outdone themselves tonight. Everyone was relieved that the first part of Granny's plan had been accomplished. My mind was now readying itself for tomorrow.

"Lily your grandmother would be so proud of you kids," Uncle Dillon said lovingly. I was about to respond when I heard it.

"Not long now boys and girls," his playfully taunting voice carried across the orchard. My head whipped in his direction. He was standing in the light of the almost full moon. The coven gathered around as Mason took point with me. He couldn't get to me yet. The wards would hold until tomorrow night. With the Goddess' help, there would be no fight. I would be able to reinforce the wards, and Dax would just lose. However something told me that it wasn't going to be quite that easy. The noises were now coming from all around me. I whispered behind me to my scared family.

"Go back to the house! Now." I heard the scurrying noise of their footfalls. "Mmm…you look delicious Lily, and tomorrow I'll have you and your little cat too." His eerie laughter filled the night. Izzy was all fluffed up and hissing as she wound herself protectively around us. I turned to face my coven. "The vampires are on the farm."

TWENTY-ONE

Ciaran and I walked into the kitchen after I had changed into jeans and a sweater. We were discussing the preparations for tomorrow. In the event that I couldn't perform my first Wiccan duty as a newly initiated witch. Aunt Rae was standing in front of the breakfast nook holding out two mugs of coffee for us.

"Thanks mom. You might want to brew a lot more of this," Ciaran said before chugging it down. No one in the house was in the mood to sleep. There was a very somber feel to this once, light and happy house.

"Thank you Aunt Rae. You've been a lifesaver. Feeding us, helping me get ready, and not to mention, you make the best coffee in the state." I hugged my favorite aunt.

"Let's do it." Riona said seriously. She had the bag of wooden pieces that my dad had brought. They still needed to be blessed in order to be truly lethal, plus we wanted to bless extra stakes. Mason looked on as Riona, Cormac, Ciaran and I raised our hands, holding the bag above our heads.

We called out in unison, "Goddess come to you daughters and sons, and bless this wood with your power." We repeated the spell over fifty times. Mason finally joined me.

"How are you feeling Angel?" I feel tired, scared, physically sore, and like the clock is in fast-forward.

"I'm fine. I just need to keep guzzling coffee." I rested my head on his shoulder. "Mason?" He gave a little, "Uh-huh?"

I continued, "Are you scared?" He wrapped his arms around me and answered.

"I'm not afraid for myself, but yes, I'm scared to death for you. Dax isn't messing around Lily. I've been scanning the trees, and he's brought an army." It was as if his words had gotten their attention, because the noises and yells ensued.

"Lily we're waiting for you."

"The Moon coven ends tomorrow."

"We'll drain the lot of you!"

Mason ushered us inside. "You need to stay focused." He spoke to the coven as our parents listened. "You have trained hard. All of you. Now it's time to put your training to use where it really counts. Tomorrow, if we have to fight, then we do it to protect everyone. When Granny and I fought together I learned what it truly meant to be good. She fought to protect innocence. You guys have to fight for your lives first, because people that don't even know about the real horrors in our world will surely die at the hands of one of those beasts. Ciaran, you're fast and strong. I want you to position yourself around Shannon." She looked up. "Ah, before you get upset. You're good, really good. You're also small, and they'll definitely try to ambush you." Her face became serious as she nodded.

"Lily, you have a bull's-eye on your back. I want you to fight, but I really want you to bounce around with your elemental power. Braden and Declan, shoot as many as you can. Mr. Lochlan, will be assisting you from inside of the circle. Duncan, you're a hunter. This is going to be unlike any other hunt that you've been on. The vampires are going to hunt you. And you're not going to have the rest of the hunters there to watch your back. Stay alert! Luke will be inside of the circle keeping everyone else away from the wards. I never watched Granny perform the rite, but I know that the vampires cannot cross the line." My boyfriend was making direct eye contact with all three of the men that he spoke to.

"Allow Lily the opportunity to cast the spell. The rest of the coven will be working with her to make the wards as strong as possible, which in turn makes them stronger." He went over to Cam.

"Your job is to stay in the circle. Lily can't be distracted, and we all would be if something happened to you and the baby. The dead will find you, and they may have information for us. Can you handle this Cam?" She stood up proudly.

"This is my family too. I can handle anything for Lily, but I'm still scared."

Mason went to each person in turn explaining to them the importance of their role in the fast approaching event. I wandered through the house finally making my way to my bedroom. I opened the door and was shocked to see the coven. From the looks of it, they had been waiting for me.

"Lily, close the door and come over here," Ciaran whispered. I did as I was told. Aidan scooted over to make room for me on the bed.

"What's wrong now guys?" My heart started beating a million miles a minute.

"Nothing's wrong, aside from the waiting bloodsuckers. We wanted to tell you that we believe in you and to give you this," Shannon handed me a long thin piece of wood. My confused eyes searched the faces on my bed.

"Um...Thanks...I...I should put this up somewhere it'll be safe," I said examining the stick.

"You're out of it Lily!" Declan laughed. "It's our family's wand. You'll need it to do the wards." I felt like an idiot.

"Guys, I'm sorry, I totally forgot. Wait, where did you find this?" Seamus beamed.

"I found it upstairs in the attic when I was working on the runes." When we couldn't locate it earlier, Seamus whittled us a new one from elder wood. We had blessed it for tomorrow. I thought that our family's original wand had been lost forever. My mood changed instantly. Our family might have a chance at a happy ending after all.

The night turned into the early morning hours of Halloween. The day had come. I moved through the house gathering my weapons. I had grabbed my favorite jeans, and sweatshirt to work our magick, and if all else failed fight for my coven's life in. I grabbed the piece of tartan cloth that once belonged to Ana and shoved it in my pocket. Jessie french braided each of the girls' hair, to keep it from flying in our faces. I had my athame, wand, and plenty of blessed stakes. I also had my bowstaff. Mason felt that that was the weapon for me after the way that I had weilded his deathblade.

The kitchen was buzzing with nervous activity. Cam and Luke were cuddled up together on the sofa, lost in their own little world. That made me happy. I wanted to cast glamour on them and sneak them out of this house, far away. Mason was going over fight tactics with my brother in the corner. My father caught my eye. He inclined his head in the front porches direction. I nodded my understanding, grabbed a cup of coffee and followed him.

His back was to me, "Lilyann." I moved closer to him and placed my hand on his shoulder. He turned around. Tears were falling from his tired blue eyes.

"Dad, please don't cry. I'm going to do everything in my power to save them. I promise I won't let the vampires touch you." My father struggled to speak.

"I've always been harder on you than the others. I knew that you were strong, but I never realized how strong you truly are. I feel like the weight of the world is on your shoulders, and not once have you complained. You trudge forward. All the while, you've had no support from me. You have always has your mothers' strength." He lowered his head.

"I can't even remember the last time that I told you how much I love you." The tears came heavily now from him and I both.

"Dad, I know that you love me. You know what? I'm glad that you were hard on me. It made me toughen up, and that's helping me now. So you have supported me. I love you Daddy." I hugged my father for what I prayed to my Goddess wasn't the last time.

I put my empty mug in the sink, and glanced at the clock. It was five o'clock, and the only light outside was from the full moon. It was time to try my Wiccan hand at putting the wards up. I turned around to gather everyone, only to find them staring back at me. They were ready. The center of my grandmothers' property was only about twenty yards from the back door. Everyone started setting up there. The vampires were visible, even in the dark. After seeing us in the open yard, one of the vampires ran toward us only to be pushed back by the invisible barrier.

"See what I mean," Mason said helping my father get settled. I grabbed our family's ancestral wand, and the Book of Shadows. The coven joined me at the northern most part of the circle that I had cast. Mason ran over.

"I want you guys to stay back about five yards from the markers. The wards are going to start coming down fast. If you're too close, they're going to grab one of you. Let's get started." I took a deep breath, centering myself, and released it. Vampires began leaving the cover of the tree line. POP! I spun around. My dad had shot on of those beasts.

"Breathe Angel" Mason whispered in my ear. This was all happening too fast. I forgot what I was supposed to do.

"Lily we're here too," Cassie said calmly. My head turned in her direction. The coven stood unified by my side. "It's okay, remember." I nodded my head. She was right. I knew what I had to do, and I was more than capable. I shot up a prayer, 'Goddess protect them.'

I raised the wand and began, "Goddess protect us. Surround us with your loving glow. Earth empower us, as above so below." I traced the rune for Fehu in the air. It resembled a crooked F. It symbolized new beginnings. I turned clockwise. My wand held high.

"Goddess protect us. Keep us safe from harm. Air empower us with communication and shield this farm." Again the wand whipped through the night. I now traced the rune for Eihwaz. The crooked backward Z was completed. I moved clockwise once more with my wand still raised.

"Goddess protect us. Fill us with your deepest desires. Fire empower us with the knowledge to suffer this situation so dire." My hand was zooming through the air. I traced the rune for Elhaz. It sort of looked like an upside-down broom. I turned on my heel for the final time. The popping sound from my fathers' gun was driving me bonkers, but he was killing our enemies. So I dealt with it. I glanced in front of me quickly to see the vampires getting closer. Goddess please let this work! I raised my wand again.

"Goddess protect us. Keep us close to your side. Water empower us with compassion, loyalty and pride." My wand slashed downward, marking the I in the sky. It was the runic symbol Isa. It stood for unity, our coven. "On all Hallows' eve I send you this plea. Enforce the wards to keep this sacred space in harmony. This property no one enters with evil in their heart. By the power of the Goddess they will be torn apart!" I yelled into the night. I had completed the spell.

I looked all around me. Nothing had changed. The vampires were getting closer by the minute! "Oh no...I had to have messed it up," I cried. My family would die, because I couldn't follow instructions. "Granny you choose wrong. I'm not a super witch." I had to catch my breath.

"She didn't choose who became a spirit user Angel, the Goddess did," Mason spoke. "We have to fight. The wards are going to box us in soon, and then there will be no hope of surviving this. Get your stakes ready!"

I scanned my area. No sign of Victor or Dax, but I knew that they were out there somewhere. Declan and Braden were sending blessed stakes through the chest of vampires, one after another. There were two vampires closing in on Mason. He had jumped into the fight. His death blade slashed through the air. I turned my focus to the vampire directly in front of me. The time had come for me to cross the wards. "Fire!" I hurled my element at the abnormally tall man. He tried to duck out of the way. The flame caught him on the shoulder, and I didn't hesitate. I plunged one of my stakes through his heart. A shadow in my peripheral vision caught my attention. A man and a woman raced toward me.

"She's mine!" The woman roared. She had a long Burgundy ponytail that whipped around her heart shaped face as she leapt at me. I waited until the last minute before spinning to the left, out of her reach. She recovered her balance quickly. We circled each other, trying to gauge the others' strengths and weaknesses.

"Lily, I've come for you. Good job Lacey." His words had distracted me. The woman took advantage of my momentary lapse of concentration. She was on top of me in a split second. Her fangs were bared and her red eyes were crazed. I continued to fight the insane red head now perched on my chest.

"Stopadh" I yelled. My spell had no effect on him. I struggled with my attacker as Dax moved toward me with immeasurable speed.

He was only a short distance away when Mason and his sword slashed down from the sky meeting his brother's own death blade. When they collided, it sounded like one of those knights of armor in the museum had crashed. Mason's sword kept his oldest brother busy long enough for me to throw a freezing spell at the fiery red head.

"Cuiro!" I had escaped, and was running through the invisible barrier of the wards. I collided with my father, causing him to hit the trigger accidentally.

"Lily are you hurt?" He looked me up and down. I was panting, but I was physically fine.

"Sorry Dad! Yeah, I'm fine. I need to check on everyone else." Each member of the coven was fighting. Ciaran and Declan were battling two vampires a piece, and holding their own. Everyone else was dealing with the immediate threats in front of them. Shannon and Jessie had the blessed stake nunchuks that Mason had made for them twirling in the air. Both girls ended a vampire's life in that moment. Luke was doing the job that Mason had assigned him. He had the parents huddled together.

Luke continued to call out warnings to us. Cam was sitting Indian style on the ground. I got her attention.

"Anything yet?" She shook her head. Damn!

My dad was picking vampires off left and right. Thank the Goddess Granny had left him this weapon. We would have been in a world of hurt right now without him. I tried to find a hole for me to plug when I heard him again.

"Mason, you do realize that I am going to rip your throat out, don't you?" Dax laughed. Both brothers had bared their fangs. The hatred between them was more than normal sibling rivalry. It was clear that both vampires were fighting for...me. Mason was meeting every one of his brothers' strikes with ease. Mason would be fine. I needed to get back out there. I spotted just who I wanted, Victor. He and another vampire were getting ready to double team Seamus.

"Not today, you little weasel!" Without missing a single beat I started throwing different spells at him. "Stopadh! Cuiro!" My magick slowed him only slightly, but it was enough to plant a kick to his chest that sent him flying through the night.

"Lily behind you!" Cam screamed from inside the circle. I thrust my sharpened bow-staff behind me, and right into the chest of another vampire. He fell dead. Victor had taken off again. The situation was getting more chaotic by the minute. Duncan had just staked another vampire. The hunter was agile in his attacks. But he was effective. We had to have collectively killed over fifty of the bloodsuckers, but more poured from the trees. "Goddess! How many are there?" I asked. The vampires were like cockroaches, they were everywhere and into everything.

Cassie was now fighting the crazed red head, Lacey. She was throwing magick, and punches at the woman. My sister was holding her own, but just barely. Cormac had cast a blinding spell to help Cassie out. I was fighting an older vampire whose skills were impeccable when I heard him again.

"How about I take your head now, I'm tired of this game little brother." Mason's words caused a lump to form in throat.

"Take my head Dax, she'll still never be yours!"

"Lily, she's here!" Cam yelled louder than I had ever heard come from her tiny frame. I was in the middle of fighting two vampires now. I had just planted a stake in one's chest, and jumped out of the way of the others fangs. Declan, and Riona were tag teaming a rather large vampire to my left.

"Lily, go find out if Granny can help us!" Ri screamed. I was still spitting spells at my remaining threat. My hand flew out in front of me.

"Earth, Air, Fire, and Water do my bidding!" I commanded the elements. They came in force. The elemental storm that I had created held the beasts contained, but the Goddess was the only one who knew for how long. I turned and ran to Cam. Sweat dripped down my back, underneath my sweatshirt. The continued sound of fighting hurt my head.

"Where is she Cam?" My best friend pointed off to a spot close to my father. Well, I already thought that I was crazy. I might as well act the part.

"Granny, help us! I don't know how to touch spirit. Help me save them. Please help!" I cried.

Cam nodded her head. "She said you need to allow your emotions to take over, and call to it." What?

"Okay, I'm pissed! Spirit!" I looked around me and all that was visible was the downfall of the coven. Jessie was lying on her side in the circle. The carnage was epic! Everyone was taking a beating. I wasn't sure how much longer they would last, before one of them was really hurt. Or even worse, killed.

"Lily she said for you to remember the inscription on the back of your amulet." Cam called over to me. I had bent down to check on my sister. She was banged up, and bleeding. "Lily! Mason!" Multiple voices pierced the night. What was going on? I turned around. My worst fear realized. Mason was stumbling across the wards, holding his neck. Blood poured heavily from the wound Dax had inflicted with his blade.

My family had retreated back inside of the wards. My boyfriend fell to the ground. I pulled his limp body onto mine, cradling him. I checked his neck. "Goddess. NO!" Dax had practically decapitated Mason. "Cam you ask her if my blood will fix this! ASK HER!" I sobbed. "Mason stay with me, okay. I can't lose you. I love you." I begged him. Aunt Rae ran over with a towel, and put pressure on his neck to try to slow the bleeding.

"Yes Lily! She said it will heal his wound immediately. Your blood has healing qualities." Thank you Goddess!

"Mason did you hear that? You're going to drink a little of my blood and you'll be okay again, better than okay." The ache in my heart stopped. His voice was hard to hear over the vampires still trying to throw themselves at the wards to get to us. "I can't hear you sweetie. What did you say?" I lowered my head to his mouth.

"No. I will not drink from you. I'm so sorry Angel." His green eyes closed.

TWENTY-TWO

"I told you Lily that I would kill him. Now it's only a matter of time before you are mine," Dax cackled. "The wards that protect you are almost gone, and when they are I'm taking you with me." I looked down at Masons' gaunt face. I gave him no options! It was now or never. He was the love of my life. He was not allowed to leave me here alone. We we're in trouble, and only he could help me save my family. I slashed my athame over the fleshy portion of my wrist. Crimson liquid began falling from the gash. I shoved my wrist up to Masons' mouth.

"No! Someone stop her!" From somewhere behind me, Dax screeched. He was furious. Vampires ran at the wards from every direction. They were unable to reach me, yet.

"Dammit Mason drink. If you don't drink from me, we're all going to die! Please!" I cried to him. He was so pale. My fathers' voice rang out next to me.

"Mason! Do you hear me?" he barely moved his head. My dad continued angrily. "You told me that you would always take care of Lily! That you loved her more than yourself. Was that the truth? Damn it son. You need to save her. I gave you my blessing to marry her when this was all over. Mason please!" His eyes fluttered open. He nodded his head more aggressively. I was in shock at my fathers' words, but I offered Mason my wrist again, and this time he drank, and drank well. I felt a little weak, but the adrenaline rush wouldn't allow my body to give out just yet. I searched for Dax. I spotted him about ten feet from us.

"Hey Dax, your baby brother is going to rip you apart. How does it feel to be the mouse?" Within a minute, the wound on his neck had closed. He leaned over and kissed me passionately. As he rose he winked at me. Mason was okay. He was on his feet yelling commands.

"Mr. Lochlan, shoot as many as you can! Aunt Rae, get Lily's bleeding to stop! Declan, watch yourself." He was faster and stronger than ever, and to think that my blood did that.

Wow!

I felt my amulet warm against my skin and it hit me. Of course!

Aunt Rae tried to fuss over me, but there wasn't time. I wrapped Ana's tartan cloth around my bleeding wrist, tying it with my teeth.

"Aunt Rae, keep everyone in the circle. I think that I just figured the wards out." I ran to the center of the property. I raised the wand, and closed my eyes. "Goddess, I'm ready. Send me the words. I am with you in Spirit!" I felt like someone had just wrapped me in a warm blanket. In my head I heard a woman's voice and it was beautiful. I repeated what she offered me.

"Spirit protect us. Under the blanket of the moon, stars, and our Goddess who is all seeing. Spirit empower us with your entire being." I wove an intricate pattern under the full moon. "I call the spirits of my ancestors to me. Through the night you will fly, and be visible to our eye!" I hadn't noticed the silence before that was now deafening. All eyes, including the vampires, were now focused on me.

White wisps were flying toward the circle. The vampires were backing up.

"Lily you did it! The wards are pushing the vampires back," Ciaran exclaimed. I didn't have time to enjoy the fruits of my labor. I noticed that if a vampire wasn't fast enough to get away from the wards, it trapped them inside of the wards. There were about fifteen hungry vampires trapped inside of the protective wards with my non-supernatural family. Victor was one of them, and he was mine. Dax ran screaming from the scene.

"Victor get out! We'll get the stubborn little witch another day." Mason charged after him. The coven stood together facing the beasts. I tore after Victor. I had summoned spirit, and it filled me with love for my family, and shear rage for this monster. He dodged around me. I had just missed hitting him with a freezing spell when he was headed back towards my father. The next few minutes were a blur. The sound of flesh being opened, metal clanging, and a pop from my fathers' gun were all I remembered. Somehow I had grabbed Victor by the arm and spun him into my stake. After it was embedded in his chest, I threw him to the ground and jumped on top of him to make sure my stake had gone all the way through his heart. I stared blankly as he began to disintegrate.

"He's dead, love."

I looked up into those green eyes that were my world now.

"Everyone else?" I managed to choke out.

"The vampires are gone. You saved everyone Angel." He helped me up off of the ground. I was sore everywhere, but especially my wrist. Mason ran his finger over the tartan cloth.

"Ehhh.." That didn't sound good. I whipped my head in the direction of the moan and saw people gathered around my sister.

"Oh my goddess, Cassie!" I broke out into a sprint. I dropped to my knees when I reached her. My father had just left my brother lying on the ground.

"Dad, go see Cass. I'm fine, it's just an ankle." Cam had my sister's head cradled in her arms. Duncan and Luke took turns speaking.

"Ay lass your sister was fighting that wild eyed red headed woman after the vampires got trapped inside the wards."

Luke began, "Lily, Cassie was fine until she tried to stake her vampire, and protect Cam and me. Another vampire was headed straight for us, and Ciaran was coming to save us. Cassie didn't know that, and the red head kicked her in the chest. She's breathing hard. I think that her rib may have punctured her lung."

I lay my body on the ground next to her. "Cassie I'm so sorry. It's my fault. I should have killed her when I had the chance."

Aunt Rae started crying softly, "Lochlan, she's bleeding out. She won't make it to the hospital." Cassie coughed, and blood dripped from her mouth. Wait…if I could save Mason than I could surely save my sister. I jumped up from the ground.

"Granny! I know that you're here. Come to me now, all of you. Cassie's hurt. Mom I need you!" I allowed spirit to call for them, from within myself. Wisps of smoke zoomed through the air. They weaved themselves all around us. The spirits of my grandmother and my mom settled in front of us, followed by about fifty other family members. "Granny how do I save my sister?" I demanded. I watched my mom's pearly figure float to her middle daughter.

"No Leeny. That would be messing with the balance. If Cassandra is destined to die then she will return to our Goddess' side. Blessed be." Goddess grant me strength.

"Look I don't know who you are, I really could care less," I screamed at the nosy ghost. I turned my attention back to my grandmother. "Granny. Please. She's going to die! Hasn't this family lost enough?" My grandmothers' face fell.

"Leighann" my father whispered. He and my mothers' spirit had locked eyes. She glided over to her husband, hovering over my sisters quivering body.

"I'll tell you how to save her." A beautiful woman with long curls floated to the front. She looked like me or I looked like her.

"You're Ana." She seemed shocked that I knew of her.

"I am, but now is not the time if you want to save your sister. Do you have our wand?" I pulled it from my back pocket showing it to her. It must have been a trick of the light. But I thought that I saw a glimmer of a devious grin flash across her beautiful features."Good. You'll need to give her your blood also." I just kept nodding. "Okay Lily, the Moon coven's new Spirit leader, repeat after me. With this witch's blood so pure, give her the strength for her life to endure." I stopped repeating after Ana because different words were being given to me in my head. I spoke loudly.

"I give of myself and ask nothing in return. From all experiences, wisdom I will earn. My Goddess saves my sister Cassie this night, with the hopes our family learns wrong from right." I tore the tartan from my wrist. "Cass, I'm pretty sure this is going to be gross, but drink." I tilted my wrist up for the second time this evening. I hoped that I wouldn't run out of blood. A moment later my sister's breathing calmed down, and she was regaining a little color in her cheeks. Cassie was going to be okay.

"Mom, Granny I miss you guys so badly." I sniffled.

"My little lady, I am so proud of you. I have been watching you all the time. You are strong, loving, courageous, and beautiful. Please never think that you are alone, because I am always with you. By the way, Mason has my approval to marry my daughter. I love you my sweet. I'll give you a few minutes with you grandmother while I check on Cassie, and the others." My mother was still just as beautiful as ever as she floated toward the house. I turned back to Granny, and smiled.

"So, had my life mapped out for a while have we?" I laughed. She pondered her words.

"Lily-Bug you were the only choice that our Goddess could have made. As far as Mason goes, I just knew that it was the two of you forever. I'm so sorry that I can't give you answers that you want or need, but the Goddess wants to see you work. You know that a Christmas wedding would be magickal." She smiled at me and then past me as Mason came walking back outside. He had carried my sister into the house so that everyone could start babying her.

"Granny, I am so sorry that I failed you." He said morosely. My grandmother glided up to him and looked into his eyes.

"Mason James Shaw. You did not fail me. You have helped Lily keep the coven alive. More importantly you have taught my granddaughter that love is real, and it doesn't always leave us. I am so proud of you both. Keep me in your heart, and remember I am always with you in Spirit." She floated toward the house. The old ghost who gave me a hard time earlier beckoned me to her.

"I'm sorry Lilyann Kathleen. I had to see how you would use you gifts. You will set the Moon family's reputation right." She smiled softly through her opaque eyes. She turned and I called out, "Excuse me, but who are you?" She smiled even brighter.

"I am your great grandmother Rose Moon, and I love you child. Blessed Be." She disappeared.

Ana was looking for me. "Lilyann I am happy that you were able to save your sister." Her eyes found the tartan cloth wrapped around my wrist. "You know I wouldn't have done that for Landon if I knew then what I know now." I smiled at her.

"I know Ana. I hope that you find your Landon one day up there with the Goddess. Blessed Be." She too floated away.

I leaned my back up against Mason. "This feels amazing. Just you and I under the stars, and no one is right around the corner trying to kill us." He pulled me into his warmth.

"We have lots of these nights on the horizon, and I have an Angel to share them with." He spun me around and kissed me. Now that there was no danger, maybe he and I could concentrate on us, just a little bit. Probably not.

Two weeks later, we were having a party to celebrate Rionna's birthday. Family and friends were in abundance. So was food, drink, and happiness. Aunt Rae had planned this little shindig. Purple streamers and balloons were draped over everything. It was totally Riona.

"We're going to play football. Who's in?" Liam proclaimed jovially. The men in my family were finally letting their guards down a little. My boyfriend was outside with the rest of the guys. Declan leaned on Ciaran. He had a badly sprained ankle. Cassie and Mason had both healed fully from their wounds. The rest of the coven including myself had wounds that were all but scars now. It would take a lot longer for the ones on the inside to heal. My family had finally decided that Ri's new boyfriend John was worthy of her. So now he joined the festivities, just not the supernatural ones.

I ran back into the house and grabbed my coat to get the mail. I had seen the truck and I was expecting paperwork from my school. I was planning on taking a few classes online. I was joined by the love of my life.

"Where do you think that you're going without my protection, Angel?" He joked. I took his hand and we finished the short walk to the box. I grabbed the mail inside. I flipped through each piece, but one stood out. It was a handwritten address. Obviously not a bill. I slid my finger under the flap and pulled out a sheet of folded paper. I read the note.

'Lilyann, I have not given up on making you mine. I will have you sooner than you realize. Tell my brother that we will have to "catch up" in the near future. Oh and I have a question for you. Why didn't you ask me who the 2nd man in your dream was? Ha-ha. Sleep tight, Dax' My eyes flew up to meet Masons'. "Dax." I handed him the note. His eyes flashed dangerously.

Our heads turned in unison at the sound of kicked up stones. The coven came running toward us. Riona looked dizzy. "Ri had a vision." Aidan announced. Riona addressed all of us.

"I hope everyone has their passports in order. Because according to my vision, we're going to need them."

Kymberlee Burks-Miller is a wife, and mother. She lives in PA now where she and her husband have an interdivisional NFL rivalry. She is a die-hard Ravens fan, and her husband and son are Steelers fans. If you can't find her on the sidelines of her sons' football games, baseball games, online, cooking, cleaning, shopping, or on the phone wandering through her house, than she's probably tucked herself away in her cave. Kymberlee's positive attitude, and absolute fun-loving approach to life makes it easy for the voices in her head to take over on a regular basis. Enjoy the journey~Kymberlee

For more information on Kymberlee Burks-Miller and her books follow her on facebook at www.facebook.com/CompulsionSeries

Conversion~the second book in the Compulsion Series coming October 2012

CPSIA information can be obtained at www.ICGtesting.com
Printed in the USA
LVOW120904200212

269507LV00016B/220/P